MORGAN'S MISCELLANY

ANTHOLOGY

AN INSPECTOR MARSHALL MYSTERY

Emma Melville

ISBN-13: 978-1-8380344-4-3

Book of golden stories
Days of open roads
Now the autumn leaves are falling
We'll meet on the edges
Memories, no regrets

Runrig.

CONTENTS

ACKNOWLEDGEMENTS...i

FOREWORD 1
PART 1 MORGAN'S MISCELLANY.. 2
Thought Crime 2
The Camera Never Lies... 42
Hindsight 76
Déjà vu.. 128

PART 2 OTHER MARSHALL SHORTS...................................... 147
Ill Met by Moonlight.. 147
Ghost of a Rose 169
The Tide Comes; The Sea Calls Out.................................... 184
Penance... 203
The Wrong Train 226

PART 3 OTHER SHORT STORIES IN SETTING...................... 239
The Little Red Book.. 239
After the Flood 260
The Enemy Within.. 269
Midnight Treat 289

ABOUT THE AUTHOR 300

ACKNOWLEDGEMENTS

Thanks to Paul for his wonderful artwork again. Also to Toby who continues to correct my medical details without being too sarcastic. Thanks to Mum, Dad, Hazel, Faye, Jack and Alan for all the help and proofreading and continued support of my writing. And always, and forever, to Jon.

FOREWORD

This is an anthology of short stories involving the strange town of Fenwick. Most involve Inspector Marshall. Part one is a set of four linked stories involving the Inspector and part two is an assortment of further stand-alone stories concerning Marshall and crimes he has to solve. Part three is a collection of other stories set in Fenwick which star various of the cast of characters/settings met in the tales so far.

Many of these short stories have been published previously in anthologies in their original form. They have been adapted here to run coherently together rather than left with their initial storylines which introduced the setting of Fenwick and its strange library every time.

Versions of the following have been published:

'Thought Crime', published in *Open and Shut* (short story anthology edited by 221B magazine), 2011; 5800074704409.

'Déjà vu', published in *Nightbird Singing in the Dead of Night* (short story anthology edited by Jeff Dennis), Nightbird Publishing, Sep 2009, 978-0-9819572-0-3 (USA).

'The Wrong Train', published in *Invisible Ink 2* (short story anthology edited by J Arnold and FM Foster), Baineth Publications, July 2008, 978-0-9557593-2-1.

'Hindsight', published in *With Islands in Mind* (short story anthology edited by Kay Green), Earlyworks Press, 2006, 978-0-9553429-4-3.

PART 1

MORGAN'S MISCELLANY

Thought Crime

Dawn Sabeena had been bludgeoned to death in her bed while, according to his story, her husband, Carlton, had been playing Call of Duty in total oblivion in the lounge.

Marshall, looking at the absolute carnage in the bedroom, couldn't believe for a moment that the husband was telling the truth.

"He did it, do you suppose?" Mark had also been dragged from his bed at three o'clock in the morning to view the corpse. "All fired up from the computer game."

"Can't see how—"

"No," Dr Trent said sharply from where she knelt beside the bed, "not a drop of blood on him as far as I could see."

"He got changed," Mark argued.

"She's still warm, Mark. This is two hours old, if that. He seriously hasn't had time to do anything clever. I don't believe he did it. Not totally impossible but highly improbable."

"So, someone breaks in or walks in, passes hubby playing games, kills her, walks out again and then he only discovers it when he comes up to bed?" Mark shook his head. "Pull the other one."

"I know," the doctor said, "but he would be covered. I can't make it fit either way."

"Do you know what she was hit with?" Marshall asked before Mark could argue further. "Might help if we know what to look for."

"Hammer, I think," she said. "I'll give you a better idea once I've looked closer at the lab. Shape of bruises gets a bit more lost against dark skin and surrounded by this much blood. Let me clean her up."

"We'll talk to the husband then," Marshall said, leading the way back downstairs.

The husband's obliviousness became slightly more understandable in the lounge. The television had to be six feet across and equipped with a massive set of turquoise headphones as well as being plugged into all sorts of boxes which Marshall failed to recognise. Some video game which involved people shooting each other was still providing a distraction on the screen though Carlton Sabeena was obviously too shaken by the actual violence he had discovered (or committed) to be taking part in the virtual recreation. He sat in an armchair, turned away from the display, cradling a mug with an attendant young WPC making small talk. As far as Marshall could tell, it was a fairly one-sided conversation but she was managing to fill all the silences with pointless and meaningless chatter.

Marshall smiled at her. "Thank you, Constable. Well done. I don't suppose you could rustle up a coffee for Sergeant Sherbourne and I?"

"Certainly, sir." She turned to her seated companion. "Can I get you another drink, Mr Sabeena?"

At his vague nod she relieved him of his empty cup and headed for the kitchen, leaving him alone with Marshall and his sergeant.

"So, sir," Marshall angled the other armchair so he could see the man's face while they spoke, "tell me about what happened."

Mark pulled out a notebook and perched on the third chair in the room. Marshall noted the lack of settee; this was obviously not a room designed for its occupants to sit cuddled up watching television of an evening. He wondered whether the victim had been as obsessed with computer games as her husband seemed to be.

"So much blood," Carlton said, sounding spaced out, "everywhere."

"We noticed," Marshall said, keeping his voice soft. "Tell me about your evening, before that."

"I was playing Call of Duty," Carlton said. "They'd released the new season and I was working through the new maps so it was about two before I got up to go to bed."

Marshall ignored the game stuff; it had never interested him and he couldn't see that it was relevant. "Your wife went up before then?"

"Oh yes, she usually does," Carlton agreed. "She needs to get up early to get in to work."

"Where does she work?"

"Bank in town, catches the bus in about eight."

"And you, do you work?"

"I drive a taxi, mostly later hours, though I sometimes do the school runs."

"So," Marshall summarised, "about two a.m. you went upstairs and found your wife dead?"

"Yes." Carlton's voice shook. "So much blood," he said again.

"And you didn't hear or see anything?" Marshall failed to keep all the scepticism out of his voice.

Carlton had the good grace to look embarrassed. "I don't hear much when I'm in the zone on the game," he admitted. "Dawn used to complain about it until I…" His voice tailed off.

"Until," Marshall prompted.

"I, well, I, she, well…" Carlton put his hands to his head. "She can't be gone."

Marshall could recognise distraction tactics when he heard them. "Until," he said again.

After a pause, Carlton whispered, "Until I taught her not to."

Out of the corner of his eye Marshall saw Mark's hand tighten on his pen and the young WPC pause as she re-entered the room bearing a tray.

"Was tonight a lesson as well?" he asked softly.

"No, no." Carlton half stood, uncurling his giant frame out of the chair. "Lord, no. I tell you truth. I was playing. I heard nothing. I didn't… I couldn't… I know I… but no, not that. I love Dawn." He subsided back into the chair. "I didn't do that. Please believe me."

Marshall took his coffee. "Give me a reason to," he said bluntly.

"I went upstairs and she was d… like that," Carlton said, leaning forwards and then – as if it had just occurred to him, "I phoned you. I wouldn't have done that if I'd done it, would I?"

"Unlikely," Marshall admitted.

"I didn't touch anything, I remembered that from the telly."

Marshall nodded. 'No blood on him,' Liza had said.

Before he could ask further, Craig Hickson, Fenwick's leading forensic scientist, stuck his head round the door.

"Evening, John, well, probably nearer morning actually. What have you got for me this time?"

Seeing the horror on Carlton's face at this jovial greeting, Marshall ushered the forensic specialist back out of the lounge. "Tact, Craig," he admonished. "There's plenty of blood for you, but I want some evidence of who did for her. Either to show the husband managed it somehow, whilst staying clear of any of the blood, or a way someone else could enter with the husband hearing nothing."

"Got you, I'll see what I can find. Liza here?"

"Upstairs."

Hickson nodded cheerfully and started upstairs slowly, his careful eyes checking every corner as he went.

Marshall went back to the lounge to finish his coffee.

"Can you think of anyone who might want to hurt your wife, Mr Sabeena?" he asked as he handed his cup to Mark to take away.

"No." The big man shook his head in a slightly dazed fashion. "No, she didn't really go out much. She wouldn't hurt anyone."

"She hadn't had an argument with anyone recently, or a disagreement."

"No, of course not, she wasn't the arguing kind."

Marshall had a nasty suspicion that, even if she had been, her husband may well have knocked it out of her. He paused but then decided there was nothing more he could get at the moment. He advised Carlton Sabeena not to go anywhere. "We will take a proper statement at the station later today," Marshall told him, adding, to himself, *Possibly under caution.*

"Constable." He turned to the young woman who was clearing mugs.

"Ashton, sir, Gillian Ashton."

"Good to meet you, Constable. Can you help Mr Sabeena to find somewhere he can go to stay for a while, maybe someone he can be with?"

"Of course, sir."

Marshall and Mark left the house and took a look round outside as they headed back to the car, taking care not to disturb anything which might be evidence. Marshall hoped Hickson could see something more obvious as a way in than he could.

"He must have done it," Mark said as Marshall started the car.

"But Liza says not."

"Who else—"

"I know," Marshall said, "but this is Fenwick and, if experience has taught us anything, it is that we shouldn't discount impossibilities just yet."

*

Mark got nowhere the following morning. Carlton Sabeena, upon direct questioning, admitted that he occasionally hit his wife to teach her the proper way to behave but he was absolutely adamant that he hadn't killed her. His unchanging account was that he was playing Call of Duty until two in the morning and he had then bored Mark with detailed accounts of the new season's battle pass. He seemed more animated and worked up about changes in maps and gun specifications than about his wife's death.

Finally, Mark gave him his statement to sign, cautioned him not to leave town and went in search of coffee.

"Total washout," Mark told Marshall as they made coffee in the tiny station kitchen. "I can tell you more than I ever wanted to know about pump-action shotguns on Call of Duty but I'm not really sure he will notice, until his tea doesn't arrive when he wants it, that his wife isn't there any longer."

"So, you you're no longer convinced that he did it?"

"No, can't make it fit and Hickson says categorically no blood on the husband's clothes. Liza was right about that. Hickson did find some blood on the stairs but that could have been Carlton tramping back to the lounge once the police had arrived. Nothing to indicate who killed her."

"Any definite ideas yet, on what was used to kill her?" Marshall asked.

"Liza says hammer, so we'll scour the house for one but I don't hold out much hope. Liza also says there are old bruises; I think he hit her more than the odd time he is suggesting."

*

Elsie Beck's husband, Donald, had finished his late shift at two, so, when he discovered his wife's body, it had been getting on for three in the morning.

Marshall was, therefore, dragged from bed in the middle of the second night running to go and stare at a woman's bloody corpse.

"Same?" he asked Liza Trent who was carefully examining the sprawled figure.

"I'd say very probably," the pathologist said. "Bruises much the same – more towards the head and very brutal. Uncontrolled,. really. Happened after midnight but not long past."

"Ugly," Mark said from where he stood behind Marshall in the doorway. "You didn't call Helen in, then? I had to get up again!"

"Probably misplaced chivalry," Marshall said, "and she won't thank me for it."

"Same in other ways too," Liza Trent said. "Mrs Beck has several bruises from before tonight."

"I really don't understand some relationships," Marshall said. "Let's go and talk to the husband, though if he is confirmed to have been at work then he couldn't have done it however much he might have hit her at other times."

"If it's the same," Mark said as they headed downstairs, "then it sort of rules out Carlton Sabeena for the other."

"Or makes him guilty of both," Marshall said reflexively, though he couldn't see it being so. "More likely not, I have to agree."

*

Donald Beck was a small, wiry, grey-haired gentleman who worked as a night-watchman at an industrial estate on the outskirts of Fenwick. From what Marshall had seen of the victim, it looked like she had been the larger of the pair. Mr Beck was sitting in an armchair that almost drowned him in a living room crammed with chintz and ornaments. The television got lost in one corner behind several pictures of wedding couples and a pile of knitting magazines. The contrast to Mr Sabeena's high-tech gaming room leapt out at Marshall.

"Can you confirm your whereabouts tonight?" Marshall said, having introduced himself.

"I was at work." The man had a very nasal voice. "I do the late shift."

"Can anyone confirm that?"

"Oh yes, we have lots of deliveries and collections at night, that's why we need someone on the gate at all hours. There were lorries coming and going all the time. Probably over twenty people saw me."

Marshall nodded; the voice was really going to grate. "So, when you came home? Any sign of a break-in?"

"No," Donald Beck said sharply, "she'd left the front door unlocked again. I keep telling her she shouldn't. I have a key and if she's in bed it's not safe. Well, it just proves my point, doesn't it?"

"Bit of a drastic lesson," Marshall said, feeling any sympathy for the man ebbing away.

"I told her!"

"Hit her about it as well?" Mark asked.

"I…" Donald Beck paused and then breathed out sharply through his nose. "It was the only way the silly cow learnt anything. She never complained."

"So perhaps you hit her tonight to teach her the lesson," Marshall suggested though, unfortunately, the evidence didn't seem to be making the case that simple.

"Of course not," the small man snapped, "I was at work. And I never draw blood, just a slap." He seemed quite proud of the fact which meant his probable innocence of the murder annoyed Marshall even further.

"Well," Marshall began and then his phone rang. It was Helen, which was a surprise; she was supposed to be asleep.

Stepping out into the hall, he answered the call. "Helen, what are you doing up?"

"Looking at a woman's corpse," she said briskly. "They asked me as it seems you and Mark already had your own."

"Another one? Where are you?"

"Riverside, about two streets over from you. If you've got Liza or Craig there then you could send them this way when they're done."

"I'll come and have a look as well; it will save me from trying to throttle the husband here."

Having obtained an address, Marshall left Mark dealing with Donald Beck and walked the half mile to where Helen was.

*

A young woman was peering over the front fence of seventeen Trent Road when Marshall got there. He recognised her as Maggie Arkwright, a reporter from the local paper.

"What are you doing here?"

"Could ask you the same," she said, cheerfully. "Seem to have been busy round Riverside the last couple of nights."

"Ambulance chasing a bit below you, isn't it?"

"Just keeping an eye on the local police. Best way to get interesting stories."

"I'm not telling you anything," Marshall said, "you should know that by now."

"Yes," she smiled, "but neighbours will talk to me. So, you had a corpse over on Avon Drive last night, and this isn't the first place you've been tonight. More deaths?"

"I refer you to my earlier answer," Marshall said, pushing past her to go up the drive. "Go away, Maggie, please." He knew she was unlikely to do so, but news headlines about multiple corpses was the last thing he needed.

*

"We've got a serial."

Looking at the pulpy mess where the woman's head used to be, Marshall was inclined to agree with his constable. Three bodies in two nights was rather unusual. "Let's wait for the reports, Helen, before we leap to any conclusions."

She raised one eyebrow.

"All right, yes, it looks like we have a serial killer but I'd prefer not to say it in front of anyone who might quote me until we get something definite back from the labs. No point in causing a panic."

"Hammer again?"

"Looks like it but you know Doctor Trent is going to get very sarcastic if I don't let her tell me. We're not supposed to be able to make deductions like that."

"Want to interview the husband while we wait for Hickson and Trent to deal with your corpse?"

"Yeah, I suppose we'd better."

They found William Cropper sitting in his lounge, staring blankly at the wall; a cup of tea forgotten in his hand provided by WPC Ashton who, Marshall decided, had pulled a bad week for doing the night shift. Mr Cropper still wore a pair of blood-spattered pyjamas and his unshaven face was pale beneath its artificial tan.

Helen moved to look out of the window.

"Vultures are gathering, sir," she commented. So Maggie

obviously hadn't taken his advice and Helen's use of the plural suggested the reporter was no longer alone outside.

"Doesn't take long. Though God only knows how they find out. How's Mr Cropper, Constable Ashton?"

"In shock. I think we ought to send him to The Nightingale."

"Any of that blood his?"

"No, I don't believe so, sir. All hers."

Marshall crouched down in front of the motionless man. "Mr Cropper, do you feel up to answering a couple of questions for me?"

Blue eyes slowly focused on Marshall's face. "What?"

"Do you think you could answer a couple of questions for me?"

"Yeah, I s'pose."

"Did you hear anything last night? Can you tell me anything about the person who did this to your wife?"

"No, no, nothing. I was asleep and then I woke up and… and… and…" The man began to shake.

"Okay, maybe we'll try again once you've seen someone." Marshall pushed himself upright. "Helen, get him an ambulance. We'll get nothing out of him in this state."

"Already ordered, sir," Gillian Ashton said.

"Thank you, Constable. I want him checked over and see if anyone can tell me if he took anything… or… I don't know, was drugged. Meanwhile, we'll start some house-to-house. See if anybody saw anything during the night. And I want this place gone over with a fine-tooth comb."

"What are we looking for?" Helen asked.

"The way he or she got in, possibly the murder weapon," Marshall frowned, "and, assuming a serial killer – which I know I said we weren't yet but if we were – this woman must have had something in common with the other two. Let's see what we can find."

"Could be random," Helen pointed out.

"God, I hope not. Let's have a pattern then we can make some predictions."

The paramedics arrived and escorted the shaken husband from the house.

"So, we don't consider him a suspect?" Gillian Ashton said having watched him go.

"No," a voice said from the doorway. Craig Hickson had arrived. He was a slim, neat man in his early forties, third generation British from an Afro-Caribbean heritage, and his forensic ability was the most reliable Marshall had ever known. "Blood spatter in the bedroom and on the back of Mr Cropper's pyjamas suggests to me that he was lying on his left-hand side facing away from his wife while she was killed. There is no way he could have been holding the murder weapon. The murderer stood by the wife's side of the bed and brought the weapon down from above."

"He or she will have got blood on them?" Marshall couldn't see how the murderer could have avoided it.

"Undoubtedly. Drenched in the stuff all down his front," Hickson said cheerfully. "Doc's upstairs with her if you want a chat."

Marshall went back upstairs. Liza Trent smiled up at him as he entered. "Don't need me to tell you this is the same, do I, John?"

"No. Can you give me a time?"

"Four to six hours ago. Like the others, I'd say it happened between about midnight and two. Hammer again, like the others. I'll have a better idea once I've done your post mortem but I'd say probably the same hammer. Wielded two handed and all blows aimed at the head. There's not a mark on the rest of her. Actually," she went on before Marshall could say a word, "that's not strictly accurate. Our murderer left no other marks but she is riddled with old bruises and scars. I'll make a list for you, shall I?"

"Her as well?"

"Yes, funny that. All your victims seem to have been abused, John. Possible link there?"

*

The huge board along the side of the incident room now had three faces staring from it – Mary Cropper had joined Dawn Sabeena and Elsie Beck.

"Is there anything to link these three women other than they all seem to have been battered wives?" Marshall wrote that up on the board. There was no obvious similarity in looks and their ages ranged from late twenties to early sixties.

"Hobbies?"

Mark shook his head. "Not really, and nothing outside the home. Got the impression they weren't encouraged to go out."

"Ties in, I suppose, with the battered wives bit," Marshall said. "Frequent the local with their other halves or anything like that?"

"According to the delightful Mr Beck, his wife stayed in her place in the kitchen to make his meals while he went to the pub." Mark rolled his eyes. "Some people still seem to be living in the nineteen fifties."

"Place of work?" Marshall tried, having exhausted all other avenues he could think of.

Helen answered. "Elsie was retired, Dawn worked in a bank. Neighbour suggests Mary worked in a shop in town; said she recognised the uniform. We're checking that out but with Mr Cropper still sedated we're having to send someone into town to find out." Helen checked her notebook. "I did find one possibility."

"Go on."

"Well, this same neighbour said she saw Mary Cropper take the bus in every morning – the bus stops right outside her house – and back every evening. The thing is, Dawn took the same bus in according to her husband. They live further back along its route."

"And Elsie?"

"I was coming to her. She was a woman of habit; went into town twice a week – Tuesdays and Fridays – on the bus."

"Same route?"

"Yes, sir. Didn't go in until lunch time after she'd cleaned but she came back late so she may well have been on the same bus as Dawn and Mary."

"Do we know what time that was?"

"Dawn finished work at five thirty and dashed to the bus stop to catch the five thirty-nine home. One of her colleagues said Dawn once admitted that her husband hit her if she missed the right bus."

Marshall shook his head; it never ceased to amaze him that men could hit their wives and did so over such pointless things.

"All right. Helen, catch up on a bit of sleep this afternoon and then I want you to catch the five thirty-nine tonight and see if anyone on there can throw any light on this. Were these three friends? Is there any link? Collect the names of all the regulars on the service as there's the possibility that one of them is either a killer or a potential next victim. See if you can also get a list of the regular drivers on the route." Marshall turned to his sergeant. "Meanwhile, if neither of you object, I'm going to transfer WPC Ashton for a secondment. She seems efficient and we could do with the help in getting some statements from neighbours and chasing up records."

"Go for it," Mark said. "Try PC Nick Sharp as well. I was quite impressed with him this morning on the house-to-house and I get the distinct impression we could be doing a lot of that."

"By all means. Take Sharp on the buses with you, Helen. Mark, you and I are going to track down the other link. I want you to talk to the victims' doctors and see if they ever reported the abuse. I'm going to go down to Cooper Street and visit the refuge, they might have stopped there."

*

"No, I'm sorry, Inspector; I can't find any records for any of these women." Sally Bingham shook her neatly coiffured head.

"Maybe under different names? Do you recognise the pictures?"

"No, truly, Inspector. I'm sorry. It is a very sad fact that we only see a tiny percentage of abused women here. Most are too scared or too… loyal to come forward." She sighed. "Rather too many, Inspector, feel they deserve what they get. If I had a pound for every time I've heard '*If I'd done this right he wouldn't…*' then I'd be a very rich woman by now."

"And they really believe that?"

"Oh yes, abuse can be psychological as well as physical, Inspector. If the abuser can convince his – or her – victim that they have deserved it then they effectively trap them into conspiring or… agreeing… to the abuse. That's not quite the right word but…"

"No, I understand. So my women may never have officially reported their abuse to anyone?"

"No, I'm afraid not."

"Well, thank you for your time anyway."

*

Once outside, Marshall phoned his sergeant. "Any luck, Mark?"

"Not really. Same story in all three cases. The '*well, I had suspicions but she claimed she fell*' sort of thing. Nothing concrete, nothing reported and definitely no referrals anywhere."

"Same doctor?"

"Not even the same surgeries. To be honest, John, I'm not sure where we're going with this. Surely anybody who knew all three women were being abused is much more likely to have hammered the husbands to death?"

"I would agree but then we're rational people." Marshall sighed. "I really don't like coincidences but I think I may have to admit that this is one. Let's hope Helen is doing better."

*

WPC Gillian Ashton and PC Nick Sharp had taken up residence in the CID office when Marshall made it back there. Nick Sharp was in his mid-thirties, a close-cropped beard highlighting a strong chin beneath twinkling green eyes. Gillian Ashton was significantly younger, short blonde hair in a pixie bob framed a thin face. Her eyes were a pale blue, behind frameless glasses she was using to read through information.

"I can't find other links," she reported, looking up from the sheaf of documents. "They worked in different places, had different hobbies, were different ages, nothing I can find in their histories to create links. I'm not sure their paths would ever have crossed."

"The refuge was a bit of a washout too," Marshall admitted. "I hope you're having better luck, Helen."

Helen Lovell had just returned with two lists: one of regular passengers on the five thirty-nine service of the number five bus and a shorter – though not by much – one of drivers on the route.

"They work shifts, change routes and God knows what. We're going to have to talk to most of the company's drivers, I'm afraid."

"And passengers?"

"Across the length of the route from the town centre to where the first of them – Dawn – got off there was about thirty people today who claimed to be regulars on the route and saw all three of the victims on a weekly or even daily basis," Nick Sharp reported.

"Any way of narrowing it down?"

"Only if someone can tell us the gender of the murderer. We can cut the combined lists in half if we knew that."

"It would also help to look for opportunity," Marshall said. "Sorry folks, but tomorrow we're going to have to interview everyone on those lists to find out where they were on Tuesday and Wednesday nights and then we'll have to check their alibis. We need to start eliminating people. Helen, you and Gillian take passengers and Mark and Nick can start on drivers."

"So, we definitely think—" Gillian Ashton began.

"No, lass, we don't," said Mark, "but currently it's the only concrete link we've got so let's see what we can turn up before we have to face the fact we might have a random killer out there."

*

"Is she on the list of bus passengers?" Marshall turned away from examining body number four in the early hours of Thursday morning.

"No, John." Helen shook her head.

"Well, you better go and ask Mr Hart if his wife used the bus and doesn't work Wednesdays or you missed her in some way."

"I already asked."

"And?"

"Mr Hart drove his wife to work every morning on his way to *his* place of work. He told me he wasn't going to have his wife sitting on some bus rubbing thighs with strange men. Liza suggests he probably... er, emphasised this decision."

"Really?" Marshall picked his way across the carpet to investigate the bed. The blood clearly outlined where Mr Hart must have been lying beside his wife as she died a violent and messy death. "How can four men all totally fail to hear that sort of violence going on round them, in some cases, right beside them? It beggars belief. The only connection seems to be that they all abused their wives."

"Perhaps they colluded."

"What?"

"Well, if this was some form of 'hitman' and they paid him to do it without implicating them…" Helen tailed off.

"And they all decided this in the same week?"

"When you put it like that."

"Anything's possible, Helen, particularly as this just blew the bus theory out of the water. Let's start on house-to-house."

"Hasn't really been much use so far."

"I know that, Helen. Very few people are up in the early hours of the morning but I'm hoping we might strike lucky this time. Let's try where she works as well and then go back to the husbands and start a list of friends and acquaintances. There just has to be some connection."

"It could be random, like I said."

"I know that as well, Helen, and, unfortunately, though I hate the idea, it looks more and more like it is but let's hunt down every possibility first, shall we, because 'random' means 'unpredictable' and that means 'panic' and 'chaos' as soon as the press get hold of it. So let's find a pattern if it's there to be found."

*

Mr Hart was a gibbering wreck having woken to go to the toilet at four in the morning to discover, instead, what had been done to his wife. Marshall sent him off to The Nightingale after a fruitless couple of questions. As far as Marshall could tell, he now had four wife beaters, none of whom had actually killed their wives, and no other leads.

"Mark's turn for house-to-house," Helen said.

"All right," Marshall agreed. "You can come with me, Helen, and we'll visit her place of work. Then I have a dreadful feeling I'm going to have to talk to that blasted woman from The Advertiser and get them to run a warning piece on securing homes and house alarms."

"He broke the lock this time," Hickson said cheerfully from where he was measuring blood spatter on the floor by the front porch.

"Yes, thanks, was sort of hoping you could come up with something more helpful," Marshall said.

"He walked out through an open door," Hickson said with a grin, "so he might manage quiet killing but not walking through walls."

"Marvellous!"

"Though," Liza Trent added from where she was putting her instruments away, "quiet just doesn't do it justice. He does seem to be managing rather violent hammer killings so silently he isn't even waking the husband."

"He?"

"Or she, I suppose."

"Size ten footprint," Hickson said, "on the stairs of the last one. I'd go for male."

"I'll bear it in mind," Marshall said. "Come on, Helen, let's see if we can find any links to the others at her work before I have to tell the press we've got a serial killer at large."

*

Leaving Mark to supervise the house-to-house, and refusing point blank to speak to the few reporters waving notebooks who had gathered like vultures round the door, Marshall took Helen with him to the large insurance firm where Melanie Hart had worked.

This was housed in a towering glass construction on the edge of the town centre and was filled with buzzing phones and tapping keyboards.

Melanie's boss was a woman who made it clear that she had much more important places she could be. "I'm sorry, Inspector, I know very little about Melanie. She arrived two minutes before nine each day and left on the dot of five thirty. She didn't really make friends; sat and ate her lunch at her station, that sort of thing." She pursed her lips. "I'm not one to gossip, Inspector, but I did hear that her husband preferred her not to make friends."

"Do you think her husband hit Mrs Hart?"

"I really couldn't say, Inspector. It would... do you know, I never thought of that before." She sounded animated for the first time. "I was going to say that it would be hard to tell because you never saw an inch of uncovered flesh; long tops and skirts all year round. But isn't that a sign of this sort of thing? In fact, Melanie came back just yesterday from a week off recovering from a 'fall'. You make me think, Inspector, that it might have been something else."

"That's possible. Long clothing and tales of 'falls' are fairly common." Marshall made a note to get down to the mortuary and talk to Liza Trent. He needed to know what Mrs Hart showed in the way of signs of abuse and, then, murderer or no murderer, he was going to wave some assault charges round at the husbands.

Marshall and Helen had a brief look round Melanie Hart's workstation but it told them nothing; no clue as to who might have wanted to batter her to a pulp.

"Oh come on, I give up. Let's go and see if Dr Trent has found anything to make our life any easier." Marshall headed for the door and then realised Helen had stopped.

"Helen?"

"That man." She pointed to where a young man was hanging a door. "He was on the bus yesterday."

Marshall came back. "Was he now? Can you remember his name?"

"No, sorry, but he was definitely on my list."

"That's all right, Constable." Marshall drifted back to the

reception desk. "Excuse me, can you tell me who the carpenter is?"

"Carpenter? That's Bob, he's our handyman, fixes anything."

"Bob? Can you give me a full name, please?"

"Robert MacLean."

"Thank you. Is he... okay?"

"Bob? Yeah, he's a nice guy. Nothing's ever too much trouble."

"I assume he might own a hammer?" Helen suggested.

The young receptionist glared at them and Marshall could see the cogs working. He silently cursed journalists and their desire for front-page glories. "A hammer? I saw those dead women mentioned in the paper. Was it a hammer? You can't pin this on Bob. He's really nice and he's happily married."

As if, thought Marshall, that made a difference. Except it did because 'happily married' meant someone who could vouch for him having been in bed every night that week.

"Of course." He smiled at the glowering woman and headed for the door, Helen in tow.

"Aren't we going to speak to him?" Helen asked.

"No, we're going to find your list, get his address and go and see if his wife's in. If she can tell us where he was this week then we'll have no need to trouble him."

"And if we don't speak to him first then he can't warn her that we're on the way, right? No pre-arranged stories."

"Quite."

"Unless they already did that."

"Don't be such an optimist, Helen," Marshall said. "And we might be barking up totally the wrong tree."

"But he was on the bus too which means he knew all four victims."

Marshall grinned at her. "That's better; positive thinking."

*

Robert MacLean lived at twenty-seven, Orwell Drive. It was not far from the houses of the first three victims though that was to be expected if he took the same bus home. It didn't necessarily make him a killer.

His wife was young and beautiful. Long auburn hair fell in ringlets round high cheekbones and discreet make-up highlighted her full lips and green eyes. Marshall found her rather brittle and slightly phoney.

"What can I do for you, Inspector?"

"Your husband gave his name to my constable yesterday, Mrs MacLean, as a regular on the bus route used by three victims in a murder investigation. I need to eliminate him from our enquiries. I wonder if you could tell me if your husband has slept at home this week."

"Of course, Inspector."

"You share a room?"

"Of course."

"And you would know if he left your side during the night?"

"Obviously, Inspector. He disturbs me every time he snores," the voice hardened slightly before the breathless gushing was back, "though that has been better recently."

"Has he mentioned anything that leads you to suspect—"

"My husband is the most wonderful man in the world, Inspector. He would never hurt anyone. He just wants people to be happy."

"It's refreshing to meet a wife so content," Marshall said, considering to himself the evidence he had of the victims' married lives.

"Oh I am, Inspector. Do you know, for my birthday last week he even bought a charm that means he has total empathy with me. He knows exactly what I'm thinking. What other man would do that?"

"I beg your pardon?" Marshall said.

"It's a charm so he can pick up on all my feelings and make sure I'm always happy. Isn't that wonderful?"

"He told you that?" One born every minute, Marshall thought, and she had actually seemed intelligent despite the silly voice.

"Oh, I went with him. Saw an advert in the Smith Foundation Library for a small shop in Butchers' Passage. It was a real birthday treat."

"Right." Marshall abandoned that line of enquiry. "Well, thank you for your time, Mrs MacLean. Can I just ask that you be a little vigilant at present? There is a possible link to the number five bus that your husband uses so you should both take care."

"Yes, thank you, Inspector. I'll make sure."

*

"Is it me? She did just say...?"

"Don't worry, Helen." Marshall patted her arm. "There's a fruit cake in every case. This one's a new one on me, I have to admit."

"Not something you can buy off the shelf in Sainsburys."

Marshall laughed briefly. "Actually, Helen, start checking down the rest of that list of yours and send Mark to meet me at the Smith Foundation. I think I'll just go and ask Jenny a question or two. If we can discredit Mrs MacLean as a witness then her husband is still a suspect."

*

Mark met him outside the Smith Foundation on Museum Street. "Nothing from the house-to-house round the Hart place, John."

"You'd think someone needed to go to the toilet in the night and heard something," Marshall complained.

"I think it only happens that way on the telly."

"Yeah. Anything else?"

"I went to see Dr Trent. She's got a lovely impression of the

24

hammer. Same one for all four victims."

"Excellent."

"Not really. Hickson says it's a standard, 'off the shelf' variety you can buy in any hardware store. I've probably got one at home along with most of the residents of Fenwick."

"Bugger. What about the other bruises on the victims?" Marshall asked.

"Not good."

"Meaning?"

"Doctor says all four suffered abuse and it is *likely* that it is the husband in each case but without some witness statements there's no way you'll prove that. Nothing in the bruises and scars can tell you who hit them. A good defence lawyer… no, let's face it, any defence lawyer would simply claim 'no case to answer' and get it thrown out."

"Do you have any good news at all, Mark?"

"Doctor says there is a slight possibility with victims three and four that the first blow didn't actually kill them. They may have had time to scream or something."

"Right. We're going to go and talk to Jenny," he tapped the plaque on the wall which gave the librarian's name, "and then we're going to drag all four husbands in. There is no way I am going to believe that anybody slept through this so we're going to shake them all until something falls out."

"You think the murderer threatened them to keep silent?"

"Can't think of any other reason they're not talking."

"And we're seeing Jenny because…?" Mark asked.

"Loose end, Mark. I have what seems like a viable suspect who knew all four women but his wife has given him an alibi. She also seems to be a couple of sandwiches short of a picnic so if we can discredit her then… I know it's a long shot but anything's better than the current newspaper fashion for alarmist headlines."

*

Jenny greeted the two of them with a smile. "Been a while, gentlemen. Come through to the back, I'll put the kettle on."

They made their way through the high wooden shelves to Jenny's office and living space at the back and settled into armchairs around the fireplace while Jenny made coffee.

"So, social call or business?" the young woman asked as they sipped their drinks.

"I've got a witness claiming she found an advert here for a shop in Butchers' Passage where she went with her husband and picked up a charm in some way that allows him to know what she is thinking. Sounds a bit far-fetched, but I know this place has 'hidden depths', shall we say, so thought I'd better check."

"Give me a mo'," Jenny said and disappeared into the library. She returned shortly clutching a piece of paper. "This might be it. Appeared on the front desk a couple of weeks ago. No idea where from."

The paper showed the front of an ancient shop with the name 'Morgan's Miscellany' in antique script above the door. 'For all your needs' it advertised in bright red lettering down one side. The address across the bottom was 'Butchers' Passage, Fenwick'.

"Right," Marshall said. "I assume this is what our witness saw. She claims she then went to the shop."

"Quite possibly," Jenny said.

"No," Mark said sharply, "quite impossibly. There are no shops in Butchers' Passage."

Marshall nodded; the small alley ran along the back of Argos from the High Street to Museum Street.

"Can't help you," Jenny said. "I mean, I don't disagree with you, but things aren't always as they seem round here. David may know."

"He's still around?" The past librarian was also very much an ex-librarian.

"You could try in the garden, he's usually there."

Marshall and Mark exchanged a glance but they'd both encountered the strangeness of the library several times and Marshall had been in the garden before. "Open the mirror, please, Jenny," Marshall said, "we will go and see."

*

When the full-length mirror at the back of the room cleared to show the lawns and fountain beyond, David was standing waiting for them.

"I heard you, Inspector," he said. "You bring a lot of disquiet with you today."

"Must be the lack of sleep and the number of corpses," Marshall said. "It can have that effect."

"Can I help?" David asked. "From here?"

"Yes," Marshall said, "you can tell us about this shop which is supposed to be in Butchers' Passage and what I might find if I go there."

"I'm not sure I can help—"

"I am, David. You're here to work with me, to assist in Fenwick. That's what you said when we first met and what Wayland said at Christmas. So, help!"

There was a brief pause and then David sighed, a sound dragged up from deep down. "Sorry, Jenny," he said. "I should have spoken to you. I'll tell John and then you come later when you've shut up the library and I'll explain it to you. Come to the summerhouse, John, Mark."

The three of them strolled across the lawns and past the fountain, while Jenny turned back to go to the desk at the front of the library.

Beyond the greensward was a summer house of golden stone. Inside was one large, sunlit room with a sizeable desk and a couple of upright chairs beside it. A rocking chair sat in a corner beside a music stand and a couple of guitars. An easel stood in the opposite corner with a half-finished painting on it.

Marshall took a seat at the desk while Mark went to view the picture of a wolf on the easel. David took the other seat at the table.

"So tell us about this shop," Marshall said.

"I first encountered it before I became librarian," David said.

Mark let out a low whistle. "That's some time ago."

"I know. Morgan, the lady who runs it, is rather older than she appears."

"Like you," Marshall said slowly.

"I don't know. I know nothing about her, really, so I don't know how she has been around so long or where she comes from."

"All right, carry on. How do you know her?"

"I was a bit of a vagabond before I came here and I have to admit I stole from Morgan when she failed to give me what I needed. It's not something I wanted to admit to Jenny."

"You might just have shown her you were human," Marshall said.

"I am beginning to realise that. Sorry, John."

"We have a witness now," Marshall said, "who claims her husband got a charm in the shop which allows him to know what she is thinking. Is that possible?"

"I think so, Morgan provides all sorts. When I first met her it was to provide me with a love charm to try and win the daughter of a local squire."

"Did it work?" Mark asked.

"Sort of, but then I was made librarian. So I couldn't be with my love. As I said, John, embarrassing. A love potion, a theft and a fight not to be who I am – not my finest hour. Morgan reminds me of it on her visits which are, thankfully, not that frequent.

"What does she want here?"

"She sells items," David said, "to meet people's needs. It doesn't always end well. What people want and need and what is good for them don't always marry up. Morgan's interference isn't always for the best."

"I'd say so," Mark said with feeling. "Do you think she'd talk to us?"

"You can try. The shop can be difficult to find but it might help if you mention you've come from me."

"Mention where? To whom?" Marshall asked.

"When you get to Butcher's Passage."

"All right," Marshall glanced at Mark who was looking dubious, "I suppose we might give it a go. Anything else, Mark?"

Mark shook his head. "Not really, just wondering how we're going to write this one up."

*

The pair of them said farewell to Jenny and headed back outside. On the doorstep, Marshall paused.

"Butcher's Passage?" he asked.

"We can walk that way if you like."

"Oh come on, don't tell me you're not curious."

"All right, I'm curious."

They turned off Museum Street into the alley that was Butcher's Passage. St Mary's loomed on one side, the back of Argos on the other. There were no doors and no shops.

Marshall laughed. "Look at us. There's never been a shop in Butcher's Passage. God knows what David was going on about."

"Perhaps it's one of those 'only the pure in heart find it' kind of thing and we don't have what it takes."

"Really?" Marshall raised an eyebrow. "I'd say we'd just been had if I didn't know Jenny and David better than that. Maybe they've been had too—"

"John!" Mark grabbed his arm.

"Yes, I know…"

"No, John, look!" Halfway along the passage a door had appeared. It was a small shop doorway with a clouded window in the top half and peeling purple paint.

Marshall hesitated. "We are being had, Mark, I can feel it."

"You wanted to know."

"Bugger." Marshall set off for the door, fully expecting it to vanish before he got to it. He felt that he might be happier if it did; at least then he'd know someone was playing games and he wouldn't have to cope with a shop where no shop could possibly be.

The door stayed put.

It led into a small dark room full of curiosities. Large quantities of clothing, mainly black, hung from all available surfaces amidst assorted jewellery and stuffed animals. Many of these Marshall found he couldn't put a name to.

The middle-aged woman who greeted him from behind the counter was smartly attired in a dark jacket and skirt with shoulder-length curled hair and expertly applied make-up.

Marshall blinked in amazement.

"Oh, I'm sorry, Inspector. Not what you were expecting?" There was a brief shimmer to the air and she now wore a long patchwork skirt and a bright tie-dyed top. "Better? I can go for the whole 'witch' look if you prefer but it's not really me."

"David said…" Marshall struggled to find his voice.

"I know all that, Inspector."

Marshall sighed. "Humour me."

"Okay," she laughed, "you fire ahead."

"I have been led to believe that you may have had dealings with a suspect in a murder we are investigating; one Robert MacLean."

"Yes, a very nice gentleman."

"Really? I have some evidence that he may be a killer."

"Anyone can kill, Inspector, with the right motivation. Even you."

"I have never felt inclined to beat anyone to death, Miss Morgan, and I have met some fairly despicable villains in my time."

"What about if someone raped one of your daughters?" She stood up and came round the counter towards Marshall and Mark where they stood inside the doorway.

"If…" Marshall stopped. It was notoriously difficult to get rapists convicted but he had all the weight of the police force behind him which he would use if… hang on. He shook his head. "How the hell do you know I have daughters?"

The woman stopped in front of Marshall and bowed her head slightly. "I am sorry, Inspector, you are right; I don't think you would kill anyone." She patted his cheek gently. "Your poor girls."

Marshall, now thoroughly confused as well as rather annoyed, looked to Mark who shrugged and pulled an 'I've no idea either' face.

"Would you care to explain?" Marshall demanded.

"Not 'I'm a policeman, I don't kill' or 'no-one hurts my daughters' but simply a logical question which makes you the consummate professional. As your daughter, I might prefer a father who would take apart anyone who hurt me."

"All right, point taken, now how about Mr MacLean?"

"I saw him twice in two days. It's not often people are that… how shall I put it? Considerate."

"Considerate?" Mark prompted when she paused.

"I sell some very unusual talents and objects here, Sergeant. I need safeguards. No-one gets in here who does so solely for their own benefit."

"We're here."

"Why would that be, Inspector?"

"To ask you questions." Marshall felt that they were now going round in circles.

"Think deeper."

Marshall frowned. "Well, all right, I'm trying to save other women's lives, yes?"

She merely smiled.

"So, Robert MacLean wanted what?"

"He wanted to make others happy. In particular he wished to make his wife happy but also colleagues and so on. He felt that he could do this if he really knew what they felt and needed."

"He could have tried asking," Mark said drily. "It's what I do; talk to my wife."

"It was a true desire, or he wouldn't have found the door."

"So you gave him a 'charm', I'm told."

"Empathy charm."

"To know what his wife was feeling?"

"He could afford nothing so refined, Inspector."

"So… he knew what everyone was feeling?"

"Yes."

"And that's cheaper?"

"Think of it like a computer, Inspector. Access to the internet is quite cheap, it's the virus filters which cost."

It made a weird sort of sense.

"You're saying he got everything, unfiltered?"

"Yes."

"And the second time? You said you saw him twice."

"The first thing he picked up on was that his wife was unhappy as she hadn't had a good night's sleep in years due to his snoring. He wanted a cure for snoring so she would be… happier."

"Which you gave him?" Mark sounded as sceptical as Marshall felt.

"In a manner of speaking."

"Go on."

"It was cheaper just to stop anyone hearing him."

"He snores silently now?"

"Sort of."

"Go on." Marshall had a worrying feeling he knew where this was going.

"Detail costs, Inspector. A spell which only picks out snoring is quite complex."

"Don't tell me. Robert MacLean now does everything silently at night."

"Between the hours of twelve and six, Inspector. Blanket cover…"

"…Is cheaper, yes, I guessed."

"I did the best I could for him at a price he could afford."

"I'll take your word for that, Miss Morgan, as I have no idea how much of what you just told me is possible. Thank you for your time. I am going to have to ask you not to leave town at present as we may need to speak to you again once we've investigated further."

"I shall be here, Inspector, if you need me." She stressed 'need' ever so slightly.

"One last question," Mark said as Marshall turned towards the door. "Sorry, John, just curious. Do you think I would kill?"

"I think you care, possibly too much, about people."

"Really? And?"

She opened the door for them. "Oh yes, Sergeant. This is the third time in five years that your involvement in a case has meant you have forgotten your mother's birthday." She ushered them through the doorway and closed it firmly behind them, leaving Mark gaping at it.

"Bugger!" Mark hit the door frame. "I knew something was bugging me. That is one very strange woman."

"You're telling me."

Marshall led them along the small alley as quickly as he was able, feeling distinctly uncomfortable. He didn't look back. He knew with certainty that the door would no longer be there.

"So, Mark, what do you make of that?"

"That's the back of Argos, there's no way that shop is there."

"Nope."

"And *charms?*"

"Quite."

There was a significant pause.

"It explains why no-one heard him," Mark said hesitantly, "but…" He paused.

Marshall stopped and turned to his sergeant. "Go on."

"But if he was suddenly so full of empathy and knew what those women were going through then why the fuck didn't he kill the husbands?"

"Shall we ask him?"

"Have we got enough to pull him in if we ignore disappearing shops and stories of charms?"

"Same bus as three victims, same workplace as the fourth. Works with hammers. Wife's alibi to be expected and just what any loving wife would do, doesn't make it true. I'd say we've enough to question him and enough to get a search warrant and see if we can find the hammer or any clothes." Marshall clapped Mark on the back. "But let's be even-handed about this, hey? We'll pull in all four husbands too. Suspected abuse gives us good grounds to make them murder suspects. We'll question all five and see what that gives us."

They strode on in silence for a while.

"You know," Mark said, "even if Miss Morgan was telling the truth, there's no way a jury is going to believe it."

"Therefore, we need a confession, Mark, and it better be good."

Mark nodded and then paused with a slight sigh. "Meet you back at the station, John, I need to grab a birthday card."

*

Robert MacLean was brought in from work by uniformed officers. He was stockily built with broad shoulders and large, capable hands. His whole demeanour gave Marshall the initial impression of a solid, dependable man except for a small tic below his right eye which jumped spasmodically, and dark rings which suggested he hadn't slept well in days.

MacLean stood before the custody officer to be checked in beside Melanie Hart's husband and his whole body flinched repeatedly away from the other man. Then Mr Cropper arrived and Robert MacLean cowered away with his hands pressed firmly over his ears.

"Get him to an interview room, Mark," Marshall snapped. He turned to the custody officer. "Put the others in cells for now and I'll speak to MacLean first."

*

The suspect had relaxed slightly in the interview room though he still viewed Marshall with wary eyes.

Marshall started the tape, reeling off time and date and those present.

"Mr MacLean, would you like a lawyer?"

"No, I'm fine. Less people, the better."

"I have to remind you that you are still under caution."

MacLean nodded and then responded when prompted for the benefit of the tape machine.

"First, can I ask you about your reaction to Mr Cropper outside?"

"He was screaming… screaming and screaming and…"

Marshall sighed; it was going to be one of those. He leapt in with another question. "I heard nothing?"

"Inside, in my head, he just screamed—"

"Why was he screaming?"

"He's scared. Scared of going to sleep now, scared of being alone, scared of what you'll do to him, scared of being locked up, scared of—"

"How do you know that?"

"I can feel it, inside. I have this gift and I wish to God I hadn't because—"

"Did the women scream?"

"Yes, on and on, filling my head all the time and I couldn't stop hearing them. I just had to follow the screaming to find where they lived. I couldn't sleep. I couldn't watch the telly or… or anything. There was just this noise in my head going on and on and—"

"They were afraid too?"

"Yes, so scared to go home, of all the things they'd done wrong and what their husbands would do and—"

"And Melanie came back after her fall?"

"All day, in my head, all day on and on and on…" His voice rose, his hands clutching at his head. "I can still hear that man. Make him stop."

"How do you make them stop, Mr MacLean? Bash their heads in?"

MacLean looked at him helplessly. "I had to. I needed to sleep. The noise is driving me mad."

"Didn't it stop when they slept?"

"They didn't sleep, just lay awake being afraid."

"They were awake?" Marshall pounced on that. "Are you telling me they saw you coming and did nothing?"

MacLean shrugged. "You learn not to scream out loud. One of them begged but the others just watched me."

"And the husbands just ignored you? I find that hard to believe."

"They didn't hear me. No-one hears me at night. I went to this shop in Butcher's Passage and she made me silent at night. She did this to me."

"She?"

"The woman there."

Mark leant forward. "There are no shops in Butcher's Passage, Mr MacLean."

"Not any more. I tried to go back and get her to make the noise stop but it wasn't there."

"Can you tell me," Marshall said after a pause, "what you did with the hammer and the clothes you wore?" A search of both house and work had revealed nothing.

"I left them in Butcher's Passage for her to find. I left a note as well; told her it was her fault." The bitterness seeped out of the words.

"When was this?"

"Last night, after I killed Melanie."

"There was nothing in the passage earlier." Which meant either the man was lying or the woman in the shop knew rather more than she was letting on.

Robert MacLean shrugged.

There was a tap on the door. Marshall stopped the tape and let himself out. Gillian Ashton awaited him. "What is it, Constable?"

"We've got Heather MacLean downstairs. She's come in to make a statement."

"Saying?"

"Her husband never left her side on any night this week."

"Bugger. I hate misplaced loyalty. I hope you told her that all loving wives do this and it doesn't hold water?"

"Ye...e...e...s...s..."

"And?"

"She said it was more believable than her husband's tale of hearing people's thoughts and spells of silence."

"Fuck!" Marshall hit the wall beside him. "She knows and she's still doing this?"

"Looks like it."

"OK. Thanks, Gill." He re-entered the interview room. "I have a couple more questions for you, Mr MacLean. Can you tell me if your wife knew of your plans or helped in any way?"

"No, she was asleep."

Misplaced loyalty all round then.

"All right, finally – and this has really been bugging me – I have been told by several people today just what a nice man you are, someone who wants to do the best for everyone. So can you tell me why you killed the women? Knowing what you knew, why not stop their fear by killing the husbands?"

No answer.

"Did those women deserve that after all they'd been through?"

"Yes," reluctantly. "You only get hit if you do wrong."

Marshall and his sergeant exchanged a glance.

"Women are evil," MacLean muttered. "I hate her." He suddenly surged to his feet, his hands clamped to his ears. "Make it stop! Make it stop! Make it stop…"

*

Marshall found a PC to take the man to a cell. He thought it was probably the kindest thing to do while they planned where to go next.

"He'll last there overnight," Marshall told Mark, "while we decide what to do with this mess."

"We have a confession."

"Which a good lawyer with a tame psychiatrist will rip to shreds. His whole act in there screamed insanity. Our only witnesses are dead or resident in vanishing shops – a fact we can't admit to for fear of someone committing us to the loony farm too. We've no murder weapon and no forensics to link him to the murders. Something which I also think we have Miss Morgan to thank for. Meanwhile, the defence have the wife claiming he never left her side."

"We can't just let him out to do it again."

"To be honest, Mark, letting him out, tailing him and catching him red-handed may just be our best bet."

"So what do we do now?"

"We let him sleep – if he can – he looked like he could do with it. We'll re-interview in the morning when he's calmer and see if we can get enough detail in his confession to prove he had to have been in those bedrooms. If not, we'll have to take it to the DCI. I don't want to call on this one. While we've time, let's put the fear of God into four wife beaters and see if any of them saw anything."

*

Marshall's phone rang at ten past six the following morning dragging him out of sleep. He'd spent the evening telling Marian how much he loved her, much to her surprise, but he couldn't get out of his head the fates of four battered women.

"Inspector, it's Sergeant Wilkes here. You need to get down to the station. We've got a death in the cells. Your suspect topped himself."

*

This was something of an understatement. Robert MacLean had demolished what he could of his cell, which was little enough, but then had worked on smashing himself up. Evidence suggested he

39

must have battered his head repeatedly against the wall and bed until he knocked himself out or passed out from lack of blood.

"What the fuck were you doing? Did no-one hear him?" Marshall glared round the uniformed custody officers.

"Not a sound, sir. I don't know how we missed it."

Marshall did, he just didn't think it was a good idea to tell anyone.

Sergeant Wilkes continued. "Although, sir, Paddy was in and it was difficult to hear much else." Paddy was a regular visitor. No-one knew his real name so he'd been nicknamed for his accent. He lived on the streets and when he'd begged enough money he treated himself to a bottle of scotch and got rip-roaring drunk. He then spent hours yelling, banging and singing in a cell once a patrol had picked him up – normally after a complaint about the amount of noise he was making in some quiet suburban street.

"Paddy?" Marshall raised an eyebrow.

"In good form as well, sir. He'd got hold of two bottles of single malt this time. Said a beautiful woman on a 'broomstick' had given them to him which probably meant he nicked them, though he did actually bring himself in when he got halfway down the second bottle. He said he'd been promised a cell. Absolute pain all bloody night, noisy devil. Comatose now, of course, now he's kept everyone else up."

"One might almost think," Marshall said slowly, "that he'd been sent here to drown out any other noise." Or to hide the total lack of any other noise.

"Yes, sir," Sergeant Wilkes said dutifully.

*

Marshall left them to it and retired upstairs in search of a coffee. He'd had rather too many early starts to go and stare at blood-drenched corpses for one week.

Dr Trent joined him a while later.

"Keeping me busy this week, John."

"Hopefully that'll be the last. I'm convinced he was our killer even if I can't prove it."

"Interesting, the way he tried to smash his own head in in the same way."

"Yes, I think he was hearing things he didn't want to hear."

"Voices in the head? Could be. People do things for the strangest reasons."

Marshall snorted. "I was told by a very odd woman that Mr MacLean's sole reason was to keep his wife happy."

"You think? Now that would make some kind of sense. Felt he didn't do things right for her, that sort of thing?"

Marshall straightened in his chair. "What have you found?"

"Almost identical to your other victims, John, if you ignore the self-infliction of the final acts. Web of old scars, breaks and bruises. I'd say he was abused."

"His wife hit him?"

"Looks like. It's more common than you think." Liza Trent turned to go and said over her shoulder, "Oh, and John…"

"Yes?"

"I think she used a hammer."

The Camera Never Lies

Arthur Brock had found 3 Roman coins in the fields running alongside the River Hurne so far this month and he had vague daydreams of discovering a hoard like the Staffordshire one so, despite the gentle rain, he pulled his anorak on and headed out in the dawn light to put in another hour's metal detecting before Brenda woke up.

The detector had been an inspired retirement gift from the council though Brenda did occasionally complain about the hours he spent out with it. He had promised not to take it with them to Skegness this year after the arguments it had caused last summer. In return, Brenda had agreed to leave her knitting at home and they were actually going to spend the week holidaying together.

This was probably his last hour out before they left.

The machine began a high-pitched beeping as he swung it back and forth near where he had found the last coin. Arthur dug at the soil with a small trowel. The earth had been loosened and redistributed by spring rains and a swollen river and was easily turned.

Nothing immediately appeared but the machine kept protesting loudly so he dug a little deeper.

The gold ring he unearthed was a real disappointment – it was very dirty, very modern looking and, unfortunately, still attached to the wearer's hand.

*

Harrison Campbell stormed along the lane beside St Mary's and swung sharply into Butcher's Passage. Nothing was fair and the visit to the solicitors hadn't helped. The will simply shared everything out equally between him and Peter and didn't in any way identify who was to have what. The ancient wardrobe – source of the row – had to be decided on by the two of them. The solicitor refused to get involved; had barely stopped short of rolling her eyes and calling them children.

Harrison realised he'd come to a halt, his mind replaying the meeting he'd just left. The grown-up thing to do would be to let Peter have the sodding wardrobe but his grandmother had said in her last illness that he could have it. He was fairly sure Peter just wanted to sell it for the money it would make him, whereas Harrison had every intention of keeping it for sentimental value.

Sighing, Harrison raised his head. Now, why had he come this way? He paused in the act of moving off; he'd not noticed a shop in Butcher's Passage before.

'Morgan's Miscellany', the sign read above the leaded window and underneath in smaller letters, 'we can supply all your needs'.

"Yeah," Harrison muttered sourly, "two identical wardrobes, I don't think so."

"You never know, young man," a woman's voice said behind him. "I have all sorts of solutions to problems."

Harrison snorted as he turned to confront a woman who was barely shorter than his own six-foot-one. She had long, curly, jet-black hair and bright blue eyes. "If you can manage a Victorian wardrobe like Grandma left that would be a miracle."

"Do come in." She ushered him towards the door. The small squares of glass in the display window didn't allow him to see the interior clearly but it didn't feel like a furniture store. All the same, Harrison was shepherded quite firmly through the doorway into a veritable Aladdin's cave of items.

He looked round as his eyes adjusted to the gloom. As he suspected, there was a huge variety of hippy clothes, antique-type items and a lot of what his mum called 'tat'. Things you didn't need, didn't want, didn't have a home for and probably couldn't afford but brought back from holidays anyway.

There were no wardrobes.

"I think—" he began but the woman had hold of his arm and was steering him towards a round table at the rear of the cluttered room.

"Here you go," she said with a flourish and picked up a camera from amongst the china and pewter which littered the surface.

"A camera?" Harrison took it. "What—"

"Reproduce something identical."

"I can take a picture of the damn thing on my phone," Harrison snapped, trying unsuccessfully to hand the camera back.

"Not quite like this one will take. Try it. I'll give you three days' trial before you need to pay. Return it within the time if you're not completely satisfied for no charge." She smiled, showing beautifully white teeth.

"Really, miss, I don't—"

"Take it. Try it." She began to push him gently towards the exit. "You won't be disappointed."

Without quite knowing how he got there, Harrison found himself back in the passageway, outside the shop, staring at the door that the woman was closing firmly in his face. He heard a bolt slide and then she turned the sign that was hanging inside so that it said 'closed'.

Harrison raised his hand to knock on the door but it was still full of camera. It looked very modern – state of the art digital probably, with a polished black case. No charger with it, of course, so he hoped the battery was fully charged.

Harrison shook his head; what was he thinking? He didn't need a picture of the bloody wardrobe and, if he did want to remind himself of it because he'd lost out to Peter, then he had a phone, an iPad or a camera of his own he could use for the job.

He knocked on the shop door but the strange woman didn't return. He briefly considered leaving the camera on the doorstep but it would probably just be stolen so he decided to take it with him. Maybe he could compare its quality to his own Nikon because the will did mean he would soon have some money to play with and he could treat himself to a new camera. If this was as good as the lady seemed to suggest, maybe he could get one the same.

Cradling the camera carefully, Harrison continued on down Butcher's Passage.

*

"Professor Margaret Wilson," Craig Hickson, Fenwick's forensic expert, declared, waving his hand at the decaying body laid out on the slab. "The missing body in the Ryan Steele case." The skeletal form was still wrapped in the remaining tatters of purple tweed skirt and what would once have been a silk blouse.

"Bit of a shock for the poor guy with the metal detector," Marshall said, folding up his copy of The Fenwick Advertiser which was running Arthur Brock's story on the front page. "Didn't they lock up Steele anyway?"

"Bit of a nutcase," Hickson said cheerfully. "Did him for GBH on someone else, I seem to remember. Couldn't prove the murder without the body, though it was fairly obvious to some of us that he had done something with her."

"Before my time," Marshall said, though he had looked through the file first thing in the morning. He imagined interviewing Ryan Steele was going to be top of his list of priorities for the week, once Dr Trent and Hickson had gleaned what they could from the body.

"The flat was literally swimming in blood," Hickson grinned, his teeth very white against his dark skin, "but we couldn't find her." He sounded delighted. Marshall had noticed that Hickson enjoyed himself more, the more complex a case became.

"Knife." Dr Liza Trent was peering closely at the emaciated form from which she had stripped the remains of the purple plaid skirt and lilac blouse. "He hit several bones while going in and out. Should give Craig some good impressions. Total butchery really. Don't know why he didn't finish the job and dispose of her in several locations; we'd never have found her."

"Quite glad he didn't," Marshall said drily. "At least this way we've a chance of a conviction. Let me know if you discover anything I can throw at him in interview. I shall see if I can find where they have him locked up." He paused, thinking. "If they still have him, that is. I suppose GBH and that was three years ago, he might be out by now."

*

"Steele beat up the bloke the professor was going out with," Mark had also been through the file, "left him out cold with a couple of broken bones. Prosecution claimed Steele then killed her but there was no body. His defence made a big thing of his obsession with her and made a good case for him dealing with the boyfriend out of jealousy. Even went so far as to suggest Steele was avenging her because the boyfriend killed her. The obsession was real enough, there was plenty of evidence for that, so the defence was sufficient to raise reasonable doubt in the jury's mind."

"She was Steele's lecturer?" Marshall clarified.

"Yes," Mark shut the file, "psychology degree, would you believe?"

"Perhaps he was trying to diagnose himself." Marshall shook his head. "Not that it sounds like that was amazingly difficult. Find out where he is, Mark, we need to interview him." He sighed. "And, I suppose, the professor's boyfriend because Steele's defence is hardly likely to have changed unless Hickson and Trent can find us something concrete in the way of evidence. You could—"

The phone rang, interrupting his train of thought. Mark answered it and listened in silence for a couple of minutes.

"Novel," he said as he put the phone down. "A wardrobe has fallen and killed a guy over in Manor Estate. The PCs who went over there are concerned because the witness is babbling about it appearing from nowhere."

"Materialising deadly wardrobes?"

"Yep. Hickson will love it."

"Too much Dr Who, do you suppose?"

"Or foul play by someone with an overactive imagination," Mark grinned, "or IKEA have developed a whole new delivery system. We could ask Helen to find Mr Steele while we go and look at an invisible wardrobe."

Constable Helen Lovell was the third and youngest member of Fenwick CID, having transferred from uniform at about the same time as Marshall was appointed.

Marshall hesitated but then shook his head. "That would be mean. You take Helen, I'll find Steele and his victim's boyfriend, set up some interviews."

*

A uniformed constable – PC Nick Sharp – let Mark and Helen into the small semi on Hyacinth Avenue by the back door. He was in his mid-thirties and, according to Helen, a good, solid officer who had helped and advised her significantly when she had first been in uniform. "One of the good guys," she had told Mark on the journey there. Mark agreed, the man had been solid and reliable in collecting statements over the hammer killings earlier in the month.

"Can't get in the front," Nick Sharp explained, "I'll show you." He led them through the small, outdated kitchen into the hall. The stairs led up almost immediately inside the front door and were completely blocked by the remains of two large, solid wood wardrobes. The fall down the stairs had not done huge amounts of damage – the doors had wrenched from their hinges and the wrought metal work of the banisters had gouged holes in places. Legs and handles littered the stairs and the bottom had ripped off one. What little space there might have been was filled with the corpse of a blond-haired young man that Dr Liza Trent was in the process of examining.

"Death by wardrobe is a new one on me," the petite pathologist said with a smile, "but not really a puzzle. It is fairly obvious what killed him."

"Fall or pushed?" Mark asked.

"Well, you ought to hear what his brother has to say," Nick Sharp said. "He's in the lounge with the mother."

"Something to do with materialising wardrobes." Mark grinned but got no answering smile from the PC.

"He's deadly serious, Sarge. Mother, too."

"Okay, let's hear this fantastic story."

Mark and Helen let themselves into a small lounge. It was overly floral with a couple of chintz armchairs and an oversized television. The mantelpiece and walls were covered in knick-knacks and photos of two young men growing up. Mark suspected one of them was lying under a wardrobe in the hall and the other was the figure sitting huddled in one of the two chairs, rocking slightly and clutching a state-of-the-art camera as if his life depended on it. The other chair was occupied by a woman who Mark assumed must be mother to the two men – she had the same shape of face and white-blond hair though hers, Mark thought, probably came out of a bottle.

Her red-rimmed eyes and blotchy face suggested there had already been a lot of tears.

Both mother and son stared at Mark and Helen as they entered – two sets of unblinking, frightened, watery, blue eyes.

"I'm Detective Sergeant Sherbourne, this is Detective Constable Lovell. We wondered if you could explain the situation here. Is this your house, madam?"

"No, my mother's. We've been clearing it. She died." She rubbed at her eyes as they started to fill again.

Mark nodded. It made sense; the house definitely had the same feel as his own grandmother's in her later years.

"So, can you tell me what happened?" he asked gently as Helen got out a notepad and pencil.

The woman opened and closed her mouth a couple of times but nothing came out.

Mark sighed. "Find me a chair, Helen, I think this might take a while."

The dining room, through a connecting door, provided upright chairs the two of them could sit on and PC Sharp was encouraged to supply cups of tea too.

"Now," Mark said encouragingly once they were all settled, "let's start with names. You are?"

"Rita Campbell."

"And these are your sons?" He indicated the photographs around the room.

"Yes, Harrison and Peter." Her voice caught on the last word. "Peter," she said again, her hands clutching tighter at the handkerchief she held.

"You're Harrison." Mark turned to the young man who nodded vigorously. He still held his camera in one hand while the other held his cup of tea.

"So, you were trying to get the wardrobes downstairs," Mark prompted.

"Wardrobe," Harrison corrected.

"They'd been arguing over it," Mrs Campbell said. "Mum wasn't clear who should have it and they both wanted it."

"There were two," Helen said. "Surely they could have had one each."

"There *are* two now," Harrison said bitterly. "Why couldn't she have been more specific? I'd have taken it earlier."

"Your grandmother?" asked Mark, trying to follow this cryptic pronouncement.

"No, the woman who gave me this," Harrison snapped, waving the camera and nearly spilling his tea in the process. "I wouldn't have been taking pictures on the stairs if I'd known what it did."

"What did it do?" Helen said gently.

"Created another wardrobe," Harrison said, as if this should have been obvious. "Pete had the down end but he couldn't hold it when there were suddenly two of them."

"So why were you taking pictures on the stairs?" Mark asked.

"He was being childish," Mrs Campbell said bitterly. "Peter had won the argument, so Harrison was going for 'I better have a picture to remember it as it's the last time I'll ever see it'. Also left Peter bearing most of the weight while he fiddled with the camera, which was petty."

"I didn't know it was going to do that," Harrison almost yelled. "I didn't want this. Pete can have the damned wardrobe if he… if he… he can't be dead!" The final wail was lost, muffled against his mother's chest as she crossed the room and clasped him to her.

Mark exchanged glances with Helen and they quietly left the room to go back to the hall where Dr Trent was supervising the removal of the body and Craig Hickson had just arrived with his forensic paraphernalia.

"Well," Mark said, "I suppose he could have been angry over losing the argument about who inherited it, let go of his end in a spiteful sort of 'you carry it then' way without realising his brother couldn't hold it, with resulting tragic accident. Or he might have pushed slightly."

"And the second wardrobe?" Helen indicated the mess on the stairs which was quite obviously two wardrobes.

"Absolutely no idea," Mark said, "but we've got a camera here, Craig, that you better bag up as vital evidence and, unfortunately, you probably need both wardrobes too."

Hickson looked from Mark to the broken furniture on the stairs and back. "Seriously?"

"Yes, see if you can work out which was the original and which one materialised when the picture was taken." Mark was pleased with how straight he managed to keep his face.

Hickson didn't ask him if he was serious a second time, just rolled his eyes. "We're going to need a bigger van then."

Mark and Helen returned to the living room while Hickson began bagging pieces of wood. Mother and son had calmed down though Rita Campbell still stood beside her son, her hand on his shoulder.

"We'll need the camera as evidence, Mr Campbell," Mark said. He thought the young man might refuse but after a second's hesitation he handed it over.

"Who did you say gave it to you?" Helen asked.

"Woman in a shop in Butcher's Passage. Morgan's something. Can't remember."

"There aren't any shops in Butcher's Passage," Helen said sharply while Mark bit his tongue.

"I know," Harrison wailed, his hands beginning to shake now he hadn't got anything to hold. His mother grasped hold of them and held tight.

"We need a proper statement," Mark said, "but I think it would be easier for you if you come to the station, maybe later today once you've had a chance to freshen up and calm down."

He and Helen left, leaving instructions with PC Sharp to give what help he could and then to transport mother and son to the station.

*

"We may have an issue," Mark said to Marshall when they arrived back at the station.

"What sort of issue?"

"A shop in Butchers' Passage sort of issue."

"There isn't one," Helen said.

"Not usually," Mark agreed. "Don't you remember all that fuss with our hammer killer?"

"Yes," Helen said hesitantly, "I was never sure—"

"Us neither," Marshall said, "and we actually went to the place. What this time, Mark?"

"Suspect in this wardrobe business claims he got a camera from there that led to the extra wardrobe and the death of his brother."

"Let's see what Hickson says about it before we go trying to find the shop again," Marshall said. "I wasn't amazingly comfortable in the place."

"That's an understatement," Mark agreed. "Any luck with Ryan Steele?"

"He is still staying at Her Majesty's Pleasure though he seems to be doing well because they've moved him to Thorn Cross Open. He's likely to be out in the shortest possible time and I think he has even got some resettlement leave soon so I need to go and talk to him before they let him out on licence. I've arranged to see him this afternoon."

*

Ryan Steele's file identified him as on the autistic spectrum and the defence at his trial had made great use of this fact, and his obsession with Professor Wilson, but prison had obviously been of enormous help to him. He grasped Marshall's hand in greeting, met his eye as Marshall asked questions, and his prison reports suggested a much-changed individual. Ryan had engaged well, it said, with the High Intensity Training on offer at Thorn Cross and had also taken up construction. His attention to detail and inability to leave an unfinished job were commented on which Marshall recognised as autistic traits coming through, but not in any way negatively. The counselling session notes described Ryan's work on anger management and understanding and controlling emotions.

All in all, Marshall was impressed and he was not confronted by the thug he had been expecting but by a courteous and confident young man.

Also one who, unfortunately, wasn't giving anything away.

"I'm here to talk to you because we've found Professor Margaret Wilson's body," Marshall said once he'd introduced himself.

Ryan nodded, his eyes not leaving Marshall's face, his mouth resolutely closed.

"This may give us more evidence to bring a trial for murder," Marshall continued. When nothing was forthcoming, he decided to change tack. "You seem to have turned yourself around in prison."

Ryan again nodded silently but then relented and said, "I can control things now. My next goal is to apologise to the man I beat up. I got cross with what he did and I wouldn't do that now." He paused and then added, "I'm allowed to go and visit Mum again this weekend and I go out to work now." It sounded rehearsed.

"That's good," Marshall said, "and is there anything more you can tell me about what happened to Professor Wilson?"

"No," Ryan Steele said abruptly and then, as if working through a script, "I'm sorry, that was rude of me. I can be, sometimes, but I am learning. No, I can't help you, Inspector."

Marshall tried to get more, talking about life in an open prison, how Ryan's mum was, what he intended doing in Fenwick when he came home and – intermittently – interspersing questions about Margaret Wilson. It was no use; he got nothing except vague and banal answers.

Eventually Marshall gave up, thanked Ryan for his time and wished him luck with his reintegration into society.

He called Mark who, it seemed, had about as much success with Harrison Campbell and his mother. "Sticking to the story; took picture of wardrobe, second wardrobe appeared, whole lot landed on brother. Sounds like a fairy story but I couldn't shift either of them on it."

"I'm going to talk to Hickson," Marshall said, "see if he can give us anything for either case which might help move us forward. Currently it all seems a bit of a washout."

*

The lab looked like a small tornado had passed through it. Pieces of smashed wardrobe were piled in most corners, the skeleton of Professor Wilson was spread out on one table, the remains of Peter Campbell on another.

A rather fancy camera was sitting in a plastic bag alongside the remains of Peter Campbell's skull. Marshall assumed this was the mysterious camera that was supposed to create wardrobes. Hickson had several of his own cameras for his work but these were all carefully locked away in one of the cupboards lining the walls.

Dr Trent was absent. Hickson was studying two doors from wardrobes in a far corner.

A young, slightly plump woman preceded Marshall into the lab, her heels clicking importantly on the tiled floor as she strode in. Her shoulder-length hair was strawberry blonde with touches of ginger showing through; her two-piece suit was of a subdued green.

"Ah, Emily," Hickson greeted her, standing up from his examination. "Box on the side there. Take care; it's quite heavy."

"Cheers, Craig." She looked round. "Quite a mess you've got."

"Rarely been this busy," Hickson said, looking at Marshall. "Thanks, John!"

The young woman turned quickly, realising someone else was behind her.

"Inspector John Marshall." He smiled. "Craig thinks the sudden spurt of bodies and wardrobes is my fault."

"Emily Frazer, CPS. I've come for the evidence box for the Burton case." She looked round again. "I'm hoping we won't need to take all this wood to court at any point."

"Probably not," Hickson grinned, "just the camera which created it."

"Created?"

"Special new function, according to the witnesses. Camera doesn't take pictures, just creates wardrobes."

Marshall laughed at the look on Emily's face. "Have you tried it yet, Craig?"

"Would love to but 'somebody' keeps filling my lab with corpses.

Don't have space for extra wardrobes. What I'll need shortly is a camera which creates extra cold lockers at the rate you're going."

"Sorry," Marshall said, mock seriously.

Hickson shook his head. "No, I'm sorry, John, not being a lot of help, am I? Got a vague mould of the knife blade which cut up our professor, if that's of any use."

"Professor?" Emily Frazer asked.

Hickson indicated the emaciated form. "Professor Margaret Wilson, killed a few years back, recently discovered by some poor sod with a metal detector."

The young woman turned away from the sight. Marshall didn't blame her; sometimes visits to the lab turned his stomach a bit too. Hickson's unrelenting chirpiness didn't always help.

"I'll get out of your hair, I can see you have enough to do," she said, picking up the box and beating a hasty retreat.

Marshall went to view the moulds Hickson had created.

"Large carving knife," the forensic expert said, "and unfortunately, most people will probably have something similar in their kitchen."

"Not a good day," Marshall said. "Don't seem to be getting anywhere. Two corpses, two suspects with fairly good motives, and no evidence to be able to prove either of them did anything. I was sort of hoping you might be able to give me a bit more."

"We'll keep working on it." Liza Trent had reappeared from wherever she had been. "Miracles take a little longer, I'm afraid, John."

"One thing I did note," Hickson said, heading back towards the wardrobe he had been working on, "though I'm not sure if it's any help, is that the wardrobes do seem to be identical. Come, look."

Marshall followed carefully, stepping round the mess to where two pieces of wardrobe door were leaning against the wall. "What am I looking at?"

"Door," Hickson said, "or more precisely, the keyhole. Both scratched from where people have misused the keys."

Marshall looked and then a bit closer. "The pattern of scratches seems to be similar."

"Not similar, identical," Hickson said. "I've measured it all ways. Two sets of identical damage. Not possible to recreate."

"So?"

"So, it adds weight to the creation of a second identical wardrobe tale."

"Really?" Marshall laid the back of his hand on Hickson's forehead. "Do you need to lie down?"

"I know." Hickson grinned. "Next thing you know I'll be joining morris dance groups."

"Mark can't keep his mouth shut, then," Marshall said, smiling back. "Just a bit of a try at it but it went quite well; better than anything else has this week. Let me know if you find something actually useful."

"Will do," Hickson and Trent said in unison as Marshall left the room to head back to his office.

*

Nick Sharp was in the office with Mark and Helen when Marshall arrived back. He'd taken to popping in now and again after his short stint helping out earlier in the year and was always more than happy to run errands and take on the odd bit of legwork or paperwork.

"Had Harrison Campbell in this morning downstairs," he told Marshall, "asking if he could have the camera back because he promised the woman in the shop that he would take it back after his three days' trial. I told him it was evidence in the case but he seemed quite worried; says he hasn't paid for it."

"Excuse to visit the shop?" Mark asked.

"Maybe."

"Oh please," said Helen, "I want to see it."

"All right, the two of you go in the morning, apologise for the camera not being returned, ask if she knew what it did, that sort of thing."

*

Shortly after Marshall arrived in the office the following morning and Nick had looked in with cups of coffee – usually Mark's role first thing – the quiet was disrupted by feet thundering up the stairs.

"John!" The shout was from the doorway. Hickson had arrived in the office clutching two coffee mugs. "Someone's stolen it."

"Stolen what?"

"The bloody camera. Someone's stolen the camera!"

"What? THE camera. The one that supposedly creates wardrobes?"

"Not wardrobes," Hickson said, slamming the mugs down. "See!"

"No," Marshall said placatingly. "Calm down, Craig, and tell me what I'm supposed to see."

Hickson glared at him briefly then took a deep breath. "Sorry, John, I'm a bit annoyed; in case you couldn't tell." He gave a wry smile.

"Make it a little more obvious," Marshall said sarcastically. "Now, tell me – and Nick here – what we're looking at."

"Mugs."

"So I see."

"Same mug."

"Yes." Both mugs declared someone to be 'the World's Best Dad'.

"This," Hickson picked up the one on the left, "is mine which I got last Fathers' Day. This," he pointed to a minor chip on the handle, "is from where I dropped it."

"Yes, I see." Marshall passed the mug on to Nick who had joined him beside the table.

"Now look at the other one."

Marshall picked it up and then showed Nick where it had an identical chip on the handle.

"That one," Hickson said, "appeared when I took a picture."

"Seriously?"

"Yes, the camera seems to focus on one object when you look through the viewfinder. The background sort of blurs and then when you press the button there is a blaze of light as if the flash has gone off and, hey presto, second, identical item."

Marshall shook his head. "I'd like to see it actually happen."

"Well you can't because, at present, I don't have it because someone has stolen it," Hickson said, "and this is the lab we're talking about, so it isn't a common or garden thief. This has to be an inside job."

Marshall had already worked that much out and it wasn't a happy thought, particularly not if the camera really did what Hickson claimed. To be honest, not good for anyone if evidence couldn't be proved to be secure.

"What's more," Hickson said, producing a third mug from his pocket, "there is also an 'improvement' setting."

"Which does what, exactly?"

"No chip." Hickson handed over the third mug for inspection. Marshall checked the intact handle and then passed it on.

"Any idea who could have stolen it?"

"None. It's been a bit like Piccadilly Circus in there with the number of wardrobes and corpses you've provided me with this week and Liza and I have been out at crime scenes quite a lot. Sorry, John, know it's not helpful and you're busy too but it needs finding."

"Nick," Marshall took the mug back from the PC, "do you fancy another secondment? Are you up to leading on this? See if you can make a comprehensive list of who visited the lab, check the CCTV, question people and so on."

"Yes, sir… John."

"Good man."

"What's the problem now?" Mark had appeared with Helen following him in. Marshall and Hickson brought them up to speed and they examined the various mugs.

"I want to see it," Mark said. "Seeing is believing."

"Not possible yet," Marshall said, "but Nick's on the job. How did you manage with shops?"

"There isn't a shop in Butchers' Passage," Helen said, sounding smug.

Mark shrugged. "Sorry, John, we looked and tried sidling up on it and all sorts but resolutely no shop."

"And now no camera either," Marshall said. "Perhaps that woman came to take it back."

"She wouldn't have got in," Hickson said, "not past the security."

"Really? We're talking someone who can hide a whole bloody shop." Marshall ran his hand through his hair. "Right, let's leave the shop problem for now. Nick, more important than ever that we get some idea of who might have taken the camera. I'm going to—"

The phone rang. Marshall thought they would be twice as efficient if they just unplugged the damned thing.

Mark answered the phone and had a brief conversation. "Really," he said as he put it down. "You wonder why they don't throw away the key sometimes."

"Meaning?"

"Ryan Steele."

"Go on," Marshall felt his heart sink.

"Well, it seems he's out on home leave, getting ready to reintegrate into society."

"Yes, he said he was going home this weekend. Don't tell me, he's done a bunk."

"No, he just assaulted some poor woman outside Sainsbury's."

"Outside Sainsbury's? In broad daylight?"

"Yeah, dozen witnesses and CCTV footage. Victim ran away – not surprisingly – but some of the witnesses hung on to him. He's just arrived downstairs and is talking gibberish supposedly, so can we send someone to interview him."

"As if we weren't busy enough!" Marshall sighed. "Nick, as you were and see what you can find about a missing camera and we still need to find the professor's boyfriend, please, Helen. Mark and I are going to have a short chat with Mr Steele."

*

Ryan Steele was frightened, his hands twisting together, his face drained of blood.

He perched on the edge of a chair in the interview room and started at the least sound.

The two men watched him through the glass for a while. "Looks like he knows he's blown his chance at parole," Marshall said.

"Seems an excessive reaction from a thug like Steele. I doubt prison holds a lot of fear for him," Mark said.

"From what I could see, prison has done him a world of good," Marshall said. "He's had most of the thug trained out of him."

"Let's find out what's got him so worked up then. Have they found the woman he attacked yet?"

"No but the CCTV footage is being sent over. That should give us an idea."

"I thought we had witnesses."

"Come on, John," Mark laughed. "You know what they're like. So far I'm sure she's short, tall, fat, thin, blonde, brunette; at least cameras don't lie."

"No, they just vanish and recreate wardrobes."

Mark laughed but Marshall wasn't convinced it was funny.

*

Steele leapt to his feet as they entered the interview room, sending the chair clattering backwards.

Marshall helped him to sit down again while Mark prepared the tape machine.

"Interview with Ryan Steele commenced ten fourteen a.m. Those present are Detective Inspector John Marshall, Detective Sergeant Mark Sherbourne and Ryan Steele. Mr Steele has waived his right to a solicitor."

Marshall sat beside Mark and watched Steele's shaking hands. This was not the same young man he had seen a couple of days previously; all the self-possession had evaporated.

"Why are you scared, Mr Steele? What are you frightened of?"

"She's dead. I know she is. I killed her."

Marshall nodded as if this made perfect sense, allowing the man to settle. "Who is, Mr Steele?"

"Margaret, I killed her." Well, that solved that case for them with remarkable ease.

"Some years ago, Ryan," Marshall said, "and you have been in prison. We talked last time about how well you were doing. Didn't we?" Though the unsolicited confession had just put paid to him being released any time soon.

The calm acceptance and recitation of facts seemed to be having the required effect. Colour was returning to the man's cheeks and his shoulders relaxed gradually.

"Got a job, I believe," Mark said, following Marshall's lead and also failing to push the young man about the confession of murder.

Ryan looked at Marshall as if he was simple. "I told you that."

"Quite," Marshall nodded. "So, you were out on leave today?"

"Two days this time. I had one day last month."

"What did you do?"

"Saw my mum, had a look round town, went to the pub." Ryan shrugged. "All the usual things."

"So, today you decided to…" Marshall left it hanging, let the man talk.

"Do some shopping for Mum."

"At Sainsbury's?"

"Yes." The tension crept back into Steele's voice.

"Can you tell me what happened?"

"She was there." And just like that, the gibbering wreck was back. "I killed her and she was there. She should be dead. I stabbed her and—"

"Ryan!" Mark slapped the table with the flat of his hand and Ryan snapped his head round, wide-eyed, to stare at the sound. "Who do you think you attacked?"

"Margaret; Margaret Wilson."

*

"I suddenly realised what was freaking him out," Mark said as they stood outside the interview room supping coffee from disposable cups. "This poor woman obviously looked like his victim."

"So he thinks he's seen a ghost? That makes sense though it doesn't bode well for him coping outside if he's going to see his victim in every passing stranger who looks like her."

"No," Mark said slowly. "Odd. He doesn't seem the fanciful type. I can't imagine guilt keeping him awake at night."

"Sir." A young WPC came through from the front office clutching a small box. "These discs just arrived and Sarge says you're dealing with the attack."

Marshall took it, curious to see how close a match the victim was to Margaret Wilson. How many women were going to be put at risk once Steele was out?

Marshall handed Mark the box. "Go set that up and find me a picture of Margaret Wilson when she was alive for comparison. I'll be two minutes."

Marshall organised Ryan Steele signing a copy of the taped conversation, effectively providing a written confession of the murder. Leaving the front desk to sort a cell and Steele's return to what would be an extended stay in prison, Marshall headed back upstairs to find Mark.

"So what have we got?"

Mark threw him a picture. "From her university staff badge." Professor Margaret Wilson had been short and thin, her shoulder-length hair was mousy brown, the eyes behind the glasses a washed-out grey. She looked tired and sad, a frown creasing her forehead.

"Never flattering, are they?" Marshall said.

"What?"

"Work photos. All designed to give the impression of miserable, ugly employees."

"She doesn't look that bad." Mark took the picture back. "Probably quite pretty when she smiled."

"So how does this morning's victim compare?"

"Just trying to find it."

Mark scrolled through the file, images flashing past on the large screen of shoppers hurrying in and out of the store entrance. A sudden flurry of activity in front of the doors made him pause and rewind slightly.

When the video played it showed a woman who could have been

Professor Wilson's twin staggering in a dazed manner towards the doors of the supermarket. She was wearing only a lilac blouse and a purple tartan skirt; no coat despite the weather and no bag. Ryan Steele was coming out of the shop clutching two carriers of shopping. He stopped and stared in horror at the woman before throwing the bags down and leaping on her. The woman screamed and tried to fight back and then a couple of young men in paint-stained overalls joined the fray and managed to pull Steele to the ground. Fighting off several concerned passers-by, the woman ran off towards the car park.

Marshall rewound the film slightly until he found the best view of the victim.

Margaret Wilson stared back at them.

"Shit." Mark peered hard at the screen and the picture he still held. "Did she have a twin?"

Marshall could feel icy fingers creeping down his spine. "No, she didn't. What's more…" He hesitated.

"John?"

"I've seen the skirt before. I'd swear that's what was round the legs when Hickson had her laid out in the lab."

"Seriously?"

"Get Hickson up here with a sample. Don't tell him why."

Marshall stared at the woman while Mark phoned Hickson. If he didn't know that Margaret Wilson's body was decomposing in the lab, he would have sworn that this was her visiting Sainsbury's. A little wild eyed, perhaps, and dishevelled, but definitely the professor.

Except that wasn't possible.

He began to feel some sympathy for Ryan Steele. The sight of this woman must have given him quite a turn.

"What's so urgent?" Hickson must have run up the stairs. "Hey, where did you find that? Is that the day she died?" He held out an evidence bag holding a scrap of material. "I see, yes, that's what she was wearing. Good find, John."

"That was taken this morning," Marshall said, happier now he knew it wasn't just him seeing things.

"Bollocks."

Marshall waited.

"You're not joking. Then who the fuck is that? Because it looks... Oh, bugger, are you saying my corpse...? But DNA..." He stopped, took a deep breath. "So who the hell did Ryan Steele kill?"

"He thinks he killed Margaret Wilson. So, when he saw this woman earlier he thought he'd seen a ghost."

"Right." Hickson stared closely at the screen. "DNA for the corpse I have downstairs matched the samples taken from her apartment so my corpse is positively the body of Ryan Steele's victim. But this suggests that he didn't kill Margaret Wilson." He paused. "Though he obviously thinks he did."

"And the skirt? Why does this woman look like your corpse even down to the clothes she is wearing?"

"You need to ask her."

"We haven't got her. She ran away."

The three of them stood in silence for a minute and then Hickson slapped Marshall's shoulder. "Got it."

"Really?"

"What does Ryan do when he sees his supposed victim?"

"Attack her."

"And what does that do to his parole?"

"It'll keep him locked up."

"So, if you wanted him to stay locked up. For example, if you were annoyed that he got away with a GBH charge instead of a murder one. Wouldn't this be a great way to do it?"

"But that's a hell of a disguise. It could be her."

"Then maybe start with family," Hickson said as he left. "They'd have a head start at looking like her."

"We...e...ll, I suppose it's worth a shot." Marshall looked again at the screen. "It'd almost take plastic surgery though."

*

Before Marshall could make a start on investigating relatives, Nick Sharp stuck his head round the door, WPC Gill Ashton hesitating behind him.

"I think I've worked out who took the camera," he said cheerfully. "Take a look at this." He pushed a memory stick into Marshall's computer.

They crowded round the screen which showed CCTV footage taken from the lab entrance. A young woman who Marshall recognised was entering. She strode confidently through, empty handed.

"I know her, CPS woman, was there collecting evidence last time I went down to the lab. Emily something."

"Frazer," Nick supplied. "Now, look." He directed their attention back to the screen. "Hickson leaves shortly after." The screen showed the forensic expert hurrying from the building clutching his bag.

"I think he trusts her," Marshall said. "As CPS, she must have clearance."

"Possibly," Nick said, "but here she is leaving." They watched Emily Frazer heading towards the camera, manhandling an evidence box awkwardly with one hand so that with the other she could throw something at the camera. Whatever it was stuck and blurred the lens briefly. In the fuzz, a second person could be seen leaving behind Emily but not clearly enough to work out who.

"See," Nick said. "Why do that if it wasn't her?"

"Or, more likely, the person who left with her, because we can tell it's Emily. Which," Marshall said, "makes her an accessory."

"Any way we can clean that up to work out who it is with her?" Mark asked.

"Tried, that's probably as clear as it gets," Nick said, "but Gill and I have been working on it a little – hope you don't mind me asking her to help – and we have a thought you are probably not going to like. Thanks to Gill's detective work."

"Go on," Marshall said, glancing at where Gillian was hovering by the door and waving her in. "What do I not want to know?"

"Well," Gillian said, coming over to join them, "the name rang a bell from somewhere – Emily Frazer – but I couldn't remember where. I'd seen it recently so I went back through all the Wilson case files this morning – the ones that we pulled out when her body was discovered – and managed to track it down. Found it a few minutes ago."

"Go on."

"Emily Frazer is Professor Wilson's niece."

"Oh shit!" Mark said.

"The professor helped bring her up. Her own mother – Margaret's sister – died of cancer when Emily was in her early teens. It's a side note in the Wilson case; Emily was one of the family interviewed in passing, not really relevant, so it took me a while to find her."

"Well done for remembering the name," Marshall said, "and that explains why she was a bit put out when she saw the corpse in the lab the other day. I wish I'd known. Craig and I weren't exactly sympathetic, wittering on about cameras and wardrobes and…" He tailed off. "Tell me you haven't had the thought I just had."

"Probably," Nick said cheerfully. "Ryan Steele did attack someone he thought was Margaret Wilson outside Sainsbury's. Makes more sense if it actually was Margaret Wilson… sort of."

"Does the camera do that?" Mark asked.

"We could try asking Hickson," Marshall said.

"Will he know?"

"Probably not but he's the only one, barring Harrison Campbell, who's seen the thing in action." Marshall picked up the phone to call the lab.

"Emily Frazer," he said when Hickson picked up.

"Nice lass," Hickson replied. "You met her the other day, works for the CPS."

"Got her on screen here in the lab the day the camera went missing."

"So? She's in and out all the time."

"You left her alone. We can see you leaving before her."

"She's CPS, John, you don't seriously—"

"Margaret Wilson's niece."

There was a brief silence on the other end of the line. "Why the camera?" Hickson said in a tone of voice which said he didn't really need the answer but he didn't want to hear it either.

"To take a picture."

"Of?"

"Come on, Craig, of Margaret Wilson." Marshall waited for a response and, when it wasn't forthcoming, added, "Emily left with someone and made a point of obscuring the camera so we can't tell who it is. Why else would she do that?"

When Hickson still said nothing, Marshall looked round at the circle of expectant faces and then continued, "Could the camera do that, Craig? Has she recreated her aunt?"

"I got a mug," Craig said slowly. "I wouldn't have even thought to try a person. Oh God, why would you do that?"

"Bring back the person you love," Marshall said, "and we handed her the means and opportunity on a plate."

"Oh God," Hickson said again. "Find it and destroy it, John, we can't have people being recreated."

"No need to fear death," Marshall suggested.

"Murder without consequences," Hickson snapped back. "Ryan Steele just produces recreated victim and walks out Scot free. Or some villain makes a copy of a murder weapon – couldn't have been my gun that did it, Inspector, because I have mine here. It would absolutely crucify the justice system. John, we need to get rid of it!" Hickson slammed the phone down.

Marshall put his receiver down slowly. "I think you all probably heard that. Someone go and pick up Emily Frazer and, if our hunch is correct, Professor Wilson. Make sure you bring the camera and—"

The phone rang, interrupting Marshall's instructions. "CID," he snapped into it as he picked it up.

"Sorry, sir, Sergeant Wilson, incident room," the voice on the other end said, placatingly. "I know you're rather busy, but just had a call from a rather distressed gentleman, got a strange woman trying to get into his house. I think the description matches your woman who was attacked at Sainsbury's."

"Where?" Marshall waved his hand to stop the office emptying.

"89 Bluebell Road, Manor Estate."

"I'll send someone." Marshall put the phone down. "Need someone to go to 89 Bluebell Road."

"89 Bluebell Road?" Gillian interrupted. "Sorry, John, but I think that's Margaret Wilson's last known address."

"She's gone home," Mark suggested after a brief pause as people digested this information. "She may be new but she has old memories, I suppose. Not sure she will even know she's dead... if she is dead... has been dead." Mark sighed. "You know what I mean."

"Right," Marshall said. "Mark, with me, we'll take this one. Helen, you and Nick, track down an address for Emily Frazer and pick her up, with or without her aunt."

*

Two uniformed officers had already made it to Bluebell Road when Marshall drew up outside number 89. They were embroiled in an argument with a tall, elderly man in a cardigan and slippers, and Margaret Wilson's doppelganger.

"I've lived here for eight years," the man was saying, "and I can prove it. The woman's mad."

"This is my house," she said. "I've lived here for twenty-four years. If you'd just let me in, I can find you the documents."

Another car screeched to a halt behind Marshall's and a young woman in trainers and a tracksuit raced past them as they headed up the garden path, leaving the car door wide open. "Auntie Meg, Auntie Meg, you have to come with me." She grabbed the professor's arm.

"We'll deal with this," Marshall told the uniformed officers. "I think there's a bit of a 'misunderstanding' here." Marshall helped turn the professor away from the front door. "You need to come with us and Emily – it is Emily, isn't it?" She looked rather less professional than last time he'd seen her.

"Yes, I've been trying to find her all day. She left in the night."

"Sorry you were disturbed," Mark told the bewildered house owner. "Leave it to us, she's a bit confused."

They ushered the two women back out on to the pavement.

"But that's my house," Margaret Wilson said.

"Not any more, Auntie."

"You haven't told her," Marshall said. "Haven't explained what you've done."

Emily shook her head. "I didn't know how to. It was a spur of the moment thing."

"Why did you do it?"

"I wanted my auntie back. She's the only family I ever had. She brought me up when Mum died. And when her body was found and I heard what you were saying about that camera – it was like a gift."

"How did you know it actually worked?"

"I tried it out, photographed a stapler. I was going to put it back but she ran away in the night and I've spent the day finding her."

"So you didn't intentionally send her to Sainsbury's this morning?" Mark said.

"Why would I?"

"To frighten Ryan Steele and make sure he stayed locked up."

"What was Ryan Steele doing at Sainsbury's?"

"Never mind." Marshall was convinced; she wasn't in this for revenge. Ryan Steele running into Margaret Wilson had been a tragic coincidence. "May I suggest, Mrs Wilson, that you might find pressing charges for this morning's incident an uncomfortable experience."

"I don't understand."

"Your niece will explain, I'm sure." He didn't envy them that conversation. How do you tell someone they've been dead for years? "Miss Frazer, this is your problem, you created it. I don't want to see her again, is that clear?"

"As crystal, Inspector."

"Give me the camera."

She reached into her car and collected it from the passenger seat.

"Now take her away and convince her to be someone else and then come by the station later so we can consider what theft of evidence might do to your career." He guessed, probably nothing, as he didn't think it was anything she would ever do again and he was contemplating doing something even more serious himself.

They watched the two women drive off.

"What are you going to do with it?" Mark seemed to be trying very hard not to try and take the camera off Marshall. His hands were clasped behind his back like a naughty school child.

Marshall took a pen from his jacket pocket and placed it on the pavement and then crouched down beside it. He focused carefully and pressed the button to take a photograph. There was a small flash and an identical pen lay beside his.

"Well I never," he said softly to himself. He picked up both pens, placed them back in his pocket and then put the camera down behind the front wheel of his car. Ignoring Mark's gasp, he started the ignition and very slowly drove backwards over the camera.

"A shame, it seems to have fallen in the road while we were recovering it," he said.

"But it could have—" Mark began.

"Caused chaos," Marshall said. "Cameras might not lie, but Hickson was right; this one would have facilitated just about every other evil I can think of."

"And Ryan Steele?"

"Attacked someone while out on licence and admitted to the murder of Margaret Wilson," Marshall said. "I think it's best he stays locked up for a while longer and if his experience acts to make him a little less sure of himself, that's probably not a bad thing. Now bag the pieces and we're going to go and find a shop in Butchers' Passage."

*

Marshall couldn't have said how he knew, but he was absolutely certain the strange shop would be there this time. He strode down the small alley, clutching the bag of camera bits, his sergeant a step behind.

The door was there, where it had been last time he'd found it, set incongruously in Argos' back wall.

Marshall didn't pause but slammed the door open and waited as the slim woman rose from her seat behind the desk. She seemed unsurprised.

"Inspector, do come in."

Marshall took a deep breath and tried for professionalism. "Miss Morgan. I believe you might be able to help us in our enquiries."

"I know all that, Inspector."

"Humour me!" Marshall snapped and exchanged a glance with Mark. "Assume I'm not psychic."

The woman laughed. "Good point, Inspector, fire ahead."

Marshall paused and then decided the police rule book wasn't designed to cope with situations like this. "I believe you have had dealings with a suspect in a death we are investigating. One Harrison Campbell tells us you gave him a camera which he then used with disastrous consequences."

"Was that his name? I did indeed give a young man a camera, on trial, yes. I am awaiting its return or payment for it." She smiled at Marshall as if she already knew what he was holding. "What the young man chose to do with it is not my concern." She paused, rearranging her face to look more serious. "Unless, of course, he has tried to sell it on or dispose of my property."

Marshall ignored this hint to discuss the camera. "No, just killed someone using it." If, that was, they could prove to a court the camera's ability to recreate wardrobes now that it was in pieces. Not to mention, proving Harrison had had any idea it would do so.

"As I said, Inspector, my customers' use of what they obtain is hardly my concern."

"No, but it is mine, and this camera," he waved the bag of pieces at her, "has caused quite enough trouble in my town. I'm not convinced, madam, that you really don't know the havoc your goods create but I am returning this with explicit instructions that it will not be used again."

"It doesn't look to be in the condition I left it in."

"No," Marshall said sharply, "unfortunately, it was dropped into the road during the disturbance where it was recovered." He held the woman's eye, refusing to blink or back down.

She nodded. "I see, Inspector. As I said, I cannot be held responsible for what others do with my goods, but I do understand that some of their actions are not in the best interests of the law and order within Fenwick. Thank you for returning it. I assume you would be happier for me not to find someone who can repair it."

"You assume right," Marshall said, placing the bag on the nearest table. "Good day to you."

He turned and left without looking back, Mark matching him pace for pace up the alley.

"Now," Marshall said when he had calmed slightly, "let's take the long way home, we need to agree what just happened."

*

He used the cloned pen later that afternoon to write up the 'new' version of the day's events that they'd agreed on – it seemed appropriate, somehow.

Hindsight

Inspector John Marshall squeezed his wife's hand briefly, took a deep breath and stood up. He shared a brief glance with Sergeant Mark Sherbourne who was sitting across the table and smiled slightly. He wasn't sure whether he ought to thank his sergeant or not, it depended how the next five minutes went. It was definitely due to Mark's encouragement that Marshall now found himself about to sing in front of a room full of people – something he had never done before.

At least they were a welcoming audience and likely to be kind and positive about his attempt. That didn't necessarily make it any less frightening but he'd faced down murderers and mobs in his time so a few verses of a folk song should be manageable.

He'd picked a song he had heard in War Horse. He and Marian had seen the production in the West End just before they had moved to Fenwick and the words of this particular number had stuck in his head – 'the year turns round again'. Well, it had, twice since they'd moved and, despite the strange things he'd encountered in the town, he hadn't regretted a day of his move to Fenwick.

He glanced round the room as he sang; a room full of people, many of whom he could call friends from sharing evenings out –

something which wouldn't have happened in the capital. He had so far resisted Mark's attempts to drag him along to join the Fenwick Morris Men on all but one occasion but a lot of them turned up to sing and play at the various folk clubs and sessions which he and Marian had begun to frequent. Most were here tonight to support the newest session in the area; men he'd met through Mark and through his involvement with the Smith Foundation Library which is where they all were tonight.

He had learnt to love the music and the people were talented but modest. Even his girls were welcome though they had left them at home tonight as it was a school day. Sophie rattled a tambourine along to tunes and was picking up some song words even though Marshall seriously hoped she didn't have any idea what all the innuendos meant. Kate was attempting the violin with lessons provided by Steve, another of the Fenwick Morris Men. This had involved rather less 'strangled cat' noises than Marshall had feared.

He waved his hand in the circular motion that he had learnt indicated a reprise of the final chorus and caught Jenny grinning at him. The young librarian who ran this particular session stuck up her thumbs as she sang. Marshall looked behind her and caught sight of David, her predecessor, lounging on a chair in the corner behind the casks of beer that Jenny had laid on to encourage people to come to a session outside of a pub. Marshall was always made slightly uncomfortable by David's presence as the ex-librarian was technically deceased but tonight the older man also grinned at Marshall and raised his thumbs. Marshall felt a glow of pleasure as he came to the end of the song and applause rang out.

Marian gave him a hug as he sat back down. "See, I knew you could do it."

"Didn't go too badly," Marshall agreed. "I remembered all the words."

"Brilliant," Mark said, leaning forward. "Lovely song."

Several others added their congratulations as another tune was begun by Bob on his accordion further down the long table.

"Good key," Julian said from Marshall's other side. He was another of the Morris Men. "G if you're interested." He had a guitar cradled on his lap.

"I just sang," Marshall said. "It's amazing how you can work it out and then play along."

"Years of practise," Julian said, "and you're consistent, some people change keys all over the place. Now this one," a woman had risen at the other end of the room to begin a new song, "seems to be in E flat so is a bit more of a challenge." He moved his capo along the neck of this guitar until he was happy that he was matching what the woman was singing.

"More of a challenge for those of us without a capo," Mark said, waving his penny whistle at Marshall and then indicating the melodeons Colin and Ian were resolutely not playing, though Ian was in the process of putting his down to pick up a concertina.

Marshall wasn't really listening; the woman who was singing was a woman he recognised. A woman who ran a very strange shop that he had had cause to visit a couple of times recently. She was not a regular at the sessions. She was tall and slim with a mass of curly black hair and, today, was dressed in a vibrant assortment of colours.

"Morgan," he mouthed at Mark.

"So I see," Mark said. "Anyone know her?" He spoke to those round them.

Julian shook his head. "I feel I might have seen her before but not for a while."

"Nice song," Marshall said. The woman was singing about unicorns.

"Bill Caddick one," Steve said from the other side of Julian, pausing in trying to pick out the tune on his fiddle. "Not heard it in years."

The evening continued with a mix of songs and tunes. Many of them Marshall was beginning to recognise and be able to join in with.

"Your turn next time," he teased Marian as the final strains of 'Rolling Home' faded and they began to put coats on. She aimed a playful punch at him as they headed towards the exit.

Jenny had moved to stand near the heavy wooden door and wish people a safe journey home. The lady in the brightly coloured dress was standing with her as Marshall and Marian approached.

"Nice singing," Marshall said.

"You too." Piercing blue eyes looked into his. "I gather it was your first time – well done." She smiled and headed out before he could respond.

"Didn't know she could sing," Marshall said as he gave Jenny a quick hug.

"Who is she?" Jenny said, frowning.

"Woman from that strange shop in Butchers' Passage that you had the advert for. I did tell you about it."

"Yes, not met her before. Perhaps integrating herself. I hope she comes again, though, good voice."

*

"A good evening," Jenny said as the last guest departed and she was left alone with David who came forward from the corner he had been skulking in. "You could join in, you know."

"I make them uncomfortable," David said with a shrug. "Too many know what happened at Christmas."

Jenny opened her mouth to argue but then decided not to bother. The position of Smith Foundation Librarian was a unique one. She might understand David's position but very few would. He had died to pass on the role so the fact that, here in the library, he could still turn up to advise her was a fact that most of her friends rather pointedly avoided noticing.

"Inspector sang quite nicely," she contented herself with saying.

"Agreed," David smiled, "very human our policeman is turning out to be. Even a hug for you."

"You know who the woman was who sang about unicorns?"

"Yes," David frowned, "haven't seen her in years. Morgan. I thought she was avoiding me this time round. She has that shop in Butchers' Passage which supplies some interesting items. There is a pair of glasses in the office which I... obtained... the first time she passed through."

"Obtained?"

David didn't answer, just raised his eyebrows.

Jenny grinned. "Yes, I know, the place was involved in that case of the inspector's a few weeks ago. I assume the glasses are the item you told him you stole?"

David smiled broadly. "Good girl. And little use to me they were. What Morgan provides is only for those who really require it."

"The glasses?"

"I thought I needed them. I was wrong. Don't worry about it." He dismissed the topic. "Now let me help you clear up."

*

Ollie Ward gave a resounding final smash to the cymbal and sat back. His mum stuck her head round his bedroom door.

"Sounding good. Don't think I recognise that one. How'd it go last night?"

"All right. Josh got wasted so I had to take him home but we went down well."

"Get paid this time?"

"Yeah, not a lot, but the landlord gave us free drinks all night too."

"Hence Josh overdoing it."

"He always does, though only after we finish," Ollie admitted, "but he's a bloody good singer and he doesn't object to singing my stuff either."

"We missed you at the session. The men were asking after you." His mum smiled. "Julian even sang one of yours."

Ollie grinned. "Seriously? That's good of him."

"Told your dad he thinks you're the next Dylan."

"No way, next Rory or Calum MacDonald." Runrig had been his favourite band since the family's first trip to Skye when Ollie was eight. Hence pushing his mates to join him in a folk rock band. Fenwick's suburbs weren't as romantic as the Scottish isles but Proterra's mix of modern standards alongside fast folk tunes and self-penned songs was going down well in the local pubs and clubs.

"So, earning enough to avoid getting a part-time job yet?" His mum smiled to take the sting from her words.

"Not yet," Ollie sighed. "I've an interview in town this afternoon at Argos." Saturdays spent working would eat into valuable practice time with the band but Conlan – their guitarist – worked in a car wash on Saturdays too, so it wasn't a disaster. Ollie could still practise and perform in the evenings round his A-level work and he wouldn't complain about making a little more money than the gigs brought in. Last night had been a rare landlord; mostly what the band earned in an evening just about paid for the drinks at the bar.

Ollie had his eye on a new Zildjian cymbal which wasn't cheap and, though they were supportive, he couldn't expect his parents to keep paying to expand the drum kit. Particularly not when they'd bought him a car for his seventeenth, so he could transport the kit to bookings.

"What time's the interview?"

Ollie checked his watch. "In about forty-five minutes, I better get going." He holstered the drumsticks he'd been idly twiddling. "Which one did Julian sing?"

"May Serenade. Sounded good on the guitar."

"Bet it did. I'll get him to show Conlan what he's playing in the chorus." Julian was one of the Fenwick Morris Men who Ollie's dad danced with and he was the best guitarist Ollie knew. Luckily, Conlan happened to agree and sought out Julian's advice and tuition whenever Ollie wrote anything new for the band.

"Julian said were you going to make May Day as he'd like to hear you sing it."

Fenwick Morris Men danced in the dawn on the first of May each summer at the Five Ladies stone circle above West Cross, followed by a fry-up and breakfast session in the Highwayman.

"Wouldn't miss it for the world," Ollie said. "Now I need to get to this interview."

*

Argos, unfortunately, didn't seem hugely interested in a drum-playing college student with no shop experience and Ollie felt the interview could have gone better than it did.

Leaving the store, he turned down Butchers' Passage alongside as the fastest way to get to the multi-storey car park and, incidentally, a walk which would take him past the music store in Back Lane which had the cymbal he wanted in the window display.

The bodhran in the window of the shop in Butchers' Passage brought Ollie to a halt. He had one very similar at home which he took out to sessions. The one in front of him had a rather nice harp painted onto the skin whereas his was plain.

After a few seconds of trying to see if there was a price, a small card in the top of the window caught Ollie's eye.

'Saturday staff required,' it read in ornate lettering, 'enquire within.'

After a further few moments of considering why he'd never noticed 'Morgan's Miscellany' before, Ollie decided to step inside and see if the place was keener on a drummer than Argos had been.

A small bell attached to the door tinkled to acknowledge his arrival as Ollie entered the shop. The place was subtly lit; on the gloomy side, Ollie decided as he walked into a small table just inside the door. It was also a mix of weird and wonderful items and was stocked in no recognisable order. Ollie paused and glanced round to see if there was anyone amongst the clutter. A woman with long black hair and a multi-coloured skirt and scarf was heading towards him from the back of the shop.

"Can I help you?" She smiled. "I noticed you looking at the bodhran. Would you like to try it?"

"I was more interested in the 'staff wanted' sign," Ollie said, stifling interest in a bodhran he probably couldn't afford – definitely not if he wanted the cymbal he had his eye on.

"Staff wanted… ah yes… Saturdays only, I'm afraid, at present."

"That's fine, I need to do college work in evenings," Ollie said.

"And band practice?"

Ollie blinked in amazement. "How did you know?"

"Oh, I just assumed, when you were interested in the drum. Most lads your age with a musical frame of mind belong to at least one band." It sounded false, something she had made up to account for her definitive statement about band practice.

Ollie stared hard at the woman but she didn't say anything more so he shrugged. "Yes, and band practice," he admitted.

"Are you good?"

"We think so," Ollie said. "Getting the odd gig in local pubs."

"Folk music," she stated and then smiled, "I assume, as you were interested in the bodhran."

"Yes, well a mix, do some rock too." Ollie hesitated then added, "I play percussion, full set as well as the bodhran." The woman who had interviewed him in Argos hadn't seemed impressed by this fact but this woman nodded cheerfully.

"Excellent. Well, if you do a good job I may be tempted to throw the bodhran in with your first wage packet."

"Oh... er... does that mean I've got the job?"

"Don't see why not."

"But, don't you want a CV or to ask me some things?"

"I have, and I like the look of you, which is most important. And the shop invited you in, so that'll do for me."

"I beg your pardon?"

The woman smiled and ignored him. "I'm Morgan, welcome aboard."

*

"Butchers' Passage?" Ollie's mum queried. "I didn't think there were any shops down there."

"Me neither, perhaps it's new," Ollie said. "Called Morgan's Miscellany, real mix of weird and wonderful things it sells. Some new age stuff, some ethnic, some antiques as far as I could see. The woman in charge has offered to give me the bodhran they've got as part of my first pay packet. Don't know whether she was serious but it's a better response than I got in Argos."

"What hours, just Saturdays?"

"Yes, that's what she said."

"Contract?"

"Yes, I know, I'll make sure I get one on Saturday when I go in.

I'm not an idiot, Mum."

"I know that, sweetheart, but this place doesn't sound hugely business-like. Make sure you're covered."

Ollie sighed. "You want me to try somewhere else?"

"I didn't say that, I just meant to be careful. Don't get taken for a ride." She gave his arm a quick squeeze. "Sounds like more your kind of place, to be honest, than a big supermarket, but cover your back."

"Will do. Thanks, Mum."

So now he had a job and, hopefully, would soon have some money as well as a budding musical career. Ollie grinned and picked up his drumsticks; life was good. He'd practise May Serenade ready for May Day and maybe he could engineer it, so that he was singing when the local rag came to take pictures of the morris men dancing the sun up, and he could publicise Proterra's next gig.

*

Jenny headed back to her office and living quarters at the rear of the library to grab some lunch. It was late as she had been quite busy; something she had noticed happening each month in the day or two after the music session. Perhaps the people who came to sing and play were reminded that the library existed or spotted books they fancied reading and so came back while they remembered.

As she was eating her sandwich, Jenny had a wander round the many cases that lined the walls of her office and living space. There were several cabinets holding a wealth of curiosities and one of them contained several pairs of glasses. Two pairs were ancient, wire-rimmed affairs; one was a wraparound item that looked like something out of a sci-fi movie. Jenny could imagine it shooting lasers out of the eye slit or allowing the wearer to x-ray objects or look at them in infra-red. The last pair of glasses had a set of heavy black frames and what looked like a librarian's date stamp as part of the nose piece. They were quite frankly, ugly and probably only useful if your eyesight was in serious need of help.

Jenny couldn't imagine David wanting any of the pairs, or the woman from last night being the one who supplied them. She had been expecting something brighter coloured or flowery to suit the 'hippy' vibe the woman had given off. Nothing in the display case matched her expectations.

"Oh well, maybe they're not here," Jenny muttered and went back to her tuna sandwich. She ought to get back to the front desk and she wasn't really interested in glasses. She was more intrigued by a shop which appeared in Butchers' Passage but that was something she couldn't go and see for herself, which was probably why she was feeling a touch annoyed today. Most of the time she could cope with the limits set to her world. The people she knew and loved came to her. Jenny hoped the woman – Morgan – would come into the library again and Jenny could ask about the shop.

*

As if the desire had conjured her, the woman in question was lounging beside the counter when Jenny arrived back. Her clothing was more subdued today – a long black skirt and purple vest top – though her smile still sparkled.

"You must be Jenny," she said, offering her hand. "I enjoyed your session last night. David was librarian here last time I was in town."

"Yes, he said," Jenny replied without stopping to think.

The woman smiled again. "I thought I saw him last night, give him my regards."

"Will do." Jenny wasn't sure whether she was imagining the knowing look in the bright blue eyes. "Can I help you?"

"No, just looking round," she leaned towards Jenny and lowered her voice, "but there's a lady crying in one of the seats in the corner down the back there. I tried to help but I don't know this place like you do. You'll be able to be of more use."

"Oh, right." Jenny hesitated but as she was offered nothing more and she couldn't think of a way to introduce the issue of appearing shops she contented herself with saying, "Thanks, I'll see what I can do," and heading off in the direction indicated.

*

A trim middle-aged lady, her hair cut in a neat chestnut bob, was sitting in one of the wing-back chairs which scattered the alcoves of the library. She wasn't crying though the small pile of tissues on the coffee table in front of her suggested she had been doing so recently.

"Hi, I'm Jenny, the librarian here." Jenny pulled another chair closer. "Can I help you at all?"

"No, it's all right. I lost my husband a couple of months ago and it still hits me sometimes without warning."

"Oh, I'm so sorry." Jenny wasn't sure how she could help but she did her best. "Was it books on bereavement you were looking for… er…"

"Alison, Alison Miller. No, I didn't want anything; I just find it peaceful here."

Jenny remembered her own first days in the library, trying to get over the grief of losing her father and could understand that. "Okay, if you're sure. A lady at the desk was a little concerned and wondered if I might be of use but I don't want to intrude."

"There was a woman. She told me about some glasses she had loaned to you. I was going to find them, look at them."

Jenny frowned; glasses again, loaned not stolen? Why hadn't the Morgan woman mentioned this, and what was so special about these glasses? "I'm sorry, I believe they're in a case in the office. I don't have them on display." She had considered putting some of the items from the cabinets out in the main library but she had no idea of the provenance or history of most of them. Some of them – like the glasses – might not even belong to the library at all which could lead to awkward questions being asked of her. One day she planned to get David to explain what all the objects were so she could put together an exhibition properly, but she hadn't got round to it yet.

"Oh, right," Alison said. "I see." She smiled tremulously. "Silly thing, really, but I think that woman was just trying to take my mind off things."

Jenny nodded vaguely, feeling awkward. "Well, if there's nothing I can do…"

"No, thank you, you're very kind."

Jenny left her to her peaceful corner and hurried back to the desk but Morgan was gone so she was deprived of any chance to ask about stolen glasses or shops where they shouldn't be.

She made a mental note to track David down about both and what it all meant and then went back to cataloguing books – a challenging task in the ever-changing environment of the Smith Foundation Library.

*

Alison Miller left the main entrance of the library and hurried into the crowds in Museum Street. Her fingers were clutched tightly round the pair of glasses stuffed inside her coat pocket.

She wasn't entirely sure why she had taken them, just that any straw to clutch at was better than the wilderness inside. Very little had touched her in the last fifteen years, until Guy's death had opened the floodgates to all the pain again. Becoming a thief too hardly seemed to matter.

The strange woman had been most insistent that these glasses could help her see the past clearly and move on – a large claim for a pair of glasses but the recollection of the hypnotic eyes boring into hers wouldn't leave Alison's memory.

So she'd crept into the library's office and taken them. She could always replace them if she was being fooled – something the very small rational part of her admitted was likely – and that she was doing most of the fooling of herself.

*

Ollie put the light out and closed his eyes; he was hopefully tired enough to sleep now. Luckily he didn't have early lectures in the morning so a three o'clock bedtime wasn't too much of an issue.

Proterra didn't usually do midweek gigs but the charity event had been for a friend of Conlan's mum so they'd made an exception. The music had gone down really well and they had played through until after midnight. According to the hostess, they had raised over a thousand for the local Samaritans and Ollie didn't think it did the band any harm to be noted for 'good works', even if the fee they'd asked was a lot less than usual.

Once they'd packed up and he'd got home it had been very late and it had taken him some while to come down from the high engendered by playing. Ollie never really understood Josh's desire to drink at a gig; the playing gave him enough of a buzz so that some nights he barely slept at all afterwards.

Lying in bed, Ollie went over the evening in his head. There were a couple of songs they needed to work on – newer ones where the flow hadn't been quite as good as it should be – but most of it had sounded good. Several of the guests had said very flattering things about the song-writing as well as the playing and, gratifyingly, his new boss had been present as well. She had been most positive about the music and told him the bodhran was his to take on Saturday. Hopefully she hadn't been drinking and would remember this promise, once Saturday actually came round.

Smiling happily to himself, Ollie drifted off into pleasant dreams of crowded stadiums and headlining festivals.

*

Marshall watched the Scene of Crime team carefully manoeuvring equipment. Dr Trent crouched by the body while Hickson gingerly stepped round her, photographing bloody footprints and spatter patterns and dusting every surface for prints. It was a process he had witnessed a hundred times before and he was always slightly horrified to realise that he was bored. He wanted to get on, and though he knew this painstaking investigation of the body and its surroundings was necessary, he had long ceased to be fascinated by the technical wizardry, which told him where the killer had stood and what he had used. That was particularly the case when, as here, it all seemed blindingly obvious. The blood, the carving knife and the large holes in the victim's chest told Marshall all he really needed to know.

"Well, doctor?" Liza Trent had finished her examination.

"All done. Take him away."

"Knifed to death, I assume?"

"Looks that way. Victim is late teenage, was attacked from the front and put up some struggle but didn't stand much chance. Been dead about four or five hours. I'll have more for you after the post mortem."

"Thank you, Liza." She nodded briefly and left, her sensible shoes making no noise on the hard floor.

Marshall looked round. The back room of 5, Primrose Street was a fairly standard suburban dining room. A French window opened out onto the back garden and a hatch in the side wall allowed food and plates to be passed back and forwards to the kitchen. A small round table with four chairs sat in the middle of the room, though it had been knocked off centre by the falling victim. A dresser ran along the length of the wall opposite the hatch. Marshall would place money on it being mahogany effect rather than real wood. A single door led out into the hall.

The force of the knife blows to the victim's chest had spread blood far and wide and someone – presumably the killer – had left bloody footprints across the wooden flooring.

"What can you tell me, Craig?" The inspector had waited for the removal of the corpse before asking, to allow Hickson time to perform his intricate routine.

"Well, he was facing the hatch and the killer stood in front of him so was presumably already in the room when the victim entered. If the killer entered the room second, then you'd expect the victim to be facing the other way or to have been stabbed in the back."

Marshall had already sized up the situation himself so he nodded. "That makes sense. So, a disturbed burglar?"

"Possibly. Though we can't find any sign of forced entry."

"What else?"

"The knife doesn't match the block in the kitchen though it has the look of being from a set; therefore I think either the victim or the killer must have brought it with them. And then there's this oddity."

"Go on."

"Look at the footprints."

A line of prints led away from where the corpse had lain towards the hatch to the kitchen.

"Our killer put something through the hatch?"

"No. Come here." Hickson crouched by the wall.

Marshall picked his way carefully across the room and bent down beside the other officer. Very clearly against the wall, a heel print stood out. He frowned. "That's not possible."

"Not without taking your heel off your shoe, cutting it in half and ramming it up against the wall. Not something the average killer does in the middle of a getaway." Hickson smiled. "It gets better, follow me."

He led the way out of the room, down the small hall and into the kitchen. The line of bloody footprints continued across the kitchen, starting by the hatch, and out of the back door into the side alley. Hickson again crouched by the wall. "Here."

There, under the hatch, was a toe print.

"So what does that tell us?" Marshall was nonplussed.

"Well, judging by the regular stride length and the piece missing between heel print and toe print being about the correct width, I'd say our killer walked out through the wall." Hickson was obviously enjoying this.

Marshall nodded practically, refusing to join in the joke. "So, you're looking for a false door here, round the hatch."

"No." Hickson shook his head, suddenly serious. "We've looked. Solid brick. He or she walked out through a solid wall."

*

Marshall crossed the hall to the front room where Constable Helen Lovell was sitting with a well-dressed young woman. They were drinking tea, which Marshall always thought was no real cure for the horror of finding a corpse. He noted the contrast between the two of them, Lovell in her comfortable trousers and severe white blouse with her hair pulled back into a neat bun and the other, dressed in an expensive-looking trouser suit, glittering with jewellery and with her dyed, blonde hair hanging in beautifully sculpted waves to her shoulders.

"Mrs Sutherland?" Marshall sat on the settee next to his colleague. "This must have been a terrible shock for you."

She nodded. "Yes, I was just telling your constable. It's quite creepy because I must have been home half an hour before I found him and all the time he was lying there." Her voice shook a little but was almost immediately brought under control. Marshall judged this to be a rather capable young woman who was managing to take even the horror of finding a dead body in her dining room fairly well. Judging shrewdly, he wondered how capable. Perhaps she had found a live body in her dining room and dealt with it accordingly.

"Half an hour? What were you doing, if you don't mind going over it again for me?"

"Well, I came in and went straight up, as I normally do, to shower and change after work. I was early today because we were going out tonight to celebrate. I've just got a promotion. I took a bit more trouble over getting changed and make-up and so on. Then I came down to have a cup of tea while I waited for Jez and I thought I'd draw the curtains in the dining room. I normally do it after tea but we weren't going to be eating in there." She stopped as if realising that he probably didn't need that sort of detail. "Anyway, I went in and there he was."

"Can you tell me who he is?"

"Me? No. I've never seen him before in my life. I sort of hoped, Inspector, that you could tell me what he was doing in my dining room."

*

"Right," Marshall said, looking round his small team, "we have an unknown young man, repeatedly stabbed with some considerable force by a killer who then – according to Hickson – walked out through a wall. Our initial thought, of the victim disturbing the killer, makes no sense if the victim was the one who shouldn't have been there. Time of death is lunchtime, say midday to one o'clock so,

Helen, can we check that Mrs Sutherland was at work and didn't come home even earlier than she's making out and surprise him? Better check on her husband too and, Gill, I want house-to-house enquiries down... which flower is it today?" The town planners on the Manor Estate had obviously had a book on local flora.

"Primrose Street," Mark supplied.

"Right, Primrose Street. See if the neighbours saw the youth or anyone else entering the property or anyone leaving it. Nick, check missing persons – though after so short a time there probably won't be anything useful – and contact the press. I shall give them a statement for the late news." There was a small silence while Marshall thought through his instructions but they'd all done this before and were becoming a tight-knit team he was proud of. "Let me know what you find."

He dismissed them, leaving just himself and Mark in the office.

"I assume Hickson has fingerprints," Mark said.

"That's only useful if our victim is on the system, so we'll look at other info too while we wait." Marshall took a breath. "Unfortunately, I also think we need to run an appeal for information; anyone acting strangely in Primrose Street yesterday or acting suspiciously around Manor Estate." Marshall hated appeals; the wading through rubbish and prank calls that followed took too much time but there was the occasional nugget.

"Wonderful!" Mark said, sharing Marshall's opinion.

Marshall retired to his desk and the difficult task of drafting a statement for the press that said just enough without giving too much away.

*

The appeal made the early evening news. Marshall, feeling as uncomfortable as he always did in front of the cameras, had managed a brief statement which omitted any real facts of interest and then asked for the public's help. He thought, watching it later in the staff canteen, that he looked stilted and awkward but Mark nodded approvingly. "Good one, John. You do sound professional doing that."

He shook his head. "I hate it, Mark. That was about the fifth time I'd said it because... oh, I don't know, the wind wasn't right or the light or the noise or something. I just think I sound bored of saying it."

"You were fine, sir," Gillian Ashton assured him, not yet having been around him long enough to always remember to use his first name.

By this time they knew that Mrs Sutherland had been at work until four in an office with seven other people, that Mr Sutherland had been defending a client in court all day and that either the inhabitants of Primrose Street had been particularly unobservant or there really had been nothing to see.

"You'd think," Mark Sherbourne noted, "that a killer who walked through walls would make some sort of impression."

"Hickson work out how that was done yet?" Marshall had a worrying feeling that this was going to be one of those cases that went nowhere fast.

"Nope. He still claims the killer walked through the blasted wall."

"And no idea who the corpse is?"

No-one answered what they assumed had been a rhetorical question.

Marshall sighed. "All right, let's sleep on it and hope the appeal brings us in something overnight."

*

Gillian Ashton was in before Marshall in the morning. Marshall found her leaning back in her chair sipping coffee while the computer screen flashed through a search.

"Morning, Constable. What did the appeal line give us?"

"Three possible identifications, twenty-seven descriptions of possible killers none of whom were actually seen in Primrose Street but they were all – according to the reports – acting suspiciously at midday yesterday, and one double glazing salesman."

"No pets stuck in trees or old biddies who are convinced their neighbours have buried someone under the new patio? I am impressed."

"Oh yes, sorry sir. A librarian who thinks her glasses have been stolen."

"There's always one." Marshall sighed. It looked like the appeal line had been even less helpful than normal.

"On the other hand." Gillian peered at the computer which had stopped scrolling. "I do know who the victim is."

"Yes?"

"We have a match on the system for his fingerprints. One Wayne Bradby."

"Wayne Bradby?" Nick and Mark entered the office on the tail end of the remarks. "That's a blast from the past," Nick said. "Right little shit, he was. Loud mouthed, violent, lost his licence years before he was old enough to own one. Then he vanished."

"Vanished?" Marshall asked in surprise.

"Yep, full missing persons act, the lot. Before your time, John, I was still in uniform so it must have been… ten… twelve years ago."

"Fifteen," Gillian contradicted, still reading the screen.

"God, has it really been that long? Probably a file still open on him somewhere, 'cos we never did find the little toe-rag."

"Well we have now," Marshall told him. "He's our corpse."

"Can't be," Nick said.

"Yes, I've run his fingerprints," Gillian objected.

"But, John, you said it was a young man, a teenager."

"Yes, twenty at most."

"Wayne Bradby was about seventeen when he vanished and if that was fifteen years ago, it's just not possible," Nick said.

"Perhaps someone kept the corpse in cold storage for fifteen years," Mark suggested cheerfully.

"Liza said it had been dead a few hours, so don't think that one will wash," Marshall said. "so, who wants the job of telling Hickson he's sent us the wrong bloody fingerprints?"

"Sir," Ashton interrupted, "the odd thing is, Wayne Bradby's last known address *was* 5 Primrose Street. Lived there with his mum."

"In which case, I'll go back to Primrose Street. There could be a connection, whoever the corpse is. I'll see if I can find someone who was there fifteen years ago. Mark, I'm giving you the short straw, so once you've seen Hickson, see if you can find the file on the missing Wayne Bradby."

*

The bodhran from the window was boxed and placed on the sales counter when Ollie arrived at work on Saturday morning.

"See," Morgan said with a smile, "I mean what I say. It's yours with good wishes for a long and profitable music career."

"Thank you, that's so kind." Ollie smiled and placed the box with his rucksack on the chair behind the desk.

"Now," Morgan waved her arm vaguely at the shop, "you have probably noticed that I am not the most organised of people. I think there needs to be some more order in what we sell. If I concentrate on sales, can you do some stocktaking and sorting? Obviously, if there is a sudden rush of customers, come and give me a hand; but otherwise, see if you can make some order out of the chaos."

Ollie took a deep breath. "All right, did you have any system in mind?"

"It should be fairly clear," Morgan said with a slight smile, "that I haven't really got a system. I'll trust you to come up with something." As Ollie glanced round the shop she added, "I know it is going to take a while, possibly several weeks. I promise not to make too much of a mess of what you do in the days between Saturdays."

Ollie laughed. "You're on. I'll see what we've got and then make a start."

He took a very slow meander around the shop, looking at all the items and attempting to create a list of 'themes' or 'categories' he could group articles under. This was easier said than done as the shop stocked a huge variety of objects from the very old to the very new. After a while, Ollie paused and went back, looking more at age than at what the objects were.

"Right," he announced, "I think we'll sort by age. If the customer arrives and walks into relatively new items and technology by the door and then, as they move further into the shop, they move back through the ages. That will probably work best. Better than trying to decide if a camera needs to be placed with the laptop technology or with the artwork."

Morgan frowned at him briefly and then nodded. "I like it. Not sure I can tell you the age of everything but I will do my best."

"I'll start modern," Ollie said cheerfully. "I can recognise most of that and move it towards the door. I'll ask about things as I continue."

Ollie made a start. He decided Morgan had been accurate in her assumption that the sorting might take several weeks. Every shelf was stacked several items deep; every drawer was full of further items; everything he moved revealed something else to consider. The likely timescale was increased by his desire to investigate all the odd equipment he didn't immediately recognise, to read all the notices and to make sure he had cleaned and dusted every nook and cranny.

Almost without realising it, the morning slipped past and he only noticed it was lunchtime when Morgan placed a plate of sandwiches and cakes on the shelf he had just cleared and told him to take a break.

*

Marshall was just pulling up in front of 5 Primrose Street when his mobile rang. It was Mark sounding very subdued.

"You're not going to believe this."

"Try me."

"They're the right fingerprints. I ran down the file too and there was a picture in it that we used at the time. Our victim does seem to be Wayne Bradby."

"Okay, track down the mother for an identification. I'll ask if anyone remembers him from this end and saw him yesterday. Then we need to go through that file and locate anything which might explain this."

"Hickson also says they're the only fingerprints you're going to get as there are none on the knife that was used. All beautifully wiped."

Having rung off, he stared unseeing out of the windscreen at the light drizzle. Gaining facts normally made a case clearer but he honestly couldn't say that of this one. The identification of the corpse cleared up a couple of things. Obviously, if the victim had once lived here, then he may well still have had a key and so been able to let himself in. That explained the lack of a break-in. Judging from what they had on the lad, it might also explain the knife; he sounded like the sort of person who may well bring one with him. He made a mental note to check with Mrs Sutherland whether the door had been unlocked when she arrived home. Had she then disturbed the victim in his burglary and ended up stabbing him? Unfortunately that didn't really fit with the timing of death but her shower could have been to wash away more than the grime of a day's work. He rang Hickson and suggested he come and take a look at the Sutherlands' shower though he had to agree that it didn't explain why the footprints led out of the house and not up the stairs.

"She could have done that as a bluff and then taken the shoes off and come back in without them. You probably want to check her dustbin too," he told Hickson.

"Why on Earth would she make it look like she walked through the wall?" Hickson was not convinced. "Surely she would have walked through the hall and out of the front door if she wanted to lay a false trail. You're assuming she pretended to walk to the wall, ripped her shoe apart to create a false impression, then walked round into the kitchen without leaving any trace of blood – we checked, there wasn't any in the hall – and then she continued her charade with the shoes in the kitchen. That's just not possible, John."

"I know, but currently it's the best I've got so just go and check the shower, please?"

"Fine, but it's a waste of time." Hickson rang off.

Marshall opened the file on the passenger seat. It contained all the witness statements taken in Primrose Street the day before. Most were unpromising; married, middle-class couples who had been out at work all day. A couple were better and one stood out. Mrs Kathleen Ascott at number 12 had lived here 'all my married life' according to her statement and then on into widowhood.

"She'll do," Marshall muttered, getting out into the damp, October drizzle.

*

Kathleen Ascott was a spry eighty-year-old with white hair set in neat curls and a twinkle in her bright blue eyes. She ushered Marshall into her front room and then bustled into the kitchen to make him tea.

He peered through the window while he waited. This gave him a clear view up and down the street. Number 5 was across the street and up a little way, though it took him a moment to work out. It was quite difficult to tell the difference. Even with their individually painted garage doors and the small bits of lawn done in personal tastes, the houses still looked like identical boxes. Not like the modern roads on his own estate, where the developers had gone to some trouble to mix and match the styles and make every house different to its neighbours.

Mrs Ascott arrived back with a tea tray. "Here you go, Inspector. Do sit down."

She poured tea into bone china mugs and offered him a biscuit from a neatly arranged plate.

"Now, how can I help you? I did tell the young woman yesterday that I hadn't seen anyone. I was probably in the kitchen having lunch at about the time you're interested in."

"Yes, I have your statement. I was actually interested in something that happened fifteen years ago. A young lad went missing from number five."

"Ah yes, Inspector, I think that was the last time I had the police knocking on my door wanting my help."

"You remember him?"

"I'm afraid so, Inspector. I'd prefer not to if I'm honest with you. He was not a nice young man at all. Mind you, I think the parents are the ones really at fault when I see children turning out like that. Of course, she was distraught when he vanished but she should have expected it really."

"His mum, you mean?" Marshall noted that Mrs Ascott, despite chatting away cheerfully, also had one eye on the goings on beyond her windows.

"Let's face it, Inspector, he spent all the time that he should have been in school stealing and racing cars that he wasn't old enough to drive. It was only a matter of time before he killed himself or was locked up."

"You think he's dead then?"

"Oh, I expect so, Inspector."

"So you didn't see him here yesterday?"

She shook her head. "Of course not, Inspector."

"So his mum moved out and the Sutherlands moved in?" He tried changing tack.

"No, Inspector. It was the Fieldings who bought off Mrs Bradby. Susan and Trevor. Nice couple, they were there about ten years and then they had three babies in three years and, of course, the house wasn't really big enough so they moved on. I still exchange Christmas cards with them, which is more than I can say for the new pair. They're hardly ever here, out at work all day and keep themselves to themselves."

"And yesterday?"

"Everything as usual except I think she got home slightly earlier than normal. And then your lot started arriving." She smiled at him. "More tea?"

"I'd love to but I'm afraid I ought to get on. Let me take this through to the kitchen for you." He picked up the tray and followed a familiar route across the hall to the kitchen. Whole street, he thought, all the same inside and out, as if the builders had thought everyone was the same.

Stepping into the kitchen, he stopped in surprise.

"Mrs Ascott?"

"Yes, Inspector." She had followed him in.

"When I was in number five yesterday, there was a hatch through there." He pointed at the open archway which led through to the dining room.

"Oh yes, some people have had them bricked up. It gives you three living rooms, you see, for the estate agent brochure. Puts the price up, Sue Fielding told me."

"So the Fieldings had the arch in number five bricked up?"

"That's right, Inspector. Is it important?"

"I don't know. Probably not but sometimes little details like that give us a bigger picture."

*

By the end of the afternoon Ollie was beginning to wonder why he had been employed. It was going to take him several Saturdays to sort the shop but, unless the shop had been unusually quiet for his first day, he didn't see why Morgan wouldn't have time to do the sorting. There had been hardly any customers and most of these had been steered by his employer straight to an item she felt they needed and most hadn't spent any time at all browsing.

The only interest in his day had come late afternoon when a middle-aged lady had arrived, obviously distressed. She had hovered in the doorway until Ollie had invited her in but Morgan had swept down and hurried her away before Ollie could do any more.

Slightly annoyed, Ollie went to sort a shelf nearer to the counter to see if he could find out what the woman needed to be so upset about it. Maybe he could earn his money by finding her something to make her happier.

Unfortunately, Morgan noticed his approach and steered the lady away into an inner sanctum before he heard more than some sobbed words about 'my son' and 'the glasses'. Despite his hovering near the desk for a further half an hour, he couldn't hear what was going on and Morgan then reappeared, thanked him profusely for his work during the day, reminded him to take his bodhran and pressed some cash into his hand as she ushered him towards the door.

Once outside, Ollie counted his money and discovered he had been paid two hundred pounds for the day. He briefly considered going back in to query the amount as it seemed like an awful lot of money for a few hours but Morgan had shut the door firmly and turned the sign to closed so Ollie decided to question it the following week along with the contract that he hadn't asked about. After all, it wasn't really his job to advise the woman on running the shop though he struggled to see how she made any sort of profit from what he'd seen during the day and he ought to make sure he kept getting paid a wage.

Tucking his money into his wallet, he headed for home past the music shop where the cymbal he wanted had suddenly become rather more affordable.

*

Marshall arrived back at the station as Mark was escorting a lady out to her car. She was lighting a cigarette with shaking hands and her eyes looked red and tear stained.

He waited until she had driven off before crossing the car park to join his sergeant. "Mrs Bradby?" Somehow the dyed red hair scraped back into a ponytail and the over-made-up, haggard face had been appropriate to the picture Mrs Ascott had given him, of a mum unable to control her child. That was, he reflected, stereotyping which wasn't always helpful but, more often than not, accurate. Mark nodded to him.

"Yeah, she recognised him straight off. Said a funny thing, actually."

"Not funny, 'ha-ha' I take it."

"She said 'he hasn't aged a day' and then burst into tears."

"Has she seen him at all then in the last fifteen years?"

"She said not."

Marshall nodded. "And I suppose she had no idea what he was doing in Primrose Street either?"

"No."

"This case is full of dead ends. Let's go and have a look through Wayne's file and see if it gives us anything."

Instead, they were greeted by Gillian Ashton who was replacing the phone as they entered the office.

"Anything, Gill?"

"That was the librarian again, sir."

Marshall snorted. "Found her glasses now, has she?"

"No, but she says she knows who took them."

"Oh, for Christ's sake." Marshall laughed. "Tell uniform. Let them deal with the old bat."

"Okay, sir… John…"

"There's a 'but' in that sentence, Constable," Marshall said. "Spit it out, what's bothering you?"

"She gave me a name. Alison Miller."

"And?"

"I ran it through the system. No form but fifteen years ago her two-year-old son was run down outside their home. A hit-and-run driver who deliberately drove across their front lawn."

"Fifteen years ago?" Mark asked. "Do you have a precise date?"

"Same day Wayne Bradby disappeared and only a couple of streets away – twenty-seven Tulip Drive."

"Is there anything to suggest that Wayne was involved in her son's death?" She'd caught Marshall's interest now.

"No-one was ever caught for it, but it was a stolen car which was used and it was found burnt out at Five Oaks. No forensics to speak of and definitely no fingerprints."

"But it is his MO," Nick said from the other side of the office.

"Steal a car, do as much damage as possible and then torch it. He took to doing that after the first time he was caught and somebody made the mistake of explaining to him that he was caught because his fingerprints were all over the steering wheel."

"Does this get us anywhere?" Marshall asked, allowing them to run with it.

"I could see if I can track her down – this Alison Miller," Mark offered. "If we can get a picture of her then we could take it back to Primrose Street and see if it jogs some memories. Maybe she was seen yesterday but people discounted her. They do that if it's a respectable-looking woman."

Marshall nodded; he knew witnesses tended to look for what they wanted to see but it all seemed an awfully long shot. Not to mention, a hell of a way from a librarian who thought this woman may have stolen her glasses.

Hang on – librarian.

God, he was being slow.

"Librarian, Gillian, which library?"

He saw sudden realisation hitting Mark too.

"Er," she checked her notes, "Smith Foundation Library. Woman name of—"

"Jenny," said Mark. "Shit!"

"Sorry," Marshall said, "should have spoken to you – and Nick – about Jenny. If you get a call from her it's probably important. She has an insight into… shall we say, strange happenings in Fenwick."

"If she thinks Alison Miller and these glasses are important?" Mark asked.

"Better find the woman. Ask her where she was yesterday. If nothing else, we can eliminate her from our non-existent list of suspects."

"What are you going to do?"

"I'm going to go and ask Jenny what possible relevance her missing glasses have to our investigation and I might ask her about suspects who can walk through walls. It's her sort of thing, or the library's at any rate."

*

The Smith Foundation Library on Museum Street was a square stone building with massive oak doors and a discreet bronze plaque which told the world that the librarian was Miss J Williams. Marshall checked, every time he entered, that the library was behaving as it should do before he went in. The events of Christmas made him wary of entering without checking; a couple of days Marshall was unlikely to ever forget, hence his careful scrutiny.

Jenny greeted him with a smile. She stood behind the desk just inside the main doors; a young woman barely out of her teens. Light brown hair fell in waves to her shoulders and deep green eyes suggested a greater experience than her age would allow.

"New girl on the phone," she said, "didn't know who I was."

"Yes, sorry, we're a bit snowed under. You called about some glasses. Wondered if you would be so good as to explain why you think they're relevant to my investigations as I really am rather busy." Marshall smiled to take the sting from the words.

"Not sure they are, but they were stolen and it's all a bit strange so thought I'd let you know." She put a 'check the office' sign on the counter. "Come on through."

They walked to the far end of the library away from the entrance. The office was crowded with old books and parchments and a variety of strange items. Many were in display cabinets around the walls; the rest strewn across the various surfaces including the bed in the far corner and the top of the fridge. The ornate, full-length mirror which hung on the back wall was today being a mirror. Marshall missed the view of calm, immaculate garden that he knew lay behind the silver surface.

Jenny threw herself into a chair on one side of the large fireplace and waved her hand at the one opposite. Just the two chairs today, Marshall noted; he had been here when the room had been able to hold six times that number.

"Sit, I'll explain," Jenny said.

"So, what do you know about my investigations?" Marshall asked, sitting down and relaxing into the soft fabric.

"Nothing, really, it's just these glasses went missing. I think they're stolen and I think I know by who. David is being a little evasive, but then, I think he also stole them once upon a time and that strange woman and her shop seem to be involved. I thought you ought to know about it."

"So, I assume there is something special about these glasses, then. What do they do?"

Jenny shrugged. "No idea. Like I said, David is being evasive and I can't leave here to go and ask the Morgan woman in the shop."

"But you think you know who took them?"

"I'm fairly sure. I found a woman called Alison Miller crying in the library because her husband died recently. She said this Morgan woman had told her about the glasses and she wanted to see them. God knows why. I said I thought they were in a display case back here, not out in the library, and thought no more about it. I went back to the desk and didn't come back here until I'd closed up. Went to have a look at the glasses—"

"Why?" Marshall asked.

"Well, there are four pairs in the display cabinet – or there were. I didn't know which ones were being talked about so I was trying to guess which ones David might have got from the shop."

"I see, go on."

"When I looked, there were only three left, which told me which ones were important, but I assume Alison Miller came and took them while I was at the desk."

"How did she know which pair to take?"

Jenny shook her head. "Either she didn't, and she guessed at one, so we don't know whether these are the right pair, or Morgan told her rather more than David is telling me."

"What do the ones she has taken look like?"

"Pair of fairly normal glasses, thick black frames so rather unattractive and here," she indicated the bridge of her nose, "a white date stamp wheel like I use for stamping books."

"And you don't know what they do," Marshall checked.

"Sorry, John," she sighed. "I really have no idea."

"Right, we'll add chasing her down to our list of jobs and I think I possibly ought to visit the shop too." He sat back and briefly closed his eyes, not something he relished doing again; the place gave him the creeps.

"Hard week?" Jenny said.

Marshall nodded. "Not as bad as some but…" He paused, but the relationship he had built with Jenny over the last few months had proved her to be a confidential and supportive ally in fighting the crime and weirdness of Fenwick. "One stabbed youth who has reappeared after fifteen years' absence, no-one saw anything or heard anything and Hickson claims the killer walked out through the wall," Marshall summarised. "No insights on that, I suppose?"

"No, I'm stuck here. If I knew a trick to getting through walls I'd have tried it by now." She smiled wryly and there was no real emotion to the words. "Visiting the shop sounds like a good idea," she said and then added quietly, "if it will let you."

"Thanks," Marshall said drily. "You didn't really need to say that; experience has told me that will probably be the case."

*

"Anything for me, Sergeant?" Marshall strode back into the office.

"Jenny a washout then?"

"You know me too well."

Mark laughed. "You only ever call me 'sergeant' when things are going badly."

"She claims Alison Miller stole the glasses. She has no idea why or how they're special and suggests we probably ought to go and visit that bloody shop again."

"You're joking!"

"No. What's more, neither was she."

"Whole thing seems mad."

"The trouble is, Mark, if it is then so is Hickson, who claims our killer walks through walls and Dr Trent, who is claiming our victim is late teens when we know he has to be early thirties." Marshall slumped into his seat. "I saw that body, Mark. There was no way it was a bloke in his thirties, so maybe I'm crazy as well."

After a minute, Mark said, "Well, we did manage to track down Alison Miller. She was at work so we said we'd call in at her home later. It might give us something."

Marshall sighed. "It's probably a waste of time but we don't have anything else. Hickson find anything in the shower?"

Mark tossed a piece of paper across to him. It was a report with 'I told you so' scrawled across it.

Marshall laughed. "I suppose I asked for that. What's Helen doing?"

"Going through old files – Wayne Bradby's; Luke Miller's death."

"We're clutching at straws, Mark."

"I know."

*

Alison Miller was small and trim, her dark hair cut in a neat bob and a subtle layer of make-up expertly applied. She was dressed in the dark suit and cream blouse she had obviously worn to work. Her greeting at the door was warm but wary.

"Do come in, Inspector, Sergeant. I've only just got in myself." She led them into a large, open kitchen with a pine table at one end. This was a much larger house than the Primrose Street one, with a beautifully landscaped garden visible through the kitchen window. Marshall noted the pictures on the window ledge. One was of Alison Miller with a man who must have been her husband and which looked like it had been taken fairly recently. The other showed a much younger version of the pair of them with a small boy. The younger Alison Miller had had nearly waist-length hair and a much slimmer figure than the current version that faced him across the table.

"I'm sorry to have to trouble you, Mrs Miller, and it's probably nothing but we believe you may be in possession of a pair of glasses belonging to the Smith Foundation Library." Marshall had decided to start this way, with something he was relatively sure about, before moving on to her son's death and any link to Wayne Bradby.

"Why, yes." She got up and removed a pair of thick-rimmed spectacles from the handbag on the side. "I believe I picked them up by mistake the other day. I've been meaning to return them." She handed them over to Marshall who put them into his pocket with barely a glance as she sat down again. He was more concerned with how he ought to approach the next question, his eyes straying to the picture of the happy family group.

Mark leapt in. "This is a nice place you've got here, Mrs Miller.

Have you been here long?"

"Fourteen years now. We moved after the accident. We couldn't bear the memories there."

"Of course." Mark nodded and Marshall was impressed anew by the effortless way his sergeant could approach sensitive topics with such delicacy. He had attempted to push Mark, a number of times in the past couple of years, into going for promotion but mostly he was glad that Mark remained with him, bringing his gentle fatherly air to these difficult questions with fragile witnesses. Mark continued gently. "In fact, we have had a development in the case. I wonder if you remember anything that might help us about the driver of the car?"

"I told the police at the time. All I remember is seeing this bright red car leaving the road and then Luke flying through the air. I rushed out as he started to scream and then I sat holding him in the road until the ambulance came. I don't know what happened to the car and I don't even know who phoned the ambulance. People kept saying things to me but all I could hear was Luke—"

"I'm sorry," Mark said softly.

"…and the dog."

"What dog, Mrs Miller?" Marshall asked curiously.

"Our dog, well Luke's really. She was barely a puppy and she was shut in the garden when I rushed out and she just howled and howled. I'm sure she knew something was wrong; animals do, you know, but I couldn't get up. Funny isn't it, Inspector, the things that hurt most? I can forgive myself for his death because he should have been safe playing in our garden while I made a drink but I can't forgive myself for not letting Poppy out to say goodbye. She just howled and howled and howled and I couldn't move. I'm not sure she ever forgave me either."

"I'm sorry." Marshall repeated his sergeant's words but it seemed such an inadequate thing to say.

She nodded. "Don't be, I live with it." They sat in awkward silence for a minute and then she said brightly, "You said there might be a lead. To do with this driver?"

Mark drew a picture of Wayne Bradby from his pocket. "Do you recognise this man at all?"

She looked at it for a long moment before handing it back. "Should I?"

"We really don't know, Mrs Miller. This man was found dead yesterday but he vanished on the day your son was killed and he did have a record for stealing cars and wrecking them. There is a possibility that he was the driver of the red car."

She gave a small smile. "I told you, Inspector, I didn't see the driver."

Inspector Marshall stood up. "Well, thank you for your time, Mrs Miller. One further thing, would you mind telling us where you were yesterday lunchtime?"

"I was at work, Inspector."

"Would you mind if we borrowed a photograph, Mrs Miller? Just so we can check your story."

"By all means." She handed him the one from the window ledge. "I had this taken with Robert a couple of months ago, shortly before he died. It's probably the most recent I've got. I will get it back, won't I?"

"Of course." He shook hands and followed Mark out of the house.

"Well," he told Mark as they got into the car, "you better check her alibi but I imagine it will stand up."

"Back to Primrose Street?" Mark asked. "Now we've got the picture?"

"Not really sure why," Marshall said, repeating, "I think her alibi will probably hold up. Let's go back to the office first."

*

Gillian greeted them when they arrived. She was clutching a large folder of papers. "I found some things of curiosity in the Wayne Bradby file."

"All we got was a pair of stolen glasses," Marshall put them on the desk with Alison Miller's picture, "and a picture of a respectable woman, who I really can't believe did anything more than walk off with a pair of glasses for some undefined reason. So, anything you can give us must be better than that."

"Here." Gillian handed Marshall a photograph. "This is a picture of the knife block in Wayne Bradby's kitchen on the day he disappeared. His mother identified one of the knives as missing, when she was asked if it looked like her son had taken anything when he vanished." She pointed to the pictures displayed on the board next to Wayne Bradby's corpse. "I'd say that knife – which killed him – is the missing one. Same handle, looks to be the right size."

"Good work." Marshall looked from one photo to another; the knives shown had identical wooden handles inlaid with a mother of pearl design. "So, did he keep hold of the knife for all this time? Fascinating."

"And," Gillian said, pulling another piece of paper from the file, "seeing this photo of Alison Miller, I think there might be something else. Here is a statement from a Mrs Ascott on the day Wayne disappeared claiming she saw a strange woman leaving number five that day. No woman has ever been found but there is an artist's impression."

Gillian put the paper down alongside the picture of Alison Miller. Allowing for the slight distortions created by a police artist drawing from someone else's memory, the two women were fairly obviously the same except the artist's impression showed Alison Miller wearing the glasses which were also sitting on the desk.

"That's not possible," Mark said.

"No," agreed Marshall.

"She didn't look like that fifteen years ago."

"No," Marshall said again.

"And she didn't have the glasses until—"

"Mark! I'm agreeing with you. Stop stating the bleeding obvious."

"So?"

"So, I need to speak to Mrs Ascott again; looks like I asked the wrong questions last time."

"And if she sticks to her story?"

"Fuck knows. I suppose we need another, slightly more interesting discussion with Mrs Miller and, probably, with someone who can explain the glasses if we can find anyone."

"Honestly?" Mark said, making it more a statement than a question.

"There's a shop – or possibly not – on Butchers' Passage which I think we need to visit. Definitely, according to Jenny. All right," Marshall said, rubbing his eyes, "let's sleep on it tonight and we will see how much else of this mess we can untangle tomorrow." He knew, if he was being honest with himself, that he was merely putting off the issue of trying to find a shop that might not want to be found.

"Coming out to the pub tonight, John?" Mark said. Fenwick Morris Men were doing their first summer dance out, in preparation for the dawn display on May morning.

"Don't know, I'm tired."

"Change as good as a rest," Mark said with a grin. "Come and forget all these complications for an evening. Beer on me."

*

The light went fairly early in the evening so there wasn't a lot of dancing.

"Stick dancing a bit of an issue at twilight," Mark explained to Marshall, "but it didn't go badly. Coming in for a song and a tune?"

"Maybe for a little but I promised Marion I'd not be too late, having spent most of the weekend at work."

"You could repeat your singing success," Steve said as he passed.

"You all heard it the other night," Marshall said. "I think I ought to learn another song before I try again."

"I didn't," a young man said cheerfully. "You could sing it for me."

"Evening, Ollie," Marshall said. "You write things and everything, not sure you want to hear my meagre efforts."

"Of course I do." The young man grinned at Marshall. "Only way to improve is to practise."

"How's the band doing?" Mark asked. "Making your millions yet?"

"Overnight success is going to take a little longer," Ian said cheerfully. "He's even had to take a 'proper' job."

Marshall laughed as Ollie gave his dad a friendly slap.

"At least she is paying me in musical instruments," he said.

"Really," Mark said. "Unusual job."

"Unusual shop, place in Butchers' Passage. She doesn't seem to have any idea of the going rate for Saturday work and she threw in a bodhran too, so I'm not complaining."

"Butchers' Passage?" Marshall exchanged a look with his sergeant.

"Yes," Ollie looked from one to the other, "is that a problem?"

"I don't think so," Marshall assured him, "but I wouldn't mind having a chat about the place."

"With your official hat on?" Ian said, standing protectively beside his son.

"Semi-official hat. Ollie hasn't done anything wrong and I don't think there is anything criminal about the shop either, it just came up in something we were investigating today as a possible source of information so I wondered what he could tell me."

"That's okay." Ian gave his son a quick hug. "Trust the Inspector, he knows what he's doing, Ollie. Was an absolute star at Christmas. Tell him about the place. To be honest, John, it sounds a little odd from what Ollie has said to me."

*

Marshall found himself and Mark a table in the corner away from the music so they could hear what Ollie was telling them. "Just a couple of questions," he said, "and then you can join the playing and singing."

"You too," Ollie said with a smile. "Call it my fee for answering questions. I want to hear you sing. Dad says you did well."

"All right. So tell us about this shop."

"Not sure there is a lot to say. I've only worked one Saturday there so far. I spent most of it sorting the most amazing load of... not junk, exactly, but half of it you wouldn't want and the rest is fairly specialised. There's no order to it or sense to some of the things she is selling. And then when the customers do arrive she just takes them straight to an item and they never look at anything else."

"She? Morgan?"

"Yes. Nice woman if a little odd. She said the shop had given me the job and I always feel she knows more about me than I've told her."

"That doesn't surprise me," Marshall said. "I assume you know about your dad's experience over Christmas. I think Morgan comes under the same heading, so be careful."

"Will do." Ollie nodded seriously. "She had some woman in tears on Saturday afternoon, though I couldn't work out what it was all about. Something to do with her son and glasses but I couldn't get close enough to hear properly. Do you want me to keep you notified if I notice anything else odd?"

"That would be good," Mark said, "though don't get yourself into trouble by being nosey. John and I will probably drop in at some point to talk to this Morgan about her involvement in the cases we are looking into."

"Is it this dead guy that was in the paper?"

Marshall laughed. "You know we're not going to answer that, young man."

Ollie nodded and stood up. "Time for a song, then."

*

Mrs Ascott was more than happy to see Marshall again and ushered him and his sergeant through to the front room.

"Can I be of further help, Inspector?"

"We hope so, Mrs Ascott. Would you look at this picture for us, please, and tell us if you've seen the woman in it before."

"Oh yes, Inspector."

Marshall exchanged glances with Mark. They were getting somewhere. "She was here yesterday, in the street?"

"Yesterday? No, Inspector."

"No?" Marshall swore inwardly; so much for that idea.

"No, but last time the police were asking questions, when the Bradby boy went missing. She was here that day."

"Are you sure? That's a long time ago."

"Oh yes, she was at number five. She followed the lad up the street and into the back alley at about half twelve and then came out again about ten minutes later."

"She had longer hair then?" Marshall hazarded.

"No, Inspector. She looked just like your photograph except for the glasses she was wearing. Large, dark things which were much too big for her face. I'm glad she took them off for the picture."

Marshall took the glasses from his pocket and showed her. "Like these?"

"Precisely those, Inspector, I remember noticing the odd white blob on the nose piece and thinking that I would have got them mended if I were her." Marshall took a better look at the glasses. They had thick black rims and there was a white dial on the nosepiece. It looked like the scrolls used on library date stamps before computers took over.

"You're absolutely sure?"

"Yes, Inspector. I saw her as clearly as I'm seeing you now."

"Thank you, Mrs Ascott, you have been a great help."

*

"Just how is that a help?" Mark leant against the car. "Fifteen years ago Alison Miller was sitting three streets away caring for her dying son. There's no way she was here killing Wayne. She didn't even know it was Wayne who had killed her son. In all honesty, neither do we. Not to mention the fact that if she did it fifteen years ago, what happened to the body for all that time, how come Liza said it was still warm, how did she preserve it and—"

"Hold it, Mark. Mrs Ascott didn't see the Alison Miller of fifteen years ago. She saw the one from the picture."

"That makes even less sense."

"I know. I have a dreadful suspicion that it all comes down to these glasses. Sorry, Mark, we need a trip to Butchers' Passage. If I read what Ollie said last night correctly, it sounds like Alison Miller was in there with these."

"You had to say it," Mark said sourly. "Let's go and see if we can find the damn place again. I'm getting rather sick of that woman and her interference in people's lives."

"You and me both."

*

The shop was there. For a change, its door was standing invitingly

119

open which, perversely, made Marshall even more reluctant to enter.

Taking a deep breath, and wondering if the woman had forgiven him for what he'd done to her camera last time, Marshall took a step through the doorway.

He took a moment to be impressed with Ollie's handiwork as the place seemed rather tidier and ordered than the last couple of times he'd been.

"Inspector." Morgan was behind her counter, dressed in a wide array of bright colours.

Remembering past encounters, Marshall decided not to beat round the bush. "You know why I'm here," he said bluntly. "I want you to tell me about these glasses."

She smiled at him. "You're learning, Inspector. The glasses are mine; they were stolen many years ago – it seems to be the way they move on."

"Though I'm told you encouraged the theft this time," Marshall said.

She shrugged. "One to you, Inspector. It could be interpreted that way. I spoke to a grieving woman and offered her a remedy."

"So what do they do that makes a pair of glasses a remedy for anything, apart from poor eyesight?"

"They see in to the past, Inspector, something some people need."

"See into? Like through a window?"

"Not as such. They can take you there." Morgan smiled. "Like everything I provide here, Inspector, they are to meet a need. They would not work for everyone. Or in the same way for everyone. David found they didn't work at all for him."

"What was his need?" Mark asked, curiously.

"It wasn't a 'need', Sergeant, just a desire to be in a past where he wasn't stuck in the library."

"Alison Miller?" Marshall prompted.

"Had ghosts to lay to rest, Inspector. More than that is her story, not mine." She paused and then gave a small smile. "The shop is closing now, Inspector."

"Not a hugely subtle hint, Miss Morgan. I have more questions."

"I have no more answers for you," she said, "not at this time." She headed for the door purposefully. "Goodbye, gentlemen."

Marshall and Mark exchanged glances and then, nodding to Morgan at the door, left. The door was closed and locked behind them.

"Okay," Marshall said as they looked at the closed door, "let's just suspend our disbelief for a moment. Let's consider what fits the facts. If these glasses really can take you into the past then we solve an awful lot of our problems. Alison uses them, puts them on and discovers she is there with the man who killed her son. So she follows him and kills him. The footprints therefore go through the wall because there was no wall fifteen years ago. The knife vanished because it reappeared here next to the body. It explains why Mrs Ascott saw her wearing them—"

"But it doesn't explain how she knew it was Wayne who was driving the car, or how the corpse ended up here and not fifteen years ago and as your original premise rests on being able to step into the past..." Mark shook his head.

"I'm going to go and check something out, Mark, you take me to Manor Estate and then will you go and bring Alison Miller in."

"You want to arrest her on *that* sort of evidence?"

"No, I just want to ask her a few questions." He paused. "I tell you what. Take her to the library. Jenny might be able to help, maybe even David. More reassuring ambience than an interview room at the station for now." He ignored Mark's look of concern. "I'll join you there."

"I'm not sure—"

"Trust me, Mark."

*

Mark took the car, dropping Marshall off at Tulip Drive where, fifteen years ago, a small boy had been run over. The houses here were almost identical to Primrose Street. A whole estate of sixties houses built to replace the bomb damage of the war.

Marshall stopped outside number twenty-seven. The front lawn was now a block-paved drive and the garage door painted a bright blue. Feeling a little silly, he took the glasses from his pocket. The date on them was already set to the 4th June, fifteen years earlier. Taking a deep breath, he put them on.

The air shimmered and then he was looking at a neatly trimmed lawn surrounded by an ornamental mini fence across which two tyre tracks ploughed a dark scar. A woman sat sobbing in the road, her arms wrapped around a still form in her lap and somewhere a dog howled.

As he watched, Alison Miller – the older version – appeared in front of him watching the tableau in the road. She stood there for half a minute and then reached up to remove the glasses he was now wearing and vanished. After a few seconds she reappeared, let out a little sob and vanished a second time. Barely any time later she again arrived in front of him and vanished again almost immediately. Marshall waited but nothing further happened.

He nodded. He'd seen enough and now he needed some answers. He reached up to remove the glasses and then hesitated. With sudden resolution, he walked over to the side gate and pushed it open, allowing the young Labrador on the other side to charge out into the road.

*

Mark was just pulling up outside the library when Marshall stepped from the taxi he'd called. Alison Miller sat beside the sergeant looking as neatly turned out as before though she had had time to change into a more casual skirt and top.

Marshall held the car door for her and then ushered her into the library.

"John." Jenny Williams came round from behind the desk. "I was about to close for the day. Please go through to the office."

"A bit late to be open."

"I don't keep very regular hours. Who knows when the library might be needed?"

He nodded; considering why he was there, he couldn't really argue with that. He led the way to the office at the back. It was tidier than his previous visit and there were already four comfortable chairs set around the fire place to one side almost as if they had been expected. Marshall found he was unsurprised.

Jenny joined them almost immediately. "What can I do for you, Inspector?"

"We found the glasses." He removed them from his pocket but didn't hand them over.

"Thank you, Inspector. Did you bring Mrs Miller here just to apologise?"

"I want to ask her some questions but I don't think we need an interview room. You've always said the library was here to answer needs."

She looked at him thoughtfully. "You know that. Should I call David?"

He nodded briefly. "If you like."

Mark, who had sat in silence watching this exchange with a look of concern, leant forward while Jenny moved to the mirror with its garden beyond. "John, are you sure this is wise?"

"Yes, Mark. Put your notebook away and keep quiet. You're just here as a witness to this." He turned to Alison Miller who sat silently watching the fire. "Mrs Miller, I have a few questions for you."

She nodded but didn't take her eyes from the dancing flames, so missing the shimmering mirror clearing to allow David to enter the room.

"You went out to Five Oaks?" He had taken a slight detour on his way here; he knew she had.

"Yes, Inspector."

"You knew that was where the car had been found?"

"It was in all the papers at the time, Inspector."

"You followed Wayne Bradby home?"

"Yes."

"Did you plan to kill him?"

"No, Inspector, I just wanted to tell him what he'd done to me, to my son, but then the knives were there as we went through the kitchen and something just snapped."

"The perfect crime because, at the time of death, you were known to be at the hospital with your son."

"I suppose so, Inspector, I didn't really think." There was no life to the voice or the answers.

"So how did the body end up here?" The only question he couldn't yet answer for himself.

"He caught hold of me and we struggled. The glasses got knocked off. I found myself back here but I had hold of him so he was too. It was too late by then as well, he was already dying. So I left him and fled."

"You cleaned the knife?"

"No, Inspector, I just left."

"You put the glasses back on to leave?"

"I'm not totally stupid, Inspector." She glanced briefly at him. "I couldn't be seen leaving a house where a corpse was about to be found so I left in the past."

"You *were* seen." Though, Marshall thought, she may as well not have been for all the help it had done either investigation.

They were all silent for a couple of minutes.

"One last question, Mrs Miller. If you knew you could go back, why did you not save your son?"

Then she did look properly at him. "Don't you think I tried? I set the date and it took me back to midday. I tried several times and it was always midday, always ten minutes too late. So revenge was all I had." She burst into tears, burying her face in her hands.

Jenny Williams crossed quickly and placed her arms around the shaking shoulders of the older woman.

*

They sat by the fire half an hour later once Marshall had sent Mark to take Alison Miller home.

"You'll let her go then?" Jenny Williams had made coffee for the three of them.

"I'll try for a conviction – that's my job. See if I can find the clothes she was wearing, look for blood, that sort of thing, but I think I might have trouble finding any. Whatever she says, Hickson found no prints. The CPS would laugh me out of court if I produced just that story as evidence. I also think she's probably suffered enough so it may just have to go on file as an unsolved crime." He held out the glasses to David. "I believe these are what you stole."

"Thank you." David shook his head. "They should probably go back to Morgan but for now, put them away, Jenny."

She took them and went to replace them in the display case. A slight cough made them turn to the doorway. Morgan stood, leaning on the frame.

"I think I will take them," she said. "I have some loose ends and the Inspector is distinctly uncomfortable, I believe, with their presence."

Marshall snorted.

"And with mine," she added before he could voice the words. "But you have a solved case, Inspector."

Marshall nodded. "I suppose so." He sighed and then asked something which had been bothering him. "Is it always midday?"

"For some people, Inspector, life doesn't move forwards past a certain point and they cannot see back beyond it."

"The glasses work like that?"

"Humans work like that, Inspector."

They stared at each other in silence for a while.

"Loose ends," he said after a while, replaying her words in his head.

She gave a small smile. "You don't want to know, Inspector, but I believe there is a knife to clean."

Marshall half started from his seat and then collapsed back down again; what was the point? Was he really going to try and wrestle the glasses off her? He really wouldn't put it past her to vanish if he moved towards her – possibly by putting the glasses on. He changed tack.

"I thought you said, Miss Morgan, that the glasses gave people what they needed."

"What they need, Inspector, is not always what they think they want." She paused. "Perhaps it was not Alison Miller's need that was answered here. Maybe this youth needed to pay or maybe the two of us needed to appreciate each other's skills." She smiled. "Or maybe it was her need after all."

"But what did Alison Miller need if not to save her son?"

"I think she needed to lay her ghosts to rest and, possibly, to forgive herself."

"But she said, when we first met her, that…" He looked into the very blue, very knowing eyes of the strange woman.

"You did let the dog out, didn't you, Inspector?"

Déjà vu

"John, letter for you." Sergeant Mark Sherbourne threw a pastel pink envelope on to his superior's desk. "Hand delivered last night."

"Oh God." Inspector John Marshall picked it up gingerly. This was one of the unforeseen side effects of being the 'face' of the local police. He had no objection to the appeals for witnesses and the statements he had to give but it did mean that every Tom, Dick and Harry in Fenwick knew his name. He ripped open the envelope and read out the enclosed letter.

"Dear Inspector, I am writing to apologise for the trouble I am about to cause. I expect my mum will visit you at some point today to report me as missing. I have chosen to leave her because I love another. I am sorry for hurting her and inconveniencing you. I am handwriting this so you can check it against things at home and know that I really did write it. Please don't look for me, I am fine. Yours sincerely, Katie Hunter."

The two men stared at each other. "Well," Mark said slowly, "either a genuine 'I don't want to be found' or a kidnapper who thinks he's being remarkably clever. What do you think?"

"I think we wait for the mother. Let's not go chasing shadows." Marshall handed the letter over. "But take a look at the watermark."

The paper clearly showed a picture of an old-fashioned shop window with the words 'Morgan's Miscellany' across it.

"Shit," Mark said. "What now?"

"Let's wait and see," Marshall cautioned again, "but I'm reaching the limits of my patience with that woman."

*

They didn't have long to wait. Mrs Margaret Hunter arrived at the front desk mid-morning. She was a small lady, almost as round as she was tall, with neatly permed grey hair and faded grey eyes, who perched on the edge of the plastic chair in the interview room looking fragile and alone.

"My daughter's gone," she said for the fifth time and eventually managed to continue without tears. "Her bed hasn't been slept in and there's this." She fumbled in her handbag and pulled a note from it. Marshall recognised the pink notepaper.

The note was briefer than his but said much the same thing. Katie had chosen to leave.

"How old is your daughter, Mrs Hunter?"

"Twenty-two."

"Normally, if someone decides to leave home willingly at the age of twenty-two there is very little I can do," Marshall said as gently as he could. "Is there anything which leads you to suspect that this is not a genuine note or that something untoward has happened to her?"

"She hasn't taken anything, Inspector. If she was leaving then surely she would have taken clothes or make-up or... well, something."

"Are you telling me that all your daughter's possessions remain at your home?"

"Yes, Inspector."

"How about this other love she mentions, have you checked with him?"

"I don't know who she means, Inspector, she's never shown any interest in boys at all. She hasn't got a boyfriend."

"No boyfriend? And absolutely nothing missing?" Marshall was already beginning to stand.

"No." She was definite and, as far as Marshall was concerned, that was not good news. In his experience, if they left willingly then they didn't leave with nothing.

"She even left her phone," Mrs Hunter continued, "and she never goes anywhere without that."

"Right, I think I'd like to take a look." Marshall held the door for her and tried to be positive. "I'm sure there's an explanation so I'll run you home and take a glance around." There was no point in frightening her unnecessarily. Bad news may be inevitable but he would try and make sure before he upset her.

Collecting Mark, he ushered Mrs Hunter out to a waiting car.

*

The house they pulled up outside was a small semi in a row of nearly identical buildings. The garden was well cared for with beds full of neatly arranged flowers. Marshall was not surprised to find that the house was as pristine inside as the plants were outside. Mrs Hunter obviously valued a tidy, precise environment.

"Can you show me your daughter's room, please?" He nodded to Mark. "Have a look round downstairs, will you?"

The stairs were decorated with family pictures. "Is this Katie?" He noted several school pictures showing a gradually maturing young woman culminating in a graduation and a couple of family groups. There were no other children in evidence; just a proud, if elderly, set of parents.

"Yes, and Bill, my husband."

"Is he at work?"

"No, he died from a heart attack three years ago. They'd just agreed he could retire at sixty, go early, and then he dropped dead at the machine." She carried on up the stairs. "Life is very unfair, Inspector." Marshall had seen too many people who had been dealt poor hands to disagree with her.

The bedroom was as tidy and uncluttered as the rest of the house.

"Have you touched anything, Mrs Hunter?" Marshall paused in the doorway. It was a very unusual young girl, he felt, who didn't have half a dozen outfits strewn across various surfaces. His own daughters seemed to live in a perpetual pigsty which, his wife assured him, would only get worse as they got older.

"I keep the place tidy but I haven't done anything this morning, Inspector. I was much too agitated to start cleaning."

Marshall nodded; he'd met 'Mrs Hunters' before. With nothing to do all day but vacuum and dust, they cleaned a house to within an inch of its life.

"So this is how it always looks?"

"Yes, Inspector, she was always very neat." Marshall guessed that the poor girl probably hadn't had much choice.

"And when did you see your daughter last?"

"Last night. We had tea and then we played Scrabble. We do that on a Tuesday because there's nothing on the television. Then we went to bed early because Katie has to get up early for work."

Marshall nodded again; parents could be illuminating. He wondered if every evening was as carefully mapped out.

"Have you actually checked whether she is at work, Mrs Hunter?"

"She wouldn't be, she didn't come down for breakfast and her uniform is still here."

"Uniform? What does Katie do?"

"She works for the hospital. She's an occupational therapist, goes out to old people to help them live on their own. She is very good at it, Inspector."

Marshall leant over the stairs. "Mark, can you phone The Nightingale and see if Katie Hunter made it to work this morning in occupational therapy?"

Under Mrs Hunter's watchful eye, Marshall checked through the room. He opened wardrobes and drawers and peered under the bed – which was spotless. The clothes all hung in neat ranks and the small dressing table held a regimented collection of bottles and lipsticks. A small handbag beside the bed contained Katie's purse, keys and mobile phone.

He flicked open the jewellery box and was about to shut it again having viewed the meagre contents when Mrs Hunter gave a gasp behind him.

"What is it, something missing?"

"The choker, it's gone."

"Choker?"

"She had a pearl choker with a sapphire set in the centre. It was a bit old fashioned so she didn't wear it much but it was valuable. I had to put it on the house insurance."

"And it was in here?"

"Yes, Inspector. I always check when I dust because I told the insurance people it was kept safe." Marshall swallowed a smile.

"And when did you last check?"

"Yesterday," she said it as if it should be obvious. "I haven't got round to cleaning this morning."

Marshall took a second look in the box but there seemed nothing wrong except for the missing item. He also checked the window but it was locked and he could see no signs of a forced entry or that a ladder had been leant against it to allow access.

"Sir?" Mark's voice came up the stairs.

"Front bedroom, Mark."

The sergeant appeared in the doorway. "She hasn't been seen in work. They tried home to check because it was unusual but they got no reply. I suppose that was while Mrs Hunter was with us. They also said they tried her mobile without success."

"No, that's because that's here." Marshall retrieved it and flipped open the cover. It showed one missed call.

"I'm going to have to take Katie's bag, Mrs Hunter, and there'll be a team coming to fingerprint the room. Do you suppose I could take a picture of Katie with me to help with enquiries?

"Certainly, Inspector."

"I don't suppose you've got a picture of this necklace as well?"

"I could give you the one of Katie at her end-of-year ball. I think she was wearing it."

"That would be ideal."

They waited downstairs in the cramped hallway while she searched through a shelf of albums in the front room to find the required picture. Marshall got the impression that only very special guests were invited in here with its shag pile carpet and crystal display cabinet. His grandfather had a room much the same, a shrine to some forgotten ideal of civility.

The picture, when she produced it, showed a tall, slim girl with shoulder-length curls of deep russet and bright blue eyes. The scooped neck of the ball gown she wore showed off her graceful neck around which she wore the missing pearl choker. Four strands of small pearls encircled her throat and a stone of the same deep blue as her eyes sat in the hollow at the base of her neck held in a silver setting in the shape of a bird in flight.

"A pretty girl, Mrs Hunter."

"That was last year, at her graduation ball." She seemed reluctant to hand it over.

"You will get it back, I promise you." Marshall put it safely in his jacket pocket. "Now, please leave everything where it is for now, especially in Katie's room, and I'll get a team round and a lady constable to sit with you."

"What shall I do?" She looked as if she might panic if left.

"Just sit and have a coffee and…"

"Maybe write down a list of Katie's friends for us," Mark suggested sympathetically. "It would really help."

They left her standing in the doorway looking lost and alone.

*

"Get Constable Ashton round here to talk to her and collect some facts." Gillian Ashton was a young WPC he had used several times recently to help out CID. She was good with witnesses and victims and had a gentleness to her that Helen sometimes lacked. "And ask for a Scene of Crime team." Marshall made no attempt to drive anywhere until his sergeant had finished phoning in the requests.

"Bit obsessive isn't she?" Mark commented once he'd finished. "Poor girl probably just needed to go somewhere she could be untidy or do something on the spur of the moment."

"What do you mean?"

"'Tuesdays we play Scrabble?' I bet every evening is planned out for her."

"Yes, some people prefer it that way." Marshall smiled; it wasn't something he was comfortable with either. His mother was one to live life for the spur of the moment; very little was ever planned in advance and even those things that were had been changed regularly to accommodate later ideas. He remembered wishing sometimes that she wouldn't just say 'yes' and then leap into the latest madcap scheme but the thought of Mrs Hunter and her regimented lifestyle made him glad his mother was so different. "I can't say I like it myself. Mum used to vacuum once a week, but we were lucky if she had time to wield a duster more than once a month."

"Oh my mum was forever at it, but then she had three of us so it was a full-time occupation keeping the house free of mud." Mark grinned. "You wouldn't believe the amount of mess three rugby kits can make."

"I doubt Katie Hunter was the type to fill the house with mud."

"No, so a definite 'missing' person then?" Mark frowned. "You're not thinking runaway?"

"Runaways take something, Mark."

"The choker?"

"It just doesn't feel right."

"So where now?"

"The Nightingale I think, Mark. Let's see if the people she worked with can throw any light on the matter."

They drove for a while in silence.

"Shall I check the bridge?" Mark said as they passed through the town centre and over the river on their way out of town.

Marshall hesitated and then nodded. "Might as well. Phone the desk and see if there were any jumpers last night. If not, get a car to drive down the embankment and check." It was sad, but too often true, that if nothing was missing except the person it was because the absentee planned to go where nothing would be needed. "While we're there, we'll check and see if A&E got anyone in last night."

*

The Florence Nightingale Memorial Hospital – affectionately known as 'The Nightingale' – was on the western outskirts of Fenwick. It sprawled across several acres and the visitors' cars covered several more. Marshall didn't like the place though he was honest enough to admit that this was mainly due to the number of times he had had to visit victims here. Too many downtrodden, scared and despairing people lying in beds on wards that lacked any sort of privacy for those in most need of it.

The young girl on reception assured them that they had admitted no females that matched Katie Hunter's description during the previous night. She then gave them totally incomprehensible instructions to the Community Occupational Therapy department.

Having mistakenly visited Physiotherapy and Paediatrics, Marshall and his sergeant eventually tracked down Francis Miller, Chief Occupational Therapist, in a small building around the back of Rheumatology. She was brisk and efficient but seemed genuinely fond of Katie Hunter.

"I'm surprised, Inspector. Katie is an absolutely lovely young lady. She's a real hit with the old folks and gets even the stubborn ones to accept the help they're too proud to admit they need. She always seems really happy and settled here, a real joy to have in the department."

"She hasn't suggested that anything has bothered her recently, possibly man trouble?"

"No, not at all, and as far as I know, there isn't a man."

Marshall sighed. "I think I'm going to have to talk to her patients, I'm afraid. Do you have a list of people she visited in the past month or so to start with?"

"Is that really necessary, Inspector? These are all elderly and infirm people."

"I have a missing person on my hands, Mrs Miller. I have to check all contacts. It is possible that, if she is having problems, she might have opened up to someone less close to her. It happens more often than you think; strangers are less judgemental and more objective. But I also have to consider more disturbing possibilities. Hard as it might be to hear, I'm afraid that age does not stop some people from being harmful."

Francis Miller sifted through the pile of papers on her desk until she found a large ledger. "Appointment book," she explained. She began writing names on a piece of paper. "I'll find you some addresses as well, Inspector. It is true that Katie has recently taken on an increased case load and so will have met some new faces. Since my promotion, I have had much less time to do actual visits."

"Always the way," Marshall agreed. "Anyone in particular that may be a concern?"

"No, they were all... now that's funny." She flicked back through several pages. "Interesting."

"Mrs Miller?"

"Well, she has started visiting Charles Anderson. I was working on rehabilitating him after surgery here. Now, I never found him to need much, he's fairly self-sufficient for his age, but it looks like Katie has been visiting him at least twice a week." She frowned at him. "The thing is, Inspector, Charles' wife vanished. It must be twenty years ago now but she was never found. If Katie was going to talk to anyone about leaving then he could be a likely candidate."

*

Helen Lovell and Gillian Ashton met them as they pulled back into the station car park.

"Mrs Hunter said she'd prefer me to be finding her daughter rather than making her cups of coffee," Gillian announced.

"You were probably making the place look untidy," Mark teased.

"Well, we've got plenty to do," Marshall said. "We've got a list of people she had contact with through work, both clients and colleagues. Did you get anywhere?"

"A couple of names and numbers. No boyfriend according to Mum. I was going to go and make some calls and see if any of them saw her last night or whether she was unhappy or having problems."

"Do that and then you and Helen can start visiting some OAPs; the gently-gently approach please, Helen." He turned to Mark. "Do you want to see if you can track down information on this Charles Anderson and his missing wife?"

"Not really." Mark grinned. "Twenty years? There's no way that'll be on the system, it'll still be paper. I could be days in that archive."

"It'll be under 'unsolved' if she was never found."

"Oh, that'll be a great help. Just half the place to search then! Do you think it's worth it?"

"Call it a hunch, Mark. It's a coincidence and I don't like them so let's check it out."

It actually took the sergeant under half an hour. "They're quite well organised." He put a yellow folder down in front of Marshall. "But, talking of coincidences, you'll never believe what she was called."

"Go on."

"Missing persons file on one *Katie* Anderson."

They pored through the limited evidence.

"This is almost identical," Mark said eventually. "Woman vanished overnight and took absolutely nothing. Nice looker as well." The picture he was holding showed a slim, blue-eyed woman in her early sixties with white hair that fell in soft curls to her shoulders. "Nothing to suggest suspicious circumstances though it looks like Mr Anderson was interviewed several times. He couldn't explain her disappearance and neither could the inspector in charge of the case."

"And now another woman he knows vanishes without trace." Marshall stood up. "I think we need to talk to Mr Anderson."

"Are we looking for a body?" Mark followed him out of the room. "Two bodies?"

"We're looking for connections first, anything that doesn't add up. Let's not rush in too hard until we have a few concrete facts."

*

Charles Anderson was a spry man in his mid-eighties. He was broad of shoulder and upright in a way that suggested 'armed services' to Marshall. This was confirmed by the display case in the hall containing half a dozen well-polished medals and a picture of a much younger Charles looking handsome and heroic beside a helicopter.

"Battle of Britain?" Mark hazarded, stopping beside it.

"Korea," Charles corrected. "I'm not that old, young man, though it is a long time ago now." The old man continued walking.

Marshall paused to look. His own grandfather had had a case much the same, though he'd been army rather than air force. They never spoke of it; the war was something that his grandfather had done his best to forget for sixty years. Marshall had looked into it when he was at university and discovered his grandfather had been a POW in Japan, so forgetting was probably for the best, from what Marshall could discover. He got the impression that his grandfather had found it a lot harder to forget as his memories of recent events dwindled, particularly once his wife had gone and he had to cope with the memories alone.

Charles Anderson ushered them towards the dining room at the back of the house, where they sat stiffly round a mahogany table.

"Who did you say you were?" Marshall got the feeling that the question was to make sure of a fact, rather than the product of any memory loss.

"Inspector John Marshall and Sergeant Mark Sherbourne, Fenwick CID."

"Yes, she said you'd come."

"Really?" Marshall was a little surprised at the ease of this, but then the girl had also shown the foresight to send him a letter. "Katie Hunter?"

"*My* Katie, said you'd come."

Marshall paused, thrown. "We're here about Miss Hunter."

"Nice girl, reminded me of my lass." The old man smiled. "She left you a letter."

"Miss Hunter did?"

"*My* Katie." He pushed himself to his feet. "I'll get it for you."

Marshall was now thoroughly confused.

"Mr Anderson, are you telling me that your wife has left me a letter?"

"Of course, that's what I said, Inspector." His tone suggested that he was having doubts as to Marshall's ability to understand simple English.

"I was led to believe that your wife had been missing for twenty years."

"Twenty-two, Inspector. She left this for you on the day she went." He left the room and they heard him going upstairs.

"Am I going mad, Mark, or is he senile do you think?"

Mark wasn't listening; he'd left the table in order to prowl the room and was looking at the pictures on the mantelpiece. "Look at this, John."

He lifted down a black and white picture of a wedding. Bride and groom smiled happily from the church steps. The groom was recognisably the young Charles Anderson in full dress uniform. The other was identical to the girl whose picture they'd collected that morning. Marshall pulled it from his pocket. The two women could have been twins.

"That's uncanny; it could be the same woman."

"Look at her neck," Mark said.

Round the bride's throat lay a choker; four strands of pearls and a large stone set in the body of a flying bird. Marshall was sure that, if the picture had been in colour, the stone would have shown blue.

They stared at the scene in silence.

"So… er…" Mark paused. "I really can't come up with anything that fits, John. Wife goes missing with necklace and then girl who looks like wife turns up with it – except Mum says she didn't wear it – and then… what?" He frowned. "Or he killed his wife and sold the necklace and then girl… except that's the same problem and I can't actually see him as a killer."

"Ah, that's me and my Katie on the day we were married." Charles had re-entered the room unnoticed. "She was a beauty."

"We were admiring the choker; it's rather a distinctive one." Marshall tapped the picture. "Is that a sapphire?"

"Yes, it was her favourite piece. The only thing she owned when I met her and the only thing she took with her when she left."

Marshall was worried by just how much of that answer he had expected. "You mentioned a letter?"

"Here you are, Inspector."

The envelope was yellowed with age but was quite clearly addressed to 'Inspector John Marshall'. Without opening it, he held it up to Mark. "Recognise it?"

"Looks like…" Mark hesitated.

"…The one I got this morning?"

"But that's not possible."

Marshall shrugged and opened the letter.

Dear Inspector, being older now and wiser, I realise that you won't respect the naïve wishes of a young girl and so, sooner or later, you will come to Charles. Having worked it out so far, I am leaving you a second letter and have asked my dear husband to pass it on to you. How much you care to explain I leave in your capable hands but I think he may know – or guess – all you could tell him.

If you have not already looked, then please find our wedding photo, it is on the mantelpiece in the dining room. That may help you to understand and to see how happy I have been. As I believe I said in my first letter, all those years ago, I left for love of another and he has been all I could wish for. I knew, as soon as I met him, that he was the man for me. The age gap was huge but he was a kindred spirit like I had never found before. And then I saw the picture – the one I hope you are holding – and I understood immediately that I was looking at myself.

The woman who helped me – answered my need – said you would know where to find her but that I shouldn't tell anyone else. I promised to keep the secret hidden and so I have through all these years, even from he who I love most. Let me just say that not all doors in Fenwick open onto the room you expect behind them.

I made a further promise when I came, which I now need to keep, though it is hard. I have to leave here in the same way I entered.

You see, I cannot be where I already am and today I met my mother. She is nearly to her time, heavy with child – the only one she will ever have. Tomorrow I will be born and so, for my dearest husband, tomorrow I must die.

Ask my mother, Inspector, how she came by the choker she now claims is missing.

I am not sure where I will go now. I cannot return to either home but I have had forty years of joy and do not regret a single second. There is a shop in Butchers' Passage, or there was forty years ago, or possibly in twenty-two years' time, where I may find another door to open.

Well, there you have it. I can't honestly say I expect you to believe it and I understand that your job is to look for me but please don't be disappointed when you fail.

Yours sincerely
Katie Anderson (née Hunter)

Marshall finished reading and handed the letter to Mark.

"Do you know what this says, Mr Anderson?"

"Katie never told me, just asked me to pass it on." Marshall, watching him shrewdly, noted that 'Katie never told me' was not actually an answer to his question. The old man handed over a second letter which was much briefer.

My darling Charles, I am sorry for causing you pain but I must leave you as I said when first we met. I will love you always and one day you may understand. Give the enclosed to Inspector Marshall on the day you eventually meet him and, until then, keep both letters your own secret. You have my heart, now and forever. Katie.

Marshall shook his head. "I really don't know where to start, Mr Anderson."

"Then don't, Inspector. I'm sure you have other things to be doing." Mr Anderson stood up.

"But…"

"I am quite busy, Inspector." It was a definite dismissal.

Marshall got slowly to his feet. "Don't you want to know what this says?"

Charles Anderson ushered them forcibly down the hall and opened the front door. Once there, he smiled suddenly. "Do you think I wouldn't know my own wife when I see her, Inspector? Keep the letter. I don't care how she managed it. I just know she loved me enough to find a way. I may have lost her twice, but I thought I would never see her again after the first, so who knows what tomorrow may bring." He very firmly shut the door behind them.

*

They visited Mrs Hunter briefly on the way back to the station.

"I just had one question," Marshall explained. "Could you tell me how Katie came by the choker that is missing?"

"Certainly Inspector, she had it from me. It was presented to me on the day before I gave birth to her. A woman stopped me in the street and told me she wanted to pass it on to another Katie." Margaret Hunter shook her head. "We hadn't told anyone we were going to call the baby Katie, we didn't even know if it would be a girl. Bill always laughed at me but I'm sure she was a witch."

"Thank you, Mrs Hunter. We'll keep you informed." Marshall turned away.

*

"So, are we believing it?" Mark watched as Marshall lay the two pictures side by side – Katie Hunter and Katie Anderson. For all the age difference, the similarities were clear.

"It's obvious when you know," Marshall said softly.

"So we *are* believing it?"

"Where that shop and that woman are concerned, I don't think there is anything I wouldn't believe. I'd be less surprised if the woman in this picture had been wearing a pair of dark-rimmed glasses but I suppose she must have other resources. We'll keep our eyes and ears open for Katie Hunter in case, but I am inclined to accept it as true." Marshall pushed all the paperwork back into the yellow folder along with all three letters he had received that day. He offered it to Mark. "This needs to go away, I think, and I'm fairly sure there'll be another to join it shortly on the unsolved case of Katie Hunter."

"Unsolved?"

"You think I'm going to write that out as a solution?" He grimaced slightly. "Obviously we will do everything possible, for her mother's peace of mind as much as anything, but I really, really can't see us getting anywhere other than where we already are."

Mark nodded. "Okay, I'll put it back where I got it from." He got as far as the door before Marshall spoke.

"Then I suppose we need to pay a visit to Butchers' Passage. I think, if we can persuade her, that it is also time for Miss Morgan to leave town. I have had enough of her disruption for one year."

Mark grinned. "Be a good trick if you can manage it."

Marshall feared he might be right but decided they had to try – the outcome of cases in Fenwick was becoming less the province of the police force and more run by a strange woman and shop, in a back alley.

*

Unfortunately, there was no shop in Butchers' Passage.

Marshall and Mark strode up and down the alley several times but no door materialised.

Eventually Marshall gave up and turned his footsteps towards the Smith Foundation Library.

"Let's see if Jenny has any ideas," he said to Mark.

Jenny greeted them from behind the front desk with a smile. "John, Mark, I was going to give you a call. I have a letter for you."

"Really?" Marshall's heart sank slightly. "I've had rather too many of those today."

Jenny held out an envelope and Marshall's heart sank even further; it was the same pink paper with the same watermark.

"Oh no," Mark said. "What now?"

"It's from Morgan," Jenny said. "Ollie delivered it earlier, said Morgan had told him he no longer had a job, gave him enough money to buy a cymbal – or something like that – and she said to tell you that she knew what you now needed."

Marshall doubted that and took the letter to open it with some trepidation. It was short, and to the point.

Inspector, forgive me, I have interfered my last – for now – in your affairs. I am moving on. Katie is happy in her past, present and future. May you be so too.

Marshall passed the note to Mark, unsure quite how he felt about having his wishes pre-empted.

"Wonder where she is now?" Mark said.

"Katie or Morgan?"

"Either."

Marshall shook his head. "I don't think it matters. They've moved on, thankfully, so it's probably time we did the same."

PART 2

OTHER MARSHALL SHORTS

Ill Met by Moonlight

The body lay sprawled in the snow at the end of the alley, its eyes gaping vacantly into the cloud-heavy sky. A full moon did little to illuminate the crime scene in the gloom behind the bulk of St Anne's church.

Inspector John Marshall sidled along the narrow way, doing his best to avoid disturbing the footprints down the centre of the path.

"Mark, can you hurry Hickson along?" he called to his sergeant who was busy taping the entrance to the scene. "We need these footprints looked at before they get messed."

He bent over Doctor Trent who was squeezed into the far corner of the alley. "What can you tell me?" He viewed the greying corpse without emotion, having seen too many dead to let another affect him. This one was little different to a myriad others; items that were somehow no longer people but wearing the features of a once-loved individual.

"Male, mid-forties at a rough estimate, shot. One bullet, penetrated the heart. Death was probably fairly instantaneous."

"Shot here or dumped?"

"I'd say here. This snow's fairly fresh and there's no sign of the body being moved." She smiled up at him. "Simple one, this, I'd say. Straightforward shooting. Too much of that about these days but the bullet's still in there, so that might help. I'll have a full report for you once I've done the post mortem but I doubt it'll tell you much more."

Marshall straightened and edged back down the alley to where Hickson was setting up his equipment. The forensic expert was well wrapped against the winter's chill, the extra layers padding out his thin form.

"What can I do for you, John?"

"Get some shots of the footprints down there first before it snows again and then see what else you can find."

The winter dark was soon alive with flash bulbs and torches.

"What do we know about the victim, Mark?" Marshall turned to his sergeant.

Mark Sherbourne handed over a wallet. "Mr Simon Powell, according to his credit card."

"Is that it?"

"Afraid so, there's nothing in there with an address on."

"Oh, great! Well, let's go and see if we can start tracking him down." Marshall looked round; he couldn't see anyone in the vicinity who he didn't work with every day. "Who called it in?"

"Anonymous phone call. We're trying to trace the number."

"It's going to be one of those cases." Marshall hated it when he had to start from absolutely nothing.

*

The station was relatively quiet at 4am on a winter's morning.

Marshall went in search of breakfast while Mark put details into the computer.

"Any hits on a Mr Powell?" Marshall delivered coffee and toast.

"I've got a Simon Powell accused of stalking a couple of years ago by a Miss Edna Harvey who claimed to have seen him following her lodger on a number of occasions. He was questioned but it was never taken further. False alarm, I assume."

"Don't tell me; Edna is an elderly single lady with too much time on her hands."

"Sixty-eight, widowed," Mark said, scrolling down the screen. "Do you want me to pull the file?"

"Yes, might as well. See if we got a picture of the bloke and whether it looks like our dead Mr Powell." Marshall slumped in his chair. He wasn't optimistic. "Anything else?"

"A Simon Powell here with a gun licence. No idea if it's the same one or if it's our corpse but it gives us an address."

"And he *was* shot. OK, let's have it. I'll take Helen in case it is our guy and there's a missus. You try the credit card company; see if they're up yet and if they'll give you any details without a warrant."

*

Number seventy-three, Hayes Crescent, was a run-down semi-detached on the Abbey Estate. It was in darkness and no-one came to the door despite Marshall's repeated hammering.

"Have a look round the back, Helen. I'm going to try next door." He'd seen the curtains twitching in the front bedroom of seventy-one so he might as well talk to whoever he'd disturbed with his knocking.

A man in his early forties opened the door when Marshall rang the bell. He was unshaven, his hair unkempt above bleary eyes. He had, though, managed a dressing gown and slippers and the speed he opened the door suggested he had been waiting on the other side of it.

"Inspector Marshall, Fenwick CID. I wondered if you could tell me if a Mr Simon Powell lives next door."

"Simon? Yes, what's he done? He always seemed a nice chap."

Marshall smiled to himself. Neighbours fell into two categories – those who assumed something dreadful had happened to the person they were asked about and those who believed the worst of their neighbours. Unfortunately, it tended to tell him more about the neighbour than the victim.

"As far as I know, Mr…"

"…Andrews."

"Mr Andrews, your neighbour has done nothing. I wonder if you have any idea where he might be."

"No, I've no idea. He went out yesterday evening. We heard the car go at about nine. Hasn't he come back?"

"What sort of car would that be?"

"Small Ford, a Fiesta, red."

"You wouldn't happen to know the registration, would you?"

"No, I've never paid that much attention. Has something happened to Simon?"

"We really don't know. I wonder if you would be able to help me, Mr Andrews. I currently have a murder victim…"

"Simon?"

"As I say, we don't know. He has a credit card in that name but there are many Simon Powells. There doesn't seem to be anyone in at his place. Do you know where we might find—"

"Oh, he lives alone, there isn't anyone else there."

Marshall thought briefly and then decided he needed what help he could get. "It would help me a great deal – if you felt up to it – if you could come and look at the body."

Mr Andrews paused fractionally and then nodded. "By all means.

Glad to help. Let me just get some clothes on."

*

"Yes," he said, slowly stepping away. "That's my neighbour. That's Simon Powell... well, the man I know by that name. He looks peaceful. I thought it would be... well... messier."

Marshall speculated idly if that was why the man had come. Some witnesses were distressingly voyeuristic.

"Who could have wanted to shoot him?"

"A good question, Mr Andrews. Can you help at all? Do you have any idea about what he did for a living or..." Marshall left it hanging. People tended to ramble if given space and it could often prove more productive than asking specific questions.

"No, we didn't know him well. I think he worked shifts. He went out at odd times and had the curtains shut during the day."

"Any family, do you know?"

"Didn't seem to have. As I say, he lived alone and we never really saw visitors."

"OK, thank you, you've been most helpful."

Marshall arranged a car to take Mr Andrews home and went in search of Mark. "Any luck?"

"Bank want a warrant but this," he waved a yellow file, "shows the same address on the suspected stalker as for the gun permit."

"Who was also probably the victim. Neighbour just identified him as the person from next door who he knows as Mr Powell. Did the victim have any keys on him?"

"House and car."

"Put out a search for a red Fiesta and then bring the house keys. Let's see if we can work out why someone wanted to kill Simon Powell."

*

151

The evidence suggested that Simon Powell barely lived at seventy-three, Hayes Crescent. The minimal furniture downstairs meant he could sit or cook but little else. The only luxurious item was a state-of-the-art computer.

"Funny," Mark said, "he looked a bit fit to be a geek."

"Obsessive of some sort," Marshall said. In his experience they were the most likely to have so little. All the money went on the addiction. "Let's try upstairs." He led the way up the dimly lit staircase.

There were two bedrooms. One with a single bed and half empty wardrobe.

The other…

"Shit!" Mark's mouth dropped. Row after row of weapon cases lined the walls.

"Well I guess we know what he spent his money on," Marshall said. "I don't even recognise half of these."

"And the other half shouldn't be legal." Mark made his way round the room, peering into cases. "Swords, daggers, guns, rifles, crossbow," he identified as he moved round. He paused to stare into a case. "God knows what this is. We need to get someone down here to bag this lot." He continued his circuit of the room. "Case here with two items missing. I'd say guns from the shape of the holder."

"Conspicuously not found on the body," Marshall said. "Any sign of a catalogue so we can tell what's missing?"

"Probably on the PC."

"We better get that taken in too." Marshall looked round; he had a feeling that the victim had been a very lonely man. But then, his sort usually were.

Marshall's phone rang.

Checking the caller, he flicked it up. "Alex, what's up?"

Doctor Alex Ranald was a friend of long standing and one who would only ever phone him at work if he needed him in an official capacity.

"Have you had a shooting, John?"

"Last night. Why?"

"I've got a man just come in to A and E with a graze on his arm. He says he witnessed a shooting and one of the bullets caught his arm."

"Right, be straight over. Did he say if he'd recognise the shooter?"

"Didn't ask, John, that's your job. I was too busy trying to save the arm."

"Save the arm? Some graze."

"That's the thing and the reason I phoned straight off. I thought I ought to warn you; his arm has swollen up considerably and is red and inflamed. The infection seems to be tracking at remarkable speed. It's really nasty. I think there might be something on the bullet. I wouldn't touch it with bare hands."

"Right, thanks, I'll tell forensics and you keep hold of your patient. I'll be right with you."

Marshall signed off and immediately dialled Dr Trent. "Liza, have you started on our shooting victim yet?"

"Give me a chance, John."

"No, no, I wasn't nagging. There might be something nasty on the bullet."

"You mean apart from the victim's insides?"

"Yeah, something nastier, dangerous. Don't touch it without gloves."

"I wouldn't, John, but thanks for the warning. I'll be careful. Any idea what I'm looking for?"

"None. Might have more for you later. We think we've got a witness." Marshall rang off. "Get this lot to the station, Mark. I'm off to The Nightingale. Might be an idea to send me a couple of uniform in case this bloke is more involved with the shooting than he is letting on; maybe see if Ashton or Sharp are around. You better put out an 'all units' too – suspect is armed and we have no idea with what. Then get into the computer. If the victim was shot with his own gun then that machine might tell us what he put on the bullets."

*

Alex met him as he arrived at the Accident and Emergency Department. The tall doctor looked worried.

"Bad?" Marshall asked.

"Don't know. I've got him on anti-inflammatories and antibiotics but, as to whether it's working, I'm not sure. I wish I knew if there was some sort of antidote. His arm's a right mess."

"Can I talk to him?"

"Oh yes, by all means, the rest of him is perfectly fine."

Alex led Marshall to a small cubicle among the bustle of A and E. Nick Sharp was already standing outside the cubicle and greeted Marshall with a grin.

"Here we go," Alex said. "This is Joseph Short. Joe, this is Detective Inspector Marshall, he wants to know about what you saw."

"I'm afraid I can't tell you much, Inspector. I was passing St Anne's in town and heard a noise. A man ran past me down the alley at the side of the church and then I heard a shot from behind and felt this pain in my arm. I looked round and this other man was running away. I didn't get much of a look at him."

"Ran past you?"

"Yes."

Marshall logged that as suspicious in his own mind; what had Joseph Short been doing in a dead-end alley that late at night? He wasn't sure he was getting the full story. "Definitely a man running away?"

"Oh yes… and he had a sort of limp when he ran as if he had a problem with his leg. Probably about your height, Inspector."

"Well, that's something to go on. Thank you, Mr Short." Marshall took a full name and address. "If you think of anything else then give me a call. Hope the arm improves and, once it does, if you'd like to come down to the station we can take a full statement."

*

"Joseph Short?" Mark said. "That name rings a bell. I've seen it somewhere else today. Hang on." He searched through the paperwork littering his desk while Marshall watched. "Ah-ha, this is it. You know the old dear who accused the victim of stalking her lodger?"

"Go on."

"Lodger was one Joseph Short."

"Interesting, so he may well have known the victim?"

"Possible." Mark scanned the paper he was holding. "There was another man – Carl Vince – identified by the woman as well. She couldn't give us anything concrete except that she'd seen the pair of them standing outside her house and following Joseph when he left a couple of times."

"Hmmm, not much to go on."

Marshall's phone rang. It was Hickson.

"I hear you're interested in this bullet."

"Yes, what have you got?"

"Nothing. No coating, no radiation, no substance. I'll keep looking but it doesn't seem to have been treated with anything."

"But I've got a witness with a swollen arm."

"Witness? Man out walking a dog, yes?"

"Er, no, not as far as I know."

"Then you've got another witness somewhere; perhaps the person who called it in. Those footprints I mapped for you show that a man of about your height went down to look at the body along with a dog."

"My witness said he thought the shooter was about my height. He didn't mention any animals though. Big or small dog?"

"Large, nothing smaller than a retriever."

"He's unlikely to have missed that. Well, thanks. Keep working on that bullet."

Marshall perched on the edge of his sergeant's desk. "That alley was busy last night; the victim, Mr Short, the shooter and now a man walking his dog. Not to mention whoever called it in who might be any of those or someone else entirely. Any luck tracing that yet?"

"Helen's working on it. It was a mobile rather than a phone box which is something."

"I hope so. It just seems at the minute like the more we learn, the less we know."

"So where next?"

"Well," Marshall grinned, "daft bat and then sinister friend."

"Give me a sinister friend any day."

"I know, but we have to check out her too, I'm afraid. See if Helen can find an up to date address for Carl Vince and then we'll go and pay Edna a visit."

*

Marshall expected a doddering old dear who saw sinister echoes in her own shadow. The woman who opened the door was small, sprightly and surprisingly shrewd.

"What can I do for you, Inspector?" she asked once Marshall had introduced himself.

"Does Joseph Short still live with you, Mrs Harvey?"

"Of course." There was a moment's silence and then she said, "Is he all right?" as if it was something she thought was expected of her.

"He's fine, Mrs Harvey. He witnessed a shooting last night and got caught by a bullet but he's having his arm seen to now."

She nodded calmly. "I see. So how can I help?"

"The victim of the shooting was Simon Powell who you reported two years ago for acting suspiciously."

She looked at him with very sharp blue eyes, almost as if she was looking through him. "Oh, but I was just 'imagining' that, Inspector. The police at the time were quite clear."

"It just seemed to me to be an amazing coincidence that a man you thought was stalking your lodger is dead and your lodger happened to witness it."

There were none of the denials Marshall was expecting; nothing defensive. "There were two men following Joe, Inspector."

"Are you suggesting the other is in danger too?" Somehow the thought of a white-haired old lady threatening death wasn't silly when she did it.

Edna Harvey shook her head sadly as if he was a student who'd shown himself particularly stupid.

"No, Inspector, I'm suggesting Joe might have ducked."

Marshall almost slapped himself on the forehead. That was something he hadn't thought of.

"Thank you, Mrs Harvey, you have been most helpful." He turned away from the door and then a thought occurred to him. "Oh, by the way, does Joseph own a dog?"

"A dog?" A shadow of fear touched her eyes.

"The footprints suggest a witness with a dog may have found the body and, so far, Joseph is our only witness."

"Joseph does not own a dog, Inspector." She shut the door in his face.

*

"Well, Mark, what do you think?"

"I think she already knew about Joseph. She wasn't worried at all."

"No."

"In fact, the only time she sounded concerned – frightened almost – was when you asked about a dog."

"I noticed that. It makes no sense," Marshall said as he opened the car door. "What about her idea that Carl Vince was shooting at Short, and Powell was hit instead?"

Before Mark could answer, Marshall's phone sounded shrilly. It was Helen Lovell.

"Got a trace on who called the murder in, sir."

"Go on."

"Mobile in the name of Mrs Edna Harvey."

Marshall shut the car door again. "Let's talk to Mrs Harvey some more, shall we? Seems it was her who called it in."

They strode back up the front path. The door was open by the time they got there.

"What was the call, Inspector? Was it Joe?"

"No, he's still fine as far as I know."

"So it must be something to do with me."

"Yes, Mrs Harvey. I think we ought to come in."

She led them through to the kitchen at the back of the house where they sat round a small pine table.

"I think you haven't been entirely honest with us, Mrs Harvey," Marshall said.

"I think I have been perfectly honest, Inspector," she said briskly. "I can hardly be held to blame if you failed to ask the correct questions."

"You called us earlier to tell us about the body."

"You know that, Inspector."

"How did you know about the body?"

"I would have thought that was obvious. Joe came home. He told me what he saw and I convinced him we had to tell the police and then I sent him to hospital."

"And did Joseph tell you the shooter was Carl Vince?"

"He didn't need to."

"You mean," Mark said, "that you are assuming it was because you saw him once…"

"More than once."

"All right," Marshall said before his sergeant could argue the point further, "answer me this. Why would Carl Vince and Simon Powell want to follow or to kill Joseph?"

"I have absolutely no idea."

*

"Which was the one time I think she lied to us," said Marshall as they climbed the stairs to look in Joseph's room. "I think she knows perfectly well."

"We'll have to go back to the hospital," Mark said.

"I'm wondering if we need to provide protection, at least warn Nick Sharp that his guard duties may be rather more necessary than we first thought. If we can't find Carl Vince perhaps he is waiting to try again. If," Marshall added, "we believe it was him the first time." He paused on the landing. "That's odd."

"What?"

"This door has a bolt on the outside. Mrs Harvey can lock her lodger in."

They entered the bedroom. It was well furnished with an en-suite bathroom and a view overlooking the Abbey Park. Upon inspection, the wardrobe turned out to be full of suits, the bookshelf packed with detective fiction and the chair had a blood-stained jacket tossed across it. "Looks like he dumped it and went to the hospital," Marshall said.

"I can't see anything that would make anyone want to kill him." Mark peered under the bed. "Nothing here."

They trooped back downstairs.

"Mrs Harvey, do you lock Mr Short into his room at night?" Marshall couldn't imagine the upright old lady being afraid of anything but he supposed she might feel safer locking away the man in her house.

"Occasionally, Inspector."

"Why?"

"For his own good."

"His good?"

"Yes, Inspector." She outfaced him, her lips firmly closed, refusing to give anything else away.

Marshall gave in; now was not the time. "We may wish to speak with you again, Mrs Harvey. Please do not leave town."

"I have no intention of going anywhere, thank you."

*

Marshall's phone rang again as they headed for the hospital. It was Hickson reporting on the bullet.

"I can find absolutely nothing wrong with it, John. No poisons, toxins, radiation, foreign matter. It's just a silver bullet."

"Silver?"

"Yes, didn't Liza say? Not the normal material but it kills just as well."

*

It was getting dark by the time they arrived at the hospital. Alex Ranald greeted them in the entrance. He didn't smile, his brow creased.

"How's Joseph Short, Al?"

"Not good. I've just been discussing it with one of the surgeons;

160

we really do think we're going to have to amputate, John. Any news on the bullet?"

"It was silver. Other than that, nothing. Any chance it's an allergic reaction like people get to peanuts and bee stings?"

"No, I don't see how it can be but I can go ask him."

"We'll come too if that's all right. We've got some questions."

A sudden tremendous crash had them whirling towards the entrance. The door had slammed open and a tall man in a leather jacket staggered towards them. "Help me," he whispered hoarsely before crashing to the floor at their feet.

Alex immediately knelt beside the fallen stranger, Marshall following. The man was unshaven, the shadow of new bristle appearing on a prominent chin. His hair was nearly black, a sprinkle of grey at the temples. What caught Marshall's gaze was the left leg. The trouser was shredded revealing swollen, bloody flesh beneath. He swept his eyes across the body looking for other injuries and paused; the leather jacket bulged significantly.

Moving quickly, Marshall pulled Alex back, flicked the jacket open and removed the guns holstered inside. There were two, gleaming silver.

Doing his best to avoid the wound, Marshall patted the man down but there was no sign of other weapons. "All right, Alex, take him away but I'll stick around and you be careful; this one's dangerous. Let me know when I can ask him about these." He turned the guns over in his hands, aware of Mark's interested gaze over his shoulder.

"Any identification?" Mark asked as Alex organised a stretcher.

Marshall handed over the wallet he'd retrieved from the inner jacket pocket. "I may be wrong, but I guess that will show that this is Carl Vince."

"Yeah, two cards in his name and a driving licence." Mark handed the wallet back. "Had to be, don't usually get too many people wandering around with guns in one day."

Alex reappeared while Mark was phoning in for some more uniformed officers to help Nick Sharp with watching the suspect. "He should be all right. It looks like a dog bite."

The two policemen exchanged glances. "Can we interview him?" Marshall asked.

"I've given him something to calm him down; he's very worked up about it. He's still awake at present but try and keep him calm."

Carl Vince was a big man; at least six feet tall and running to fat around the middle. He dwarfed the hospital bed and the nurse who was cleaning the set of puncture marks on his left thigh. The size and severity suggested a large dog had bitten hard and held on for some not inconsiderable time.

Marshall introduced himself. "I wondered if you could tell me where you were last night, Mr Vince."

"Out." The brown eyes grew wary.

"Out where, Mr Vince?"

"Just out. Walking."

"Do you know a Mr Powell?"

"Yes." His mouth snapped shut on the answer.

"Did you see him last night?"

"Might have."

Marshall took a steadying breath. He often wondered what criminals thought they gained by being so obtuse.

"Mr Powell is dead, Mr Vince. He was shot and I am fairly confident that forensics will tell me that one of the weapons I removed from your coat fired the fatal shot. I also have a witness in this very hospital with a gunshot wound to his arm who, I am sure, will be able to put you at the scene. Therefore I suggest you—"

"Here? That fucking freak's here? I'll kill him!" Carl Vince pushed the nurse aside and surged to his feet only to plunge sideways as he attempted to put his weight on the injured leg. "The bastard's ripped my leg. If he's cursed me I'll—"

"Mr Vince!" Marshall struggled to help get the man back on the bed. "Are you accusing Mr Short of having something to do with the injury to your leg?"

"Fucking freak bit me."

"The doctor said that is a dog bite, Mr Vince," Mark said, holding the man's other arm. "Our information is that Mr Short does not own a dog. Are you saying this is incorrect?"

"Dog?" He collapsed into high-pitched, uncontrollable laughter which brought Alex running.

"I told you to keep him calm, John."

"Sorry, all I did was ask him about the dog which bit him."

"That's what set him off before. I thought you were going to ask about the shooting."

"Seems to be a bit complicated. He claims Mr Short's dog—"

"NO!" Carl Vince practically threw himself back off the bed with the force of his reply. "He did. He did it and now I'll be a bloody weirdo and they'll hunt me down. I don't want to die. I'm going to fucking kill him and…"

"Get out, John, while I deal with this. This isn't helping him and we do need to get the leg cleaned. Hold him down, nurse. I think I better give him something stronger too or we'll never get this leg clean." Marshall and his sergeant left the room to allow Alex to carry on.

"Now what? Do you think he is our shooter?" Mark said while they waited for the doctor.

"I'd say so and I also think, after that little outburst, that Mrs Harvey wasn't so far out when she suggested he was shooting at Mr

Short. Mr Powell looks like an innocent victim."

"Hardly innocent, John. I'd say these guns match the gaps in his weapon cases."

"So," Alex said, re-emerging, "you think the two of them went hunting Mr Short and he managed to escape while one of the hunters shot the other?"

"Sounds about right. The only thing we don't know is why. Let's go and talk to Mr Short," Marshall said.

"And the dog?" Mark asked.

"I hadn't forgotten the dog. It was a dog, wasn't it, Alex?"

"Definitely," Alex said. "No question."

Marshall nodded. "Right, so let's see what light Mr Short can throw on the matter."

*

Joseph Short was in a bad way. His arm was swollen and black, pus oozing from the open wound. His face was drained of colour, his breathing heavy.

"I am going to have to take that arm, Mr Short." A slim man who Marshall assumed was the surgeon Alex had mentioned was remonstrating with Joseph Short. Marshall got the impression this was a discussion the two of them had already been having for a while.

"It will be fine."

The two men glared at each other and then Alex intervened. "Inspector Marshall would like to ask you some more questions about last night if you feel up to it."

"Fire ahead. I'll do my best. Then you need to help me outside."

"You can't leave." Alex exchanged horrified glances with his colleague. "I won't allow it."

"I want some air, doctor, that's all."

"But it's dark and snowing again and—"

"Five minutes, doctor, and then, if you think it necessary, you can deal with the arm."

Alex paused and then nodded. "Ask quickly, John, I think delirium is setting in."

Marshall wasn't so sure; the man seemed perfectly lucid in his speech even if he wasn't acting particularly rationally. "Mr Short, can you tell me exactly what happened last night, please? A more honest version than the one you gave me this morning."

Joseph Short closed his eyes briefly. "How much do you know?"

"Can you confirm whether a Mr Carl Vince was involved?"

"Ah," he smiled, "you got him. Yes, Inspector, Mr Vince shot at me and... I managed to get out of the way. He killed his colleague instead."

"In that alley?" Mark raised an eyebrow.

"I... ducked, shall we say."

Marshall frowned. "For now. So can you tell me why Mr Vince and Mr Powell might want to kill you?"

"No, Inspector."

"Oh, come on..."

"I can show you."

"Show me?"

"Yes, help me outside."

*

It took both Marshall and Mark to support Joseph outside. Alex followed, pushing a wheelchair that the patient had refused to use.

The main car park was filled with snow-dusted vehicles and dark clouds scudded across the face of a full moon.

Joseph pulled away from their arms and stood, breathing deeply. After a few seconds, his body began to shimmer and waver as if they saw him through a heat haze. Marshall rubbed his eyes reflexively and when he lowered his hand, a large wolf stood in front of him, its tongue hanging out.

"What the fuck?" Mark took a step back and Alex gasped.

Marshall eyed the animal warily, his mind working furiously, trying to assimilate what had happened. The wolf seemed friendly enough and there was no arguing that this was Joseph Short – or had been thirty seconds earlier. But this just wasn't possible. His hand automatically crept to the reassuring weight of the guns he'd taken from Carl Vince.

"John, is it safe?"

"He," Marshall said reflexively, "is *he* safe?" He paused, realising the incongruity of his words when his own reaction had been to look for protection. Taking a deep breath, he took his hands from his pockets and held them out, palm forwards to show they were empty. "He's safe, Mark." He hoped he was right.

"But that's not possible," Mark said, staying resolutely behind Marshall.

"No, but then again, you just saw it." Marshall could feel his heartbeat returning to normal. He was a policeman – believe the evidence of your own eyes, no hearsay and don't stereotype people. He repeated the advice to himself firmly; a mantra he had had to rely on quite a lot since coming to Fenwick. "No discrimination, Mark. He's a victim whatever... well, whatever."

Mark laughed and stepped up beside him. "So now what, John?" His unflappable nature was one of the things Marshall valued most about his sergeant. They'd survived a lot together in the last couple of years.

"Can you change back?" Marshall felt silly talking to an animal but the wolf immediately began to waver again. Marshall couldn't put his finger on the exact moment when the beast became the man but one moment there was a wolf grinning at him and the next, Joseph Short stood there, swaying slightly.

"It's a popular myth, Inspector, that a creature like me has to be an animal in the full moon. The moonlight simply aids the change." He flexed his arm slightly. "More importantly, it heals."

Marshall realised that he was looking at a limb which showed no sign of infection or swelling.

"So you did bite him?" Not only a victim then.

"Self-defence, Inspector. He was trying to shoot me."

"But you would have healed. You just showed us that."

"A limb, yes. Even then, you saw what the silver did. Imagine if the bullet had pierced my heart which, I assure you, was his intent. No amount of moonlight will resurrect the dead."

"He knew what you are?"

"What am I, Inspector?"

Marshall hesitated. "In all honesty, Mr Short, I don't know. As you said, I know popular myth. The real thing is not something I ever expected. Carl Vince, though, obviously did."

"I have known him a while."

"And Mr Powell?"

"Got behind me in a dark alley. He, like you, did not understand his prey. He thought I would be unable to change out of the moon. I did not do so fast enough to avoid the bullet entirely."

"And biting Mr Vince?"

"Will make his leg hurt, Inspector, nothing more."

"Mrs Harvey locks you in—" Marshall began.

"My idea, Inspector. I mean her no harm but it helps keep her mind at rest. A pointless gesture but it carries a weight of reassurance."

They stood in silence for a while watching the snow fall past the lighted windows of the hospital on a moonlit evening.

"Am I free to go, Inspector?"

"You've broken no law that I know of." Marshall allowed himself a small smile as he imagined trying to prosecute under the Dangerous Dogs Act.

"I don't suppose," Alex began.

"I've never fancied being put under a microscope, doctor, if you don't mind." He turned to go. "I'll be at Mrs Harvey's if you need me." He strode off into the whirling snow.

Marshall watched him go, unsure now that he had seen the change at all. Absolutely positive it wasn't something he could put in a report.

"Go and arrest Carl Vince for the killing of Simon Powell, Mark."

"But..."

"A man is dead. We have a witness to say Mr Vince shot him and the forensics will identify the gun." Marshall took his sergeant's arm and led him back inside. "Get uniform to set a watch on him and charge him and then you need to buy me a stiff drink."

He looked back gratefully as the doors shut behind him. The idea of being out in the full moonlight suddenly had a slightly dangerous quality to it.

Ghost of a Rose

"Someone's been here recently," Marshall said, his voice deadened by the weight of history in the room.

A single white rose stood in the vase on the mantelpiece. It was out of place in the midst of the dust and decay.

Years of accumulated cobwebs draped the heavy furniture and crowded bookshelves; clouds of dust billowed up whenever anything was touched. The heavy velvet curtains had faded from their deep red over years of neglect. Marshall left them closed, afraid that trying to open them might bring them crashing down.

Amidst the silence of the room, the perfect, fresh rose drew the eye. No dust touched it and its delicate fragrance caught the air, diminishing the smells of age and abandonment. A single drop of dew hung on one of the petals.

"Nothing was disturbed," the WPC by the door disagreed. "Eleanor said she only came as far as the door and I called you straight away." Mark Sherbourne still also stood by the door, peering at his superior across the gloom.

"Someone brought the flower in, it's newly picked," Marshall said.

"Yeah, I suppose," Mark agreed. "Surely they would have left a trail. This dust's as good as snow."

"Hmm. Make a note of it, will you, Mark?" Marshall moved on round the room, attempting to raise as little dust as possible. His sergeant wasn't wrong; footsteps stood out like those across a winter field. "We'll get the vase bagged too; it might give us some fingerprints."

He completed his journey to the desk where the reason for his visit sat. The corpse had been there for some while; its skin taut and desiccated across the bones beneath, the clothes moth-eaten and ragged.

"I've heard of cold cases but this is ridiculous." Marshall fingered the cloth lightly, pulling his hand away as it crumbled beneath his touch. "This guy's wearing stuff you only get in history books."

"Anything to show how he died?" Mark peered into the shadows of the book-lined room.

"That'll be the four foot of steel sticking out of his back, Mark. Tends to be relatively conclusive."

"A sword?"

"Plunged in from behind."

"And then people just ignored the fact this room was here for... what... a couple of hundred years? Are you sure it's not April Fool's Day, John?"

"I wish."

"Or a film set. Perhaps we've wandered into one by mistake."

Marshall laughed. "I know. I don't understand it either but it's a murder scene so we treat it as such, however bizarre the circumstances. We'll know more once Doctor Trent gets down here and Craig Hickson with his technical wizardry. Actually, he can come in first. Get photos and the like before it's all churned up in here. I don't think it'll matter if our corpse here waits a few more minutes for the doctor."

Marshall carefully picked his way back across the room. "And bag that rose."

Something in the silence made him look.

"What rose?" Mark said, also looking at the mantelpiece. The vase was empty.

"But… you saw?" Marshall wondered if he'd imagined it but Mark nodded.

"Oh yes, I saw," the uniformed officer was nodding too, "and now I don't. Which is just another thing that's wrong about this whole set-up."

That was an understatement and a half but Marshall valued Mark Sherbourne for his pragmatism; the fact that he was solidly grounded however far a case took them from 'normal' behaviour. And they'd seen some bizarre things in Fenwick in the past couple of years; 'normal' just didn't come into it. He'd needed all of Mark's hard-headed common sense.

"Well, we'll get Hickson to test the vase anyway," Marshall said. "While we wait for the circus to turn up, I'm going to ask Miss Jenkins why this room has been ignored for what looks like centuries. Constable, do keep an eye." Though he wasn't sure what the poor girl could do about evidence that disappeared before their eyes.

*

Eleanor Jenkins was curator of Fenwick Museum, currently housed in a 1960s monstrosity on Market Street. This was soon to change with the whole catalogue to be re-housed in the old manor – a place that had stood empty for nearly forty years and now seemed to include a room that no-one knew existed, and a very dead corpse.

The woman who greeted Marshall in the grand entrance hall of the manor was in her late thirties, her brown hair clipped back from a slim face. The jeans and old t-shirt suggested this had been more than a courtesy call to see how work was progressing. Marshall knew her from Christmas and an interesting couple of days in the library. He had been impressed then by her calm, unflustered approach and hoped she could throw a sensible light on the current situation.

"Eleanor," he shook her firmly by the hand, "can you explain exactly what's happening here?" It was habit; Marshall preferred open questions, they let witnesses and suspects dig much bigger holes for themselves.

"We're opening the manor up, Inspector, and redecorating it ready to house the museum. I'd like it to look like it used to, so it'll be an exhibit in itself, if you see what I mean. The contractors have been in all month clearing rubbish and checking the soundness of walls and floors, opening up the old fireplaces that were bricked up; all that sort of thing. They've found various items of interest along the way and I've been sending in my people regularly to check it for value. It's my turn this week to make sure that some idiot doesn't consign a masterpiece to a skip."

"And this room?" Marshall nodded towards the door at the back of the hall where he and Mark had emerged.

"You're not going to believe this."

"Try me."

"It wasn't here when I arrived this morning."

Marshall regarded her in silence for a moment but her gaze didn't waver. "So when did it appear?"

"Just after lunch. I came through the hall and noticed there was a door where I'd never seen one before. It used to be a blank wall."

"So what would normally be behind this blank wall?"

"Well, if my geography is right, it should be the room – a sort of small retiring room – behind the old dining room. If you go down that passage there," she pointed away to the front left of the entrance hall, "and take the first door on the right, the dining room runs the length of the hall along the side except for the small room at the back."

"So what I've just been in is this 'retiring' room?"

"Oh no, Inspector, that room is empty. I can show you if you like."

Marshall blinked. "You mean if we go through the dining room we'll get to a different room than where I've just been?"

"Yes."

"So this new room can't be in the same place."

"Theoretically, no," Eleanor Jenkins looked rather worried, "but then again, yes. Because they are. I could show you, and the house plans if you like."

"You're trying to tell me I've got two rooms co-existing in the same place or one room which looks different depending on which door I use?"

Eleanor shrugged.

"Well then, yes, I would like to see both plans and room because that is plainly impossible." Though between the pair of them they had had plenty of experience of impossible.

The plans clearly showed that, if you took the passage along the front left of the house, the first room you came to was the dining room, which went back nearly the full length of the entrance hall and behind it was a small 'retiring room'.

When Eleanor led Marshall and his sergeant through the dining room to it, this room proved to be small and empty apart from the mound of rubble where the contractors had obviously just finished opening up the large fireplace.

Marshall stopped in surprise. A small glass vase on the mantelpiece gave off rainbows of light in the glare of early afternoon sun from the full-length window. It contained a single white rose.

"Miss Jenkins, did you put that rose there?"

"No, Inspector. How odd." She moved round the pile of bricks to look at it. "It's beautiful and such a lovely fragrance."

Marshall nodded; he recognised the scent. "See if you can collect it this time, Mark."

"John!" The call came from the front of the house. "Where are you?"

All three of them turned to the sound of Dr Trent's arrival.

"Bugger," Mark said, catching Marshall back on the point of leaving to greet the pathologist. The sergeant waved his hand at the now empty mantelpiece. "Sorry, John, took my eyes off it again."

*

Liza Trent and Craig Hickson were both waiting in the hall. Marshall considered them to be the best he'd ever worked with though he sometimes had trouble reconciling Liza Trent's delicate form with a woman who spent her life pulling corpses apart.

"Where's your body, John?" Craig Hickson's tight, black curls were going grey at the temples and he now wore glasses for the close fingerprint work but, even so, he rarely missed anything.

Marshall took a surreptitious glance across the large entrance hall. The door, with its attendant officer, still seemed to be there, which was a start. "This way," he said with some trepidation; God knows what they'd find. He'd learned the hard way that buildings in Fenwick weren't all they seemed.

He led the way in and stopped in amazement. Even half expecting something odd, he wasn't prepared. There were no cobwebs, no dust; not a trace of any such ever having been there. The room looked recently cleaned, each surface sparkling and polished.

"Bugger me," said Mark, following him in.

"I'd prefer not to," Hickson said cheerfully. "I take it something's wrong."

"This room was caked in cobwebs and dirt," Marshall said.

"When?"

"Thirty, forty minutes ago."

Hickson raised an eyebrow. "Is the body still here?"

It was, sitting at the desk with the sword pinning it there.

Except.

"This isn't right either. The corpse we saw looked like it had been dead for hundreds of years. This guy's still warm." Marshall glanced at the WPC who was looking distinctly apprehensive. "No-one came in here while we were gone, did they?" A stupid question, really. Even if someone had overpowered the woman and entered, there was no way they'd have managed the transformation in half an hour.

Dr Trent crossed the room and touched the victim's neck. "Dead less than an hour, I'd say."

"But we've been here nearly an hour, Liza, and he's been dead that long. To be honest, he's been rather more dead than he currently seems to be."

"Are you sure?"

"Of course I am. The body Mark and I saw was barely a skeleton. I know it sounds mad but it was here."

"The same man?"

"Well," Marshall paused and looked closely, "yes, I'd say so. The clothes are definitely the same though they were in rather worse condition and the height is the same and the sword in the same position. Yes, I'm sure what I saw was this corpse after a huge stretch of time."

"All right, let me work on him." Liza Trent moved them out of the way and began examining the body, while Hickson started taking pictures and measuring and fingerprinting.

"Preliminary findings for you," Dr Trent sat back on her heels. "Male, late forties, just under six foot, killed by a single stab wound from behind. Definitely murder, there is no way he could have done

175

that to himself. I'll have a better report once I've opened him up."

"Thanks, Liza. He's all yours, take him away."

Marshall noticed Eleanor Jenkins hovering in the doorway, obviously reluctant to enter without invitation but just as obviously eager to have a look round.

"Come in, Eleanor." He threw her a pair of gloves. "Careful what you touch but by all means come and have a look at this stuff for your museum."

"Isn't she a suspect?" Mark hissed in his ear.

"Possibly but I really can't see it myself. This feels all wrong."

He and Mark continued to turn over the papers on the desk and open drawers while Eleanor moved carefully around the room, investigating the larger pieces of furniture.

"Inspector," she said suddenly and Marshall thought she sounded frightened. He looked up. She was standing in front of an oak bureau.

"What is it, Miss Jenkins?"

"The museum already owns this piece."

"One like it?"

"No, this one. I remember the missing handle here," she pointed to where one drawer was devoid of a handle, "and the scratches round the lock, where a key has been misused, and the carving."

Marshall exchanged glances with Mark; duplicated wardrobes sounded like an all too familiar story. But he'd destroyed the camera in question, so he didn't see how it could be. Taking a deep breath, Marshall joined Eleanor in front of the cabinet. Someone had carved a pair of linked 'R's on the side, in the centre of a flower. To Marshall, the flower looked like a rose.

"Sure it's not just alike?" Even he couldn't see how that would be the case.

"I dropped it on my foot less than a fortnight ago whilst

rearranging the Georgian display. I assure you this is the same bureau. It is currently in room nine on the first floor of my museum."

"Except it's here," Marshall pointed out.

"Yes. How's that possible?" Light green eyes searched his face for an answer he didn't have.

"Got some letters," Mark said from by the desk, "addressed to a Mister Richard Hawkwood. Could be the victim, if this is his desk." Two policemen were currently zipping the figure into a body bag under Dr Trent's watchful supervision.

"Possible..." Marshall began.

"Hawkwood?" Eleanor interrupted. "The Hawkwoods left here in the late eighteenth century if I remember right. We found some portraits in one of the attics only yesterday."

"Wouldn't mind taking a look at those," Marshall said. "What do the letters say, Mark?"

"Threats. 'Leave my sister alone or else' sort of thing. This one seems to be the last and says, 'Dear sir, you have my final word on the subject. If you come near my sister again it shall be the death of you. Hugh Lacey.'"

"Sounds like intent and motive there. Bag them and bring them. Anything else?"

"Diary, could belong to this Richard Hawkwood. Entries here reading 'another letter from H today' and 'H came round today, R had to hide'. This one says, 'R barely hid in time today'."

"Don't know; if we assume 'R' is Richard then it sounds like someone else wrote the diary. Perhaps 'R' didn't manage to hide quickly enough the last time and so he was killed. I think we need to find this Hugh Lacey."

"I can do that for you," Eleanor said unexpectedly. "Come with me."

She led them back out into the hall and then down a side passage into a small drawing room. Framed portraits leant against the wall, three deep in places.

"Wait a moment," Eleanor instructed them and began searching through the canvases. "I'm sure I saw it here."

After a while she cleared a space along one wall and placed three portraits side by side in the gap.

"Here," she pointed to the first. "Captain Hugh Lacey, painted 1793." A young man in full regimental scarlet looked out at them. He was tall, dark and handsome and wore a sword buckled at his waist. "And here, Inspector." Eleanor directed his gaze to the next painting. A pale young woman of outstanding beauty smiled demurely from the frame. The words at the bottom declared this to be 'Lady Rose Lacey, painted 1788'.

"His sister?" Marshall peered closer. "Rose? So this could be 'R' instead?"

"I think it's his sister. It's not really my period. You should have had Percy here; he's my man for the eighteenth century. I've got a history of the manor if that will help. I can have a look for you," Eleanor offered.

"And the third?" Marshall turned to find himself looking at a beautifully rendered painting of his corpse. 'Richard Hawkwood, painted 1789'. He had been depicted standing gazing intently at what he held in his hand.

A single, white rose.

*

"So what have we got?" Marshall faced his sergeant across his desk. The two of them both held steaming mugs of coffee.

"One threatening letter possibly written by a man two hundred years ago, one room that supposedly only appeared – or reappeared –

this morning and one corpse who—"

"No."

Both men turned to where Liza Trent had appeared in the doorway. Hickson hovered behind her.

"Sorry, John. No corpse."

"What?"

"I watched it go in the body bag myself…"

"…As did we all, Liza."

"It wasn't there by the time we got back to the lab. Thought I'd better come and let you know personally. I swear I don't know how it can have vanished." She looked quite distressed.

Marshall waved his hand reassuringly. In the short time he'd worked with her he had found her to be totally reliable. He had no doubts that the vanishing body was not her fault.

"Don't fret, Liza. There's something wrong about this whole set-up."

"You're telling me." Hickson followed the doctor into the room. "Thought you might like to see these, that I took this morning. Even by Fenwick's standards we're weirding out." He waved a memory stick at them.

Marshall moved out of the way so Hickson could upload the photographs onto the computer in the middle of the desk. Then they gathered round to look. Every picture showed the starkly white retiring room at the back of the dining room with its pile of bricks. There was no sign of corpse, desk, books, heavy curtains or décor. Despite the range of angles Marshall was sure Hickson would have used, every single picture also managed to show the fireplace and – placed in a vase on the mantelpiece – the single, white rose.

"It's almost as if someone's trying to tell us something," Mark said after a moment's stunned silence.

"In Double Dutch," Marshall said sourly. "Let's go and talk to Eleanor Jenkins again and see if she can tell us the significance of this fireplace."

"Is that necessary? We don't actually have a corpse anymore."

"Probably not, Mark, but I'm intrigued and if someone is going to all this trouble to communicate let's at least make some effort to translate."

*

Eleanor Jenkins was still at the old manor sorting through what looked like the contents of several over-equipped and outdated kitchens.

"It's amazing the stuff we've found," she said, waving a lethal-looking spit arrangement at Marshall.

"So I see. Have you got a moment?"

"By all means. I found the book on manor history if you're interested. It's not really my thing, I'm more prehistoric, but it has some fascinating information in, that you ought to hear."

"I'd like to see that room behind the dining room as well; the one you showed me earlier."

They headed across the entrance hall and waited while Eleanor stopped to collect a book from amongst her things on the stairs. Marshall wasn't surprised to see that the door to the strange room was no longer present.

"Room vanished again?"

"About an hour ago," Eleanor said, "like it was never there."

"Along with the corpse," Marshall agreed, following her through the dining room.

It was precisely as Marshall remembered it, which was reassuring. Rather too much today had changed when he wasn't looking. The fireplace was a gaping hole that was going to need some restoration now it was open. A white rose stood in the vase on the shelf above the huge opening.

"The rose again," Eleanor said. "That's very weird."

"What does your history book say about this room?"

"Interestingly, it says it used to be the library until a bigger one was added with the new wing. This room was rarely used after that."

Marshall nodded; that made some sort of sense. The room that morning had looked like a library.

"And how about our corpse; anything on him?"

"Richard Hawkwood, last of the Hawkwoods to live here. Found stabbed – in his library – in 1789. No-one was ever convicted of killing him. The house passed to the Laceys in his will, specifically to Rose Lacey to whom he was betrothed except – according to the book – she vanished on the day Richard died and was never seen again. Hugh Lacey took over ownership of the manor and rumour agreed that Rose must have killed Richard and then run away."

"So we saw the ghost of an old murder?" Mark asked.

"I think we're going to be a bit pushed for evidence when it keeps vanishing on us but I'd say it looks that way and it all points to Hugh or Rose Lacey being the killer." Marshall glanced round the empty room. "Question is, why bother? It's all obvious, there's nothing we can do about it." He walked across to stand and stare at the rose which still stood on the fireplace. "I don't get it. What are you trying to tell us?" he said, feeling rather self-conscious. "Because the history books already know all this."

Mark joined him and peered into the hearth and up the chimney. "Believed in proper fires, didn't they? This is huge."

"They only finished opening it up this morning," Eleanor said. "The Smythes bricked them all up when they put in radiators."

"Hey." Mark stepped forwards into the fireplace. "Look at this, John."

Marshall stepped into the grate to peer upwards beside his sergeant. Just above eye level on the left-hand side was a carving of a rose.

"Well I never, another rose." He reached out to touch it. "It looks almost like a handle." He pushed at it. With many protesting groans a two-foot section of stone swung back, revealing a narrow opening.

Brought by the noise, Eleanor also ducked under the mantelpiece.

"Oh wow, a priest's hole. I never realised the manor had one; I don't think it's on the plans. Hang on, I'll get a torch." She was gone barely two minutes, returning with a powerful flashlight which she shone past Marshall into the hole.

The tiny room it revealed was about four foot square and most of the area was taken up with skeleton.

*

"Well, it's female," Liza Trent said, doing her best to crouch in the confined space, "but the dress probably told you that. I'd need to date her properly but I'd say this is probably a two-hundred-year-old corpse, John."

"Cause of death?"

"Can't see any trauma. I'd hazard lack of air or lack of food or a combination of both."

They stared at the sad figure in the torchlight.

"So this is Rose Lacey?" Mark asked.

"Sounds like a good guess to me," Marshall agreed.

"And her brother stabbed her lover and then shut her up in here? God, that's sick."

"No," Eleanor said from outside the small room, "I don't think he did. Remember that diary. 'R hid again'. I think this was her hiding place. Hugh turned up, got suspicious anyway and stabbed Richard."

"So why didn't she just come out?"

Eleanor shook her head. "Look at the wall. It only works one way.

Doesn't open from the inside. Someone who knew of it would have had to let her in and let her out. Priest holes were designed to be as secret as possible."

"And Hugh never knew." Marshall had a vision of the woman, waiting for release and getting increasingly panicked as she realised she was forever trapped. The cramped space felt suddenly heavy with terror.

"Let's get her out and give her a proper burial. See if you can find this Richard's grave. If no-one objects, I'm sure there'll be room in it for her."

"Sentiment?" Mark teased.

"Just feels like the right thing to do."

*

A feeling that he decided had been accurate as he stood, ten days later, beside the freshly opened grave of Richard Hawkwood and watched them lower the remains of Rose Lacey down to join her lover.

The small headstone was worn but legible and had space enough to add her name, if anyone so desired.

Except Marshall felt that probably wasn't necessary, as grave and headstone both were nearly buried beneath the weight of the rose bush which grew beside the grave.

Despite the lateness of the year it was in glorious bloom.

And each perfect flower was white.

The Tide Comes; The Sea Calls Out

The fur coat looked expensive, Inspector Marshall decided and – using a policeman's nose for these things – not the sort of item the Doyles could afford.

The coat dwarfed the girl in the picture, swaddling her up against the cold.

"Was she wearing—" Marshall began and then hesitated. Stupid question. Why would a young girl who'd vanished at the height of Fenwick's summer have taken her winter fur with her?

"Er, anything distinctive?" he settled for as a finish and then mentally berated himself again. The Doyles' daughter had vanished in the middle of the night; how on earth were they meant to know what she'd been wearing?

Mark Sherbourne, his ever-reliable sergeant, took over, speaking gently to the parents. "Have you had time to see if you can work out what she was wearing?"

"Oh, she took the fur," Karen Doyle said in her light Irish burr. "That's why I showed you the picture."

"Of course," Mark said, still gentle. "Do you know why she'd do that with the weather we've been having?"

"Took it everywhere with her, didn't she?" Steven Doyle said bluntly. "Never understood it myself."

"Like a safety blanket," his wife said. "Children need that." It sounded like an argument she'd made many times; perhaps to convince herself as much as her husband.

"Can you think of any reason she wouldn't want to come back?" Marshall asked. "Or why she would run away?"

Both parents shook their heads.

"She kept saying it was home," Karen Doyle said, a catch to her voice.

"Quite upset us," her husband added. "This is her home."

*

"My niece had a bit of cloth she took everywhere," Mark said as they returned to Marshall's car with the collected photo and a DNA sample, "but it was about the size of a flannel and she stopped before she started school."

"So not still carrying it around at the age of sixteen," Marshall said, which was the age the vanished Amelia Doyle had reached.

"And not a large and expensive fur coat."

Marshall looked back at the small semi they had just left. "It doesn't scream fur coats at you, does it?"

"No; and the girl herself."

"What about her?"

"Beautiful, very 'Celtic' colouring."

The photo showed jet-black hair, pale skin and blue eyes above sculptured cheekbones. "Yes, Celtic is a good word for it."

"Not much like blonde Mum and Dad then," Mark said.

"Oh, come on, most women's hair colour comes out of bottles these days."

"Granted, but she really doesn't look much like her parents. That and the fur almost make me think they've found a random picture of a girl they'd like us to find."

"Except for all the other pictures around the place of their daughter growing up. Not to mention the very real grief."

"Yes, yes, I know." Mark grew suddenly serious. "Actually, I didn't spot any photos of when she was younger."

"Oh, stop creating mysteries where there aren't any. We'll probably find her on a train to Cornwall. Let's go start looking."

*

The Doyles had returned the day before from their annual fortnight in a Bed and Breakfast in Falmouth. According to her parents, Amelia had thrown a real tantrum about having to come home and had then vanished during the night.

Marshall's money was on there being a boy involved; a holiday romance she couldn't bear to leave behind.

"So, have we got anything?" Marshall addressed his opening remarks to Constable Helen Lovell, the third permanent member of his team, as he entered the airy room that CID used. He'd left her behind to start some basic searches, whilst he and Mark had gone to speak to the Doyles.

"Nothing much," Helen said. "A few details on the girl. Adopted." She waved a piece of paper.

"Told you so," Mark said, smugly. "Looks nothing like Mum and Dad."

"All right," Marshall conceded, "one to you. Does it add anything?"

"Might do, whole set of things for her to be looking for," Helen said. "Particularly as she was adopted from Cornwall, sort of."

"Explain," Marshall ordered.

"Well, adopted here, but records suggest she was born in Cornwall."

"Suggest?"

"Well, maybe not born. No birth records that I can find. She was found abandoned in Cornwall as a child."

"How did she end up in Fenwick?" Mark asked.

"Don't know yet. Have asked for various records to be mailed over, in case they're helpful." Helen shrugged.

"Looks like we ought to take a trip down there," Mark suggested hopefully.

Marshall snorted. "We don't even know she's gone there and the wonders of the internet mean we can research from here."

"I'll make you a bargain," Mark said. "If I can find evidence she did, you let us have a trip out."

"I'll think about it. They do have competent police forces in the south-west too."

Mark grinned and headed for the door.

"Where are you off to?"

"Station," Mark said, whipping the photo off Marshall's desk as he passed, "see what I can find. Most likely place to start."

*

Mark was back in under an hour. "Not even trying to hide," he said cheerfully. "She caught the first train to London this morning but had bought a ticket to Falmouth. Had it on her phone."

"So we might be able to trace the phone," Marshall said.

Mark nodded. "Of course. I'll get someone to find out if Mum can give us a number and a provider."

"And see if she has any of these social media things which allow her parents, and therefore us, to see where she is."

"She'll have turned the notifications off," Mark warned, "if she has any sense."

"I expect you're right, but ask. If so, hopefully the phone

company can track the… well, whatever it is they track."

"Twenty-first century passing you by, John?"

"Knocked me down, ran me over and hurtled off into the distance," Marshall said sourly, "but should make it possible, with some technical wizardry I don't understand, to trace a missing girl as long as she holds on to the sodding phone."

"John!" Helen waved from the other side of the room where she was working at her desk beside the window. "Got some info on the adoption."

Marshall and Mark headed over to look at the document Helen had on her screen.

"Looks like she was in a children's home in Fenwick and fostered and then adopted by the Doyles," Helen summarised.

"I'll go and have a word with the home," Marshall said, "find out what the Cornish link is. Mark, contact CID in Falmouth or wherever they're based down there and see if they can find evidence of her arriving there and," he added, seeing Mark's hopeful look, "see if they would mind us heading their way. Helen, see if you can trace her phone."

*

"The problem was, Inspector, that she kept escaping and trying to throw herself into the sea." Polly Taylor was mid-thirties, bright and efficient. Her chestnut hair was pulled back into a neat ponytail and her make-up lightly applied. She ran the Fenwick Children's Home in its large Edwardian building on Museum Street and Marshall got the impression she was well loved and respected by her charges.

"She tried to drown herself?" Marshall asked, horrified. "How old was she?"

"About eight or nine, we believe, hard to be precise." She gave a tight smile. "You have to understand, Inspector, that Amelia was abandoned in Cornwall with no records. Her official details are largely guesswork."

"But surely she——"

"Afraid not. Even when she made it to us she was very withdrawn, totally uncommunicative, quite a worry to start with. I believe she was even worse when she was first found."

"Abused?"

"May well have been, Inspector. Had a couple of nasty cuts and bruises on her when she was found. Then abandoned. Something to do with a seal sanctuary, would you believe? Oh, the police did all the proper appeals and tried to trace parents and so on but had no luck. I assume if they left her, then they didn't want her back."

"Meanwhile, she tried to drown herself?" Marshall shook his head; the cruelty of the world never ceased to amaze him.

"Yes, kept escaping from the home, so she was sent here, away from the sea. Seemed to settle her and she actually turned out to be quite a good swimmer once we risked taking her near the pool."

"And the Doyles?"

"Were on our list and we thought it might be a good fit. They visit Cornwall a lot, thought it might remind Amelia of home or get her to open up; maintain the link, sort of thing."

"A home which hadn't been particularly good to her and left her suicidal?" Marshall frowned. "Was that such a good idea?"

"But she talked about the place all the time, Inspector. Not the people, but the landscape and places. Once she was happier in herself, she spoke of it with love; it seemed best."

"So how long ago——"

"She was found roughly seven years ago. The Doyles adopted her about five years ago." Which accounted for the lack of young photos Mark had noted. "She seemed very happy with them. This disappearance is such a shame."

"Do you think she is trying to drown herself again?"

"That doesn't sound like the young lady she'd become." Polly Taylor straightened her ponytail. "I really hope not. I counted her a definite success."

*

"So," Marshall said, back in the office, "let's check some news records. I can't believe a young child was abandoned in Cornwall without the papers making something out of it. Let's see if it suggests a reason why she would want to go back."

"I've heard from a Sergeant Dolan in Falmouth," Mark said. "It seems she arrived on the train. The booking clerk noted the fur coat; thought it was unusual in the height of summer."

"I'm with him there," Marshall said. "Any luck on the news sites, Helen?"

"Couple of local papers ran with it," Helen said. "Girl found on the beach with an injured seal." She flicked through various tabs she had open. "The nationals picked it up in a smaller way. Woman from a seal sanctuary got a call. When she turned up, she found Amelia with the seal. Both were hurt and there was no sign of the person who made the call. Various appeals made to try and trace her family but without success."

"And no help from her?"

"No. Various editorial pieces in the papers on the effects of trauma on the ability to communicate from all sorts of 'ologists' but basically she couldn't or wouldn't tell them anything."

"Odd that she still hasn't," Marshall said, reading over Helen's shoulder.

"Sergeant Dolan says he's quite happy for us to go down and work with them," Mark said, joining Marshall by Helen's desk.

"That is a not very subtle hint, Mark. How much persuasion did that take? Don't you think they can manage?"

"Cornwall in mid-summer," Mark laughed shortly. "They'll be snowed under with tourists. I definitely got the impression Dolan would welcome some extra manpower."

"If they've not found her by the morning then, yes, we'll take a trip." Marshall gave in. He wasn't too unhappy about the chance to get out of the office and visit the seaside. "Sorry, Helen, you'll have to hold the fort here. I'll ask uniform to lend you Gill Ashton for a couple of days."

*

The summer traffic was relatively kind until Marshall and his sergeant reached the A30 and then they joined the queues of caravans pottering through the Cornish countryside.

Eventually they gave up and stopped for a meal just outside Bodmin.

"Enjoying your trip out?" Marshall teased as Mark ladled cream onto his scone.

"Cornish pasty and cream tea," Mark said through a mouthful. "I'll cope."

Marshall checked an incoming message on his phone. "Helen says Sergeant Jack Dolan of the Devon and Cornwall Police will meet us with open arms in Falmouth."

"If we ever get there," Mark said, starting on his second scone.

"Quite, and she's sent me the address of the Bed and Breakfast place the Doyles stayed at." Marshall checked his phone. "Place in Cliff Road we can check out. Amelia may have gone somewhere she knows."

"Start at the station," Mark suggested. "No point looking elsewhere until we know if they saw where she headed."

"I think it unlikely they paid that much attention with this many people."

They were still waiting for feedback from the phone company on tracing Amelia's mobile and hadn't bothered trying to track a lone passenger's journey through London. It might become necessary but Marshall felt that there were more productive things his team could be doing, before they started on that particular needle in a haystack. She'd made it to Falmouth so, for now, he was assuming the only reason for being in London was to go through it.

*

It took them a while to fight their way to the police station through the crowds of tourists in Falmouth, but at least it guaranteed them a parking space.

Sergeant Jack Dolan was in his late twenties; tall and slim with auburn hair, freckles and green eyes. He smiled readily and grasped Marshall's hand firmly in greeting.

"What can we do for you, Inspector?"

"John, please," Marshall said. "I gather we can probably help you out. We need to visit McCuskers' guest house on Cliff Road and then track down a children's home. I think it was St Budoc's."

"And the place who found her," suggested Mark.

"A seal place?" Marshall said. "Not sure that makes much sense, maybe later."

"That'll be Gweek," Dolan said. "We can manage all that. Easiest to walk in Falmouth this time of year. We can get the car for Gweek."

*

Betty McCusker peered briefly at the photograph of Amelia Doyle before nodding briskly. "Stayed here last week, nice kid. Family come each year. I think they told me once that this was where they came on honeymoon."

"Did they seem happy last week?" Marshall asked.

"Yes," the middle-aged landlady barely paused for thought, "seemed as usual."

"Even the girl?"

"Oh yes, I told you, she was a nice kid."

"Don't suppose she had much chance to make friends here," Mark suggested.

"Couldn't say," she replied cheerfully, and then slightly sterner, "I will quite happily chat with my guests if they choose to but I'm not in the habit of grilling them for information on all their comings and goings."

Mark held up his hand placatingly. "Never meant to imply it; just wondered."

"We were curious as to whether she might have, say, a boyfriend she wanted to come back to," Marshall explained.

"Oh, I see, not that I know of."

"Have you seen her at all today or yesterday?" Dolan asked. He had ascertained for them that Amelia had arrived at Falmouth station in mid-afternoon. The booking clerk had made a note of the curiosity of a tourist arriving with a fur coat when everyone else was in shorts but hadn't been interested enough to note where she had headed from the station.

"No." Betty McCusker shook her neatly coiffured head. "Left Saturday; not seen her since."

"Well, if she does visit, could you give us a call? Her parents are worried."

"Of course." She took his card and placed it beside the phone on the front desk. "I hope you find her. Nice girl."

*

"Well," Mark said, "that got us nowhere. She made it here, but not to return to her hotel; not – as far as we know – to see anyone; and I can't really see why she would visit a care home she left seven years ago. I suppose we better check, for the sake of completeness. After that, I suppose it's everybody out looking for a girl with a fur coat."

Marshall sighed. "I'll ask Helen to get a full itinerary of where the Doyles visited last week too, we'll check thoroughly."

"Might as well visit all the tourist highlights while you're here," Dolan said with a grin. "I can point you in the direction of some good cream teas and pasties too if you like."

Mark grinned back. "Need to keep our stamina up, wouldn't you say, John?"

Marshall shook his head in mock despair. "As long as you remember we're actually at work. Don't start suggesting we paddle or anything. Actually," he turned to Dolan, "get someone to keep an eye on the beaches; Amelia's history includes attempts at drowning."

"Will do. I'll pass it on to the lifeguards and RNLI if you don't object."

Marshall seriously hoped it wasn't necessary but didn't object. "I suppose we ought to get Helen to check with the Doyles if they had problems with water with her, while they were here. Though, God knows, there are closer places to home if the poor kid wanted to end it all." The Hurne through Fenwick provided them with a small, but reliably sad, annual tally.

"So, St Budoc's," Marshall said.

"It isn't any more," Dolan said. "I've got social services to send me the records but it stopped being a children's home a while ago. It's an old folks' place now."

"Back to the office then."

They wandered back through the town and uphill to the police station, navigating the tourists still flocking towards the beach from their cars.

The social services records for Amelia Doyle added very little to their sum of knowledge. The girl, assumed to be about nine, had been found one summer's day by staff of the Cornish Seal Sanctuary in Gweek. There had been a police search for parents, a media campaign and, eventually, she had been made a ward of court. Then there were several records about the girl's escapes from the home and attempts to throw herself in the sea. All of which totally failed to include anything from Amelia herself.

In fact, when Marshall flicked through the papers a second time, there was nothing really from the girl. She had provided no information at all about her home life or family before she was found. At first she had been categorised as an elective mute, possibly due to trauma, and it had taken many months of work before social worker reports suggested they had won her trust enough to get conversation from her at all.

"Nothing in this indicates why she'd come back here," Mark said, pushing the file away. "Any sightings?" Dolan was returning with coffees.

"Nope," the young sergeant shook his head, "nothing."

"So what next?" Mark turned to Marshall.

Marshall sat back in his chair. "Let's use the local news. Put out a plea for sightings. I don't like doing it because of all the garbage you get in but we might scare up something. Keep an eye on the beaches and station. After that, no idea."

"Gweek?" Mark said hesitantly, in the manner of one expecting an explosion.

Marshall decided not to disappoint, if only mock seriously. "What the hell for? Why would she go there? Why is she here at all?"

"We don't know," Mark said evenly, "so let's cover everything." He shrugged. "We've nothing else urgent to do at present while we wait for a list of places from Helen. We've got the beaches covered and we're running a news item. Let's keep busy and out of Dolan's hair."

"All right," Marshall sighed, "we might as well. Can you provide a map, Sergeant?"

Dolan obliged and pointed them in the right direction before heading off to circulate Amelia's picture around the uniformed officers already patrolling the tourists in Falmouth centre.

*

Gweek Seal Sanctuary turned out to be in the middle of nowhere but well signposted enough that they didn't get too lost finding it.

On the way, he had received a text from Helen with a list of attractions the family had visited in the previous week. One of them was Gweek, so the visit wasn't entirely wasted.

The afternoon was drawing to an end so the sanctuary was approaching closing time. Marshall waited whilst several small children bought cuddly seals in the gift shop and then waved his badge at the young lady behind the counter.

"Inspector Marshall," he introduced himself. "We're trying to trace a young lady and wondered if she has been seen here." He thrust the picture of Amelia Doyle under her nose.

She was nodding almost before he had finished asking.

"Oh yes, she came in earlier. I remember the coat."

Marshall breathed a silent prayer of thanks for Amelia Doyle's obsession with a fur coat. "How long ago? Is she still here?"

"Well, I've been a bit busy." A small girl in the far corner of the shop started screaming about the unfairness of her mother's refusal to allow her to have more than one cuddly toy as if to emphasise the point. "But I think I'd have noticed if she'd left. She stood out."

"Can we go and have a look round, then?"

She waved them through absent-mindedly as the screaming child and her family arrived at the checkout.

Once through the entrance building, the seal sanctuary was a sprawling affair with several paths and enclosures.

"Might be better off waiting here for when she heads out," Mark said, "otherwise we might miss her."

"Agreed, except I wish I knew why she was here. She might not be—"

"There!" Mark grabbed his arm and pointed along the path. "Fur coat, surely."

"You're right." The two of them sprinted down the descending path towards the figure wearing a fur coat, its back towards them, beside one of the enclosures.

Marshall opened his mouth to yell but his brain was telling him that, fur coat notwithstanding, this was not Amelia. The stance, the hair colour, the whole demeanour – even in back view – suggested an older woman. Mark was also slowing beside him, clearly picking up the same signs.

They came to a halt one each side of the woman, who turned to stare at Marshall. "Amelia Doyle," Marshall said, though it quite obviously wasn't.

"Is that *your* coat?" Mark added.

"Of course." The woman glanced at Mark and then back to Marshall. "Is there a problem?"

"We are looking for this girl." Marshall pushed forward the picture. "You are wearing a remarkably similar coat." Which was amazingly suspicious in the summer weather. "We thought you were her," he grimaced. "Sorry if we frightened you arriving like that."

The woman looked at the picture for a long moment, ignoring the two men, and then looked Marshall in the eye and sighed. "My daughter," she said.

"Your…" Marshall exchanged glances with Mark. "Explain."

"Ah, now that might take a while."

"Is she here?" Marshall looked round but couldn't see anyone in the vicinity.

"Yes," the woman frowned at him, "but not anywhere you will… recognise her."

"What have you done?" Mark laid his hand on the woman's arm. "Where is she?"

"Sheba!" A tall lady dressed in jeans and a Cornish Seal Sanctuary t-shirt had appeared on the path behind them. "What are you doing?"

"My daughter—"

"These gentlemen don't want—"

"Actually," Marshall interrupted, "we do. Inspector Marshall, Sergeant Sherbourne, and we're investigating a girl's disappearance. I mistook this lady because of the coat she's wearing but I'm intrigued to hear why she claims Amelia Doyle as her daughter."

"Megan said there was police," the newcomer said. "I'm Sharron, manager here."

"Megan, if she was the lass in the gift shop, said my missing girl came through here earlier."

"Megan needs to learn some things about us and then she might know who to share information with," Sharron said drily.

"Sharing information pertinent to a police inquiry is—"

"Not going to help you in this case, Inspector."

"Can I be the judge of that?"

She glared hard at him, then looked at the lady in the fur coat and shrugged. "Okay, Inspector, ask your questions, let's see what you make of this but any 'wasting police time' is your own choice and not our offence."

Marshall shared a glance with his sergeant but nodded. "Agreed. I am asking for this information. So, madam, why do you say Amelia Doyle is your daughter?"

The woman in the fur coat laughed harshly. Several of the seals in the enclosure responded with their own sharp noises. "Because she is."

"You've made no claim to her for seven years."

"Couldn't." The word was bitter.

Mark mouthed the word 'prison'. Marshall considered it; the child had obviously been abused and then no-one had come to claim her. It provided an answer.

"Couldn't?" he repeated. "Why, were you locked up?"

"*She* was locked up." The answer was almost spat at him. "Old curse."

"She was being cared for. Healed. Loved." Marshall sighed. "Do you know she tried to drown herself?"

"She was just trying to get to me," the woman said. "She didn't understand."

"I don't understand," Marshall said. "Could you speak plainly, please?"

The woman stepped closer, dark eyes looking deeply into his. "She was trapped in human form. Seven years a changeling. Old curse. She was trying to get back to me, change back. Now she can. I've come to take her home. How much plainer can you get?"

Marshall stayed where he was, looking deep into the woman's eyes. There was no hint there of any lie; whatever she was saying, she believed.

"Trapped in human form?" Mark said softly behind the woman. "What form should she have?"

"Seal," Marshall said slowly. "That's what you're saying. I heard that tale once in Orkney, forget what the word was for it."

"Selkie," Sharron said.

"Seal!" the woman snapped, taking her gaze from Marshall to glare at Sharron.

Marshall took several deep breaths as the two women scowled at each other. "All right, if I remember the legend correctly, selkie can be seal as well as human. Is that what you're telling me?"

"Yes, Inspector," Sharron said. "Some of our rescued seals have that ability. Selkies, the oldest stories call them. It isn't something we necessarily advertise."

"But," Mark said, "Amelia was found as a human child."

"What they told us on Orkney," Marshall said, "is that if you find a selkie in human form and take their fur away from them then they can't change back. So they are stuck in the form."

"But she had her coat," Mark said.

"Cursed," the woman in the fur snapped. "Seven years as a changeling if the fur is taken with deliberate intent when we are in human form."

"Old curse," Sharron said, "as Sheba was saying—"

"I can tell my own tale," the other woman interrupted. "I was teaching my daughter how to change between shapes and we were seen by a couple of men. I managed to change back, she was less lucky. I tried to stop them taking the fur and got hurt in the process. So did she. A family saw them and thought they were hurting a seal – me – which, I suppose they were and they chased them off and got the fur back but by then it was too late. They called the sanctuary who came to get me and took my daughter too as she was refusing to be parted from me."

"Sheba's been here since," Sharron said, "hoping her daughter may one day return and helping me care for the others of her kind. Last week, Amelia visited."

Marshall looked round to check there were no other visitors left in the sanctuary. "Show me," he said firmly.

The woman in the fur coat looked hard at him and then shrugged, opened the door to the pool she was stood in front of and dived, fairly ungracefully, into the water. By the time the splash had died away, a seal was swimming away from them.

Sharron reached out and pulled the door to. "She won't be back, Inspector. The seal across the other side is her daughter, the lass you're looking for, arrived this afternoon."

"Well," Marshall said, "I've seen it, so I better believe it. No idea how we are going to break this to her parents. Technically, after an adoption, they probably have more rights to her than Sheba but I can't really go and hand them a seal."

"She is sixteen," Mark said, "so she has a right to make her own choice. If she stops being a seal long enough to do so."

Marshall nodded. "Is it possible for them to see her, in a form they recognise, if we bring them down here?"

"Maybe," Sharron said slowly. "I will talk to mother and daughter about it and write to these 'parents' if you give me an address. After all, it is not their fault what happened to the lass and I may be able to convince Sheba of this and that they mean no harm." She smiled slightly. "I hope they are as open-minded as you are. As open-minded as Sheba has taught me to be."

"I've seen it," Marshall said again, "so I can hardly claim it doesn't exist." A stance he had had to take more than once in his time in Fenwick. "I assume they are found in Orkney too, where I heard it told, if someone knows where to look."

"Probably, Inspector. They aren't just confined to Cornwall."

Marshall and Mark left the seal sanctuary. As they exited the shop, Sharron put an arm round the shoulders of Megan behind the desk.

"I think Megan is about to get an education," Mark said.

"Same one we just had," Marshall agreed. "Let's go say goodbye to Sergeant Dolan – maybe suggest he comes and has an enlightening chat here too – and then head home, Mark, and see if we can convince Mr and Mrs Doyle that their daughter has gone back to her natural mother, without emphasising too much the 'natural' nature of her mother. At least, not before they can come and see it for themselves."

Mark nodded. "Getting late, though, I think we can discuss what we will tell them over a meal on the way home. If I'm only getting one day of Cornish food, I'm going to make the most of it."

Penance

Mark Sherbourne crouched beside the makeshift tent to peer at the body inside. "He's been here twenty years according to the locals. Council tried to move him in the early nineties but there was a protest and in the end they let him stay."

"He was never any trouble," Helen Lovell added.

Inspector John Marshall, who was the recipient of all this local knowledge, watched the traffic charging round the island on the Fenwick bypass and wondered what could convince anyone that this was a good place to live.

"Surely there must be safer pitches... even safer roundabouts."

"Actually," Mark said, "this is large enough and the trees in the middle gave him enough protection that nothing ever hit him. The closest he came was a storm one year when a branch came down."

"He is..." Helen corrected herself. "He was quite a good witness. Sounded like a well-educated man, on the couple of times I interviewed him about accidents here."

To Marshall that made even less sense. He could understand people who got tired of city life and retired to the country. A couple he'd known for years had jacked it all in to go and run a pig farm and he, himself, had moved out of London for a quieter life in Fenwick.

Not that that seemed to be happening – Fenwick was a very strange place. But why give everything up to go and camp in a makeshift tent on a road junction?

"Alcoholic?" he guessed.

"Not as far as I know." Mark was prodding carefully at the man's shoes with latex-clad fingers.

"So why? And why here?"

Mark shrugged.

"What we got, John?" Doctor Liza Trent dumped her box down beside them. She peered over Mark's shoulder. "Oh, poor sod. Mind you, he must have been here twenty years."

"So I hear."

"Natural? The life isn't of the kindest, out in all weather."

"I hoped you could tell me. It's a bit small for us to go having a look, without disturbing the scene."

The heavy fabric was held up by stout branches but rose barely three feet off the ground.

The doctor crouched down and shuffled her way into the tent.

"Bugger!" The muffled exclamation was followed by her careful reappearance bearing a lethal-looking sword of polished metal. The tip of its four-foot blade was stained dull red.

"It's murder," she said rather unnecessarily. "People don't normally manage to remove their own heads."

Marshall looked from the blade to the tent. He imagined crawling in with it and then swinging it to decapitate. "He wasn't killed here then?"

"Oh yes, I'd say. It's soaked in blood and both bits are here."

"That's not possible unless that blade's so sharp that... no, it's just not possible. The swing you'd need to take someone's head off."

"You have experience?" Mark asked.

"Case in London, a few years back now. We had to find the head.

The experiments to demonstrate force and trajectory were quite… eye opening."

"I bet." Mark pointed to the shoes sticking from the tent which was all they could see from the outside. "So he's lying on his front and someone…"

"…Crawls over him to get into the tent, wields a four-foot blade in a three-foot tent…"

"I see. Was his head sticking out the other end, perhaps?"

"No." Helen had wandered round the far end of the structure. "The tent's too long and it's covered this end."

"No way." Liza Trent had crawled back inside. "Body finishes here." She tapped, showing a rise in the fabric less than two thirds along the ridge.

"Someone took the tent down, killed him and put it back up?" Mark didn't sound as if even he believed what he was saying.

Marshall ignored his sergeant. "See what else you can find, Liza." He strode down to the road, where Craig Hickson had arrived with his paraphernalia of cameras and powders and brushes.

"It looks like this is the murder scene, Craig. Picture it and bag it carefully. I'd quite like you to recreate it at the lab."

"Locked room scenario?" Hickson looked round. "That's quite an achievement in the middle of Fenwick Bypass."

"More, 'room not big enough for the murder weapon' type scenario. Must be a trick to it somewhere."

"Or that's not the murder weapon."

"Granted. Anything's possible. Though currently nothing seems possible."

"Okay." Hickson grinned cheerfully and set to work. Marshall had noted before that the head of the forensic team enjoyed a challenge.

"Come on, Mark, Helen, let's go. I need a history lesson and we've got some research to do."

*

"So, tell me what we know about our victim." Marshall leant back in his chair and then continued before the pair facing him could respond. "Apart from the fact that he lived on a roundabout for twenty years. I've got the hang of that fact."

"Well, he was never any trouble," Helen began.

"I think you said that before too."

"But it's important. It means he's unlikely to be on the system."

"You said he was a witness."

"Well… sort of informally." Helen looked uncomfortable.

"All right, shall we start with a name and go from there."

Silence.

"You mean you don't even know his name?" Marshall stared at the two of them in amazement.

"He answered to Leo."

"Right, so we have an unknown tramp, who has lived without bothering anyone for twenty years. So well-liked people actually petitioned to let him stay in his home, though none of them actually bothered to find out what he was called and yet somebody hated him so much they decapitated him." Marshall sighed. "One of you tell Liza the fingerprints and DNA are a priority; let's see if we can identify him that way but I have a dreadful feeling we're going to need the press. Get hold of that woman from the Advertiser."

"Maggie Arkwright?"

"Yes, her, and put out a piece asking for information about him. If you can get a time of death from Liza, then add a plea for information from anyone who might have been on the ring road at the time." He hated using the press. Pranks and cranks were the normal response, when what he really needed was information. It wasted an awful lot of time and effort but he didn't see that he had much choice this time.

"National?" Mark asked.

"No, local for now. See what response we get." There was no need to multiply the amount of hoax calls nationally, unless he really had to.

*

"Got some ID for you." Mark waved a sheet of paper at Marshall as he entered the office that afternoon. "Hickson found some dog tags on what was left of the neck."

"Soldier?" Marshall nodded slowly; it made a certain amount of sense. He'd heard of soldiers who couldn't re-adjust to civilian life. "Which war?"

"Ah, now that's where it stops being good news and gets a bit odd. According to MoD records, Matthew Alan Clarke went missing at the Somme, body never found."

"The Somme? That would make him over a hundred."

"Yes."

"Is that right?" Marshall hadn't had a good look at the victim but he was fairly sure someone so old wouldn't have been living in such a way; not as successfully as the victim seemed to.

"No, I'd have said half that at most and I always assumed he looked older than he was." Marshall agreed with that; in his experience the 'tramp' lifestyle aged people.

"Right, see if you can get some records for Matthew Clarke and then see if we can work out why our victim might have had his dog tags. Try people in his regiment, that sort of thing. If any of them are still alive."

"Will do. We've already had quite a response to the plea on the lunchtime news, by the way."

"Any of it useful?"

"Don't be silly. 'Lovely bloke', 'been there twenty years', 'never hurt a fly'."

Marshall nodded. "I could have told them that, by now."

Mark grinned. "I'll let you know if we get anything interesting. Meanwhile, Doctor Trent wants to see you about cause of death."

Marshall nodded his thanks, shuffled some paperwork half-heartedly and went to find Liza Trent.

*

Dr Trent was printing out a report in her small office.

"Just finished this for you, John."

"Thanks. Mark said something about cause of death?"

"The angle of blow and the lack of marks in the ground suggest he wasn't lying while he was beheaded. I've talked to Hickson and we're relatively sure that the angle of fall means he was kneeling."

"Kneeling?" Marshall tried to picture the scene. "An execution?"

"Looks like it. No signs of struggle or restraint so I'd say it was voluntary or, at the very least, accepted."

"Really, so the person who did it?"

"Standing over him."

"Not in that tent, he wasn't."

"Well, I'm ninety-nine percent sure the body wasn't moved but I do see the problem."

"Thanks, I'll go and see Craig; perhaps his tent reconstruction might help." Marshall took the report and idly flicked through it as he headed down the corridor. At page three he turned back.

Liza grinned at him as he reappeared in her doorway. "You got to the food."

"Yes, explain please."

"Food is unrecognisable. The meat is simply not something my system has ever encountered before, neither was the stuff we think was a type of fruit."

"Never?"

"Sorry, John."

"I've got a man wearing the dog tags of a soldier who went missing nearly a hundred years ago who had a last meal of no known food and then calmly knelt down to be beheaded in a tent that plainly isn't big enough. I hope Hickson has some good news."

*

"Afraid not." Craig Hickson looked annoyed. "I've run this thing through every test I can and it is made of no metal ever discovered." He waved the sword at Marshall as if it was somehow his fault. "It's categorically the murder weapon but it's made of something that doesn't exist."

"Any prints on it?"

"No such luck."

Marshall frowned, unsure what to say and then decided to change tack. "Is it possible," he looked to where the tent had been reconstructed, "that that was taken down for the execution and then re-erected?"

"No way. The knots hadn't been shifted in years. We had to cut two or three to get it untied from the tree."

"Bugger."

*

Marshall's phone rang as he headed back to the station.

"John, got a solicitor at the front desk asking for you," Sergeant Wilkes, the officer in charge, said. "Something to do with your dead tramp; saw it on the news."

"I'll be right with you." Perhaps this was the break he needed.

*

Sylvester Enfield, senior partner of Enfield and Hemmings, was a short fussy man in his late fifties. He sat primly across the desk from Marshall in the interview room clutching a red folder as if it was a lifeline.

"How can I help you, Mr Enfield?"

"Oh no, it is I who can help you." Marshall decided the prim manner was going to grate very quickly.

There was a short silence while Mr Enfield stared rather glassily at him. Marshall hated solicitors – they never volunteered information; it was always a bit like pulling teeth.

"About the tramp, I believe?"

"That's right."

"Do you know something about him?"

"No."

Marshall took a deep breath. "Do you have something of his?"

"I have his will, Inspector." The solicitor pulled a piece of paper from the folder and placed it on the table. With a certain show of reluctance, he turned it to face Marshall.

"All properly witnessed. I thought you might be interested as it has some unusual provisions in it."

Marshall glanced at the will and then up at the solicitor in surprise. "This was made on Monday."

"It's perfectly legal."

"I realise that, Mr Enfield. I'm just wondering if he knew he was about to die."

"Oh yes, Inspector. I think you should read it."

Marshall picked the will up and read it. The solicitor was right. It was most unusual.

"And you didn't know Mr Clarke before he asked you to do this will for him?"

"No, Inspector."

"Can you tell me anything else about him?"

"No, Inspector." He sounded quite smug about it.

"I'll have to take a copy of this."

"By all means."

*

"Mark, Helen, my office." Marshall preceded them in, clutching the copied will. "You have to hear this."

"I've got some information on Matthew Clarke from the MoD," Mark said. "There's a picture and if you aged it I suppose it could be him; definitely a relative."

"Well according to this will, our tramp was Matthew Clarke."

"He had a will?" Helen said.

"Oh yes, absolute corker." He waited for Helen to push the door to and sit down beside Mark. "Last will and testament of Matthew Alan Clarke. This will replaces all others, etc., the usual jargon at the top. The rest has obviously been dictated. 'I will die on Friday and wish to provide for the disposition of my effects. I have very little of value here but it is of great importance to he who follows me. My wealth lies in the grove and can be found for three nights at full moon. My belongings should remain intact and ready for their next occupant. My grave should be dug beneath the oak at full moon and all weapons returned to the king. I have paid full price and go in peace'."

"What the fuck does that mean?" Mark asked.

"Trip to the roundabout tonight," Helen said.

"Why?"

"Full moon."

"The guy was cracked."

"Just curious," Helen said. "Don't tell me you're not."

"I've done enough overtime this month, thank you."

Marshall raised an eyebrow and waited.

"Oh bugger, all right, I'm curious," Mark said. "It better not rain."

*

It didn't and the moon rose full and glorious above them as they stood on the edge of the road.

"How did he ever sleep?" Mark said, waving a hand at the stream of cars still passing in all directions. It wasn't as busy as rush hour but still regular enough to be noisy.

"I assume he got used to it." Marshall had lived in central London for years; you adapted to the disturbance.

They strode up the slight slope to the ring of seven trees that the developers had left while building this section of ring road.

The lights of cars flashed eerily beyond the trunks.

"Weird place at night," Helen said with feeling.

"Yes." Marshall didn't think he would have wanted this as his bedroom. "Anyone see anything that could be 'wealth'?"

The leaves above them rustled in a sudden gust of wind sending shivers racing down Marshall's spine. He glanced up to where the moon rode the clouds high above and when he looked back a man stood in the shadows in front of him.

"You have returned my sword?" The voice was deep and commanding.

Marshall swallowed, resisting the urge to step backwards. Out of the corned of his eye he saw Mark and Helen edging closer on either side.

"Who are you?" he said. "Do you know something about Matthew Clarke's murder?"

There was silence and Marshall had to peer closer to reassure himself that the figure still stood in the dark beneath the tree. "Who are you?" the man eventually said.

An irrational part of Marshall wanted to point out that he'd asked first but he merely said, "Inspector John Marshall, Fenwick CID."

"What is CID?"

"Police, law, you know."

"Law? You protect people?"

"Yes, partly. Currently we're investigating the death of Matthew Clarke; the gentleman who lived here and who was found murdered here this morning."

"You mentioned a sword," Helen said. "Was this your sword? Can you tell us anything about Mr Clarke's death?"

"He chose to die."

"Nobody chooses to have their head cut off," Helen said indignantly.

"The Lion did."

"The Lion?" Marshall asked.

"The man you are talking of," the man said impatiently.

"Leo," Mark hissed. "We called him Leo; may be the lion."

"Makes sense, I suppose." Marshall stepped forwards. "Did you wield the sword, Mr..." He waited.

"Your Highness," the man corrected, moving out of the shadows. He was taller than any of them, his hair falling in waves to his shoulders, his beard closely trimmed. He was swathed in a cloak and clutched a sword in his right hand.

"Yes, I performed the rite."

"And dropped the sword?" Marshall said.

"I placed it into the ground to complete the rite. I had forgotten that his heritage meant it would return with him."

"Rite?" Mark said.

"Return?" Helen asked.

"I'm going to have to arrest you for the murder of..." Marshall began but he was talking to thin air.

"What the...?" Mark leapt forwards, waving his hands through the space but there was no-one there. "What happened to him?"

Marshall looked round, trying to figure out how they'd been fooled. "No idea, Mark."

The three of them wandered around for a while in the dark but could find no trace of the strange man or his exit. "This is pointless. We'll come back in daylight," Marshall said eventually. "Get uniform to put a man here tonight in case he comes back. To be arrested on sight."

*

The weather was bright and cold the next morning. Autumn waved early tendrils of mist amongst the trees.

"No sign of anybody," Mark reported after speaking to the constable on duty.

Marshall followed his sergeant in between the trunks.

"We must have been about here," Marshall said. "We came from that way," he pointed behind, "and the man was under the tree in front of us." The ground still showed signs of Matthew Clarke's occupation; remains of a campfire and tattered ropes where the tent had been removed.

Mark moved slowly forwards, peering at the ground.

"There are too many leaves. I can't tell where he stood or how he left."

"Just once it'd be nice to get the line of footprints like they do in the movies," Marshall said.

Mark snorted. "Yeah, right. I think I saw a flying pig this morning. So what now?"

"Let's put a description out – man we want to interview in connection with the death, you know the format."

"As a possible suspect? He was armed."

"Yes, better make it a 'do not approach' one."

"Anything else?"

"Then go and see Hickson about that sword. He was going to get a specialist metallurgist in. I think I might shake the MoD up a bit. Let's see if they can tell me why an AWOL soldier of theirs turned up ninety years after he disappeared, with a sword made of no known metal."

"You thinking there's some sort of secret weapon project?"

"And a government who might 'disappear' people," Marshall said. "Has been known to happen."

"Damn right," Mark said. "You be bloody careful, you don't want to be next on any list."

"I just want some answers, Mark."

*

Answers he wasn't getting. Marshall spent a fruitless morning on the phone to various people.

By lunchtime he was seriously fed up.

"Either I'm being given the most almighty run-around," he told Mark over a canteen lunch, "or they really do have no idea about Matthew Clarke. How are you doing?"

"I've had a lecture on metallurgy from Hickson."

"And?"

"Didn't understand a word of it apart from the bit at the end which went 'and this bloody sword is none of them'." Mark grinned. "I'd say you're in for a call from the boss as well."

"Why?"

"They've had two RTAs and four burglaries since yesterday morning. Everyone wants forensics and Hickson's got the entire team working on your sword and stomach contents."

"Just what I need."

"Helen's been looking at the will. She says that perhaps that man last night was 'the king' who Clarke wanted the sword returned to."

"Yes, I'd sort of worked that out."

"She thinks it's important to him... the sword... and that he might come back again tonight."

"Are you proposing we go back?"

"Helen is. Observation and then catch him."

"You mean hide behind a tree and leap out on him." Marshall cringed at the thought; he could just imagine tumbling down a muddy bank while wrestling what he was sure was a government agent in the glare of hundreds of headlights. On the other hand, he wasn't having any success with anything else.

"All right. Tell Helen she can come too seeing as it's her idea. If we've got to make asses of ourselves behind trees in the middle of a bypass then she can join us."

*

There were two men this time. They appeared just after midnight though Marshall – who was watching closely – could have sworn that they didn't come up from the road. They were simply there beneath the trees.

Marshall moved to stand in front of them, his hand on his baton. The man they had seen before was still armed.

Helen and Mark also appeared, moving warily.

"This is..." Marshall began.

The second man paced to stand in the moonlit centre of the ring of trees. He looked younger than his comrade, clean shaven and slim faced.

"Hold," he said, raising his hand.

Marshall struggled to take the next step, watching Helen and Mark having a similar problem.

"You are of The Lion's home-world?" the young man asked.

"What?" Marshall frowned but Helen was quicker to follow.

"Yes," she said.

"And you wish to know of his death?"

"Yes," Marshall said. "Last night, your friend—"

"Then you may come with us," he continued, ignoring Marshall's attempts to regain some control of the conversation. "Approach."

Helen and Mark hesitated, looking to Marshall. He didn't blame them. If this was a government cover-up then they could all be in a lot of danger. Something was definitely wrong and they were without backup.

"Mark, with me," he said, thinking fast. "Helen, wait here." If these men would allow her to. "Use your judgement and call in if you think it's necessary." He trusted her not to go jumping at shadows.

The young man didn't demur at the arrangements. He held out his hand as Marshall approached. "Take my arm." The two policemen reached out, touching the silk sleeve.

With a sudden disorientating dizziness, the grove of trees swung in Marshall's vision and then settled. It was so brief he almost thought he'd imagined it but, though the trees were the same and the moon still shone, the cars and the lights of Fenwick had vanished.

Or not entirely. The noise had gone and the silence weighed oppressively but he realised that if he peered hard beyond the trees, vague lights still passed. He looked round. Helen was the barest shadow of a figure, ghost-like beneath the trees. She stared about her as if lost and then checked her watch before settling down against a trunk, her eyes glued to the spot where he and Mark must have vanished.

Marshall strode past the other men to look out between the trunks. Beyond them the bulk of a walled town loomed dark against the sky.

Castle turrets rose high above, lights flickering in tower windows.

He turned back. The two strangers stood at ease in the clearing watching him while Mark, doing his best to remain professional, was watching them.

There was also a tent though it looked grander than such a term implied. Marshall was reminded of a medieval one he'd seen at a re-enactment day at Fenwick Manor the previous summer.

A whole range of questions ran through Marshall's head but, in the end, he contented himself with saying, "It doesn't alter the fact that you claim to have killed him."

"No," the young man agreed. "We believe we understand that, in your world, such death is wrong."

"In 'our world'," Mark said, "it's murder."

"We are hoping to make you understand that here it is not considered in the same way. This was a willingly undertaken sacrifice."

"I'm listening," Marshall said. It was a courtesy he afforded all criminals. Ruthlessly he put aside all thoughts of wonder at the surroundings; first he had a felon to deal with.

"Please sit." The young man waved his hand and several tree roots rose, curving up into seats. He and his friend sat easily, Marshall and Mark following their example more hesitantly. The man then produced a small globe of light which hung above them, illuminating the glade. Out of the corner of his eye, Marshall saw Helen straighten slightly, her eyes drawn to the globe. Obviously light went both ways from wherever they were.

"This is His Royal Highness, King Karron and I am Tureg, King's Seer. You sit in the sacred grove of Arven."

"John Marshall and Mark Sherbourne, Fenwick CID." It sounded bluntly prosaic. "Now tell us what you know of the death of Matthew Clarke." He nodded to Mark who opened his notebook.

Tureg nodded. "Sire?"

"Go ahead, Tureg. These are honourable men, akin to our soldiers. Leave nothing out."

"The man you call Matthew Clarke came through to our world twenty-two years ago."

"Here?" Marshall said.

"No, far to the north. There are links here and there though less easy to find. He came from a place he called No Man's Land."

"Get the clothes, Tureg," the king ordered. "That may help them to understand."

Tureg leapt up and strode into the pavilion. After a few moments he arrived back with an army uniform. Marshall took the offered bundle and spread out the jacket. "Somme, you said, Mark?"

"I did and that looks about right but that wasn't twenty-two years ago."

"Time moves slower here," Tureg said.

Marshall glanced to where Helen could still be seen.

"Not here," Tureg added quickly. "The grove is a place where our worlds merge and time is one. Away from here, our worlds drift apart. There are tales of people who have crossed to your world and have lived fifty years in your time and have come back less than a year after they left aged beyond recognition." He paused while Marshall worked this out.

"So, it's possible that twenty-two years here could be ninety at home?"

"Much, much more," Tureg said. "We believe it is only so few because he spent the last twenty-one years here in this grove."

"Why would he do that?"

"When this man – Matthew Clarke – came to us he was near death and," Tureg frowned as if searching for the right words, "unquiet in his mind. The wounds were deep within as well as on his skin."

"I'm not surprised," Marshall said. "The Somme did that to a lot of people."

"You know this place?"

"It was an event, a battle. Thousands of young men died pointlessly over months."

"He said we saved his life," the king put in, "but this place, this battle, haunted him."

"After a couple of months with us he began to say that he owed a life." Tureg sighed. "It was hard to watch such guilt."

"How would you know?" Mark said. "You're barely—"

"I am a seer," Tureg said with a smile. "Appearances can be deceptive."

"So how old are you?"

"Old enough to have sat beside Matthew Clarke as he healed and again as he asked to die. He told me once that he had failed his men; left them to die while he was safe. Sometimes he asked to go back but your world had moved on too far."

"So how did he end up here?" Marshall asked.

"It was a way for him to return to the world he knew and, as he saw it, to repay a debt."

"Go on."

"Because of its link to your world, this is a sacred place but it also needs protecting. There are ways to stumble upon our world and… undesirable people who may wish to do so. The grove has always had a guardian. Legend has it that the first guardian was a lion." He paused and the king continued for him.

"It is an old story of the first of kings. It tells us that the grove needs a guardian and that the link is maintained by the guardian's sacrifice to the grove."

"As long as I can remember," Tureg smiled, "and you would not believe how long that is. Guardians have stood sentinel here for twenty-one years and then let their blood flow to maintain the link. They are known as The Lion while they live and are honoured for their gift to us."

"They live in both worlds?"

"If they so choose. A presence in your world helps to keep people away. There have been many hermits in the grove on your side of the curtain."

And now tramps, Marshall thought. "So someone will replace him?"

"Yes. Following three days of mourning, we will hold the ceremony and The Lion will be reborn. We need the sword for this."

"And in twenty-one years, you'll kill him again and we'll have another corpse on our hands?"

"Only, I think, if The Lion is originally from your world."

"He was killed here?" Mark said.

"Yes, about where you sit."

The four of them sat in silence while Marshall and his sergeant digested this.

"What do you want of us?" Marshall said eventually.

"I want my sword back," the king said, "and I do not want treasure seekers and the curious here."

Remembering the look on Hickson's face poring over the sword, Marshall had a dreadful feeling it might be too late.

"We would also appreciate it if The Lion... the new Lion... was left to live as he chooses in the grove."

Marshall sighed. "That's all very well but I have an unsolved murder and I'm expected to track down the killer." Feeling a little silly but knowing he had to try; Marshall stood and removed his handcuffs from his pocket.

Tureg raised a hand, almost negligently.

The blast of wind knocked Marshall back, halfway across the grove, and slammed him into the base of a tree. He lay there, winded.

Tureg was beside him, almost immediately. "I am sorry. We do understand that you need someone to hang. We would do the same to a murderer but you cannot have the king."

"Hang? No, we got rid of the death penalty years ago. They'll be locked up and probably be out in twenty years." He pushed himself to sit upright. "If you're right, that's about six months of your time."

"Really?" Tureg leant forward to offer him a hand up. "The king cannot do this but I think we can help you. If we do, will you help us?"

*

Half an hour later, while stealing a body with Mark from the deserted morgue, Marshall was having doubts.

He paused in attempting to manhandle the body bag into the back of the Ford. "What are we doing, Mark?"

Mark grinned. "Breaking the law. Fun, isn't it?"

"Tell me I didn't dream it all."

"Well, if you did then we both did." Mark shoved the door closed. "Look, we know who did it and we can't get to him. You tried and I think they'd probably have killed you too without giving it a second thought. Can you see us trying to explain to the chief why we're giving up on the case if we don't do this?"

"I'm still going to have to explain this to him."

"You said you had an idea."

He had, he just hoped he could pull it off.

*

Helen met them back at the roundabout. She was clutching the blade from Hickson's office. "He's going to be very upset to find it gone," she said as the two men dumped the body bag down.

"Yes," Marshall said, "but Tureg's right. Just imagine all the alien watchers and weirdos we'd have in Fenwick if Hickson lets on he's got a sword of no known metal."

"I'm pleased you agree." Tureg stepped out of the night. With him was a young man who flinched every time a car sped past. "This is Harril. He killed a man in a bar brawl two days ago and was due to hang this morning. I have offered him life here if he takes your justice for the death of The Lion."

Marshall nodded. "Are you happy with this?" he asked the youth.

"I don't want to die."

"Well, we'll give it a go. I'm not sure this is going to be easy." He had trouble believing this thin, scared youngster would convince anyone he was a murderer. Not to mention the question of proving who he might be.

"It will work," Tureg said confidently and Marshall wondered what the seer had done. He decided it was probably best not to find out. He was about to tell quite enough lies for one day, without hiding anything else.

"I must go before the moon sets." Tureg placed a hand on the corpse which rose into the air, turned away from them and vanished.

"Right," Marshall handcuffed the youth, "let's go and be creative with some paperwork."

*

Both Doctor Trent and Craig Hickson were with the chief constable when Marshall was called in the following morning.

"John, we have a problem. This case you're working on – death of a tramp."

"I arrested someone last night, sir."

"You did?" The chief constable paused, momentarily thrown. "But I've just been hearing reports that the body and some of the evidence went missing overnight."

"Yes sir."

"So, what am I missing?"

Marshall took a deep breath. "We had a visit from a 'gentleman' while we were investigating sights of a strange man at the roundabout."

"A gentleman?"

"Yes sir. He handed over the man we now have in custody and took the evidence."

"And you let him?"

"I didn't have much choice, sir, if you get my meaning."

"I don't think I do, John."

Craig Hickson had though. "Something to do with a sword of no recognisable metal?"

"I believe so," Marshall said.

Hickson hit the arm of his chair. "Bloody spooks. Why do they do that?"

"Believe me," Marshall said, breathing a silent prayer of thanks, "I'm no happier about it than you are."

"And we're just supposed to forget it?" Liza Trent asked.

"That seems to be the general idea." Marshall thought he probably wouldn't forget anything in a hurry.

"Then I suggest we do." The chief constable leant forwards to stare hard at Marshall. "You must have seen this before, in London?"

He had, it was what had given him the idea.

"Just drop it, John, and thank the stars they didn't think it was important enough to make you disappear. Anything else we should 'lose', as it were?"

"Mark and Helen are replacing the tent and so forth on the roundabout. There will be someone else occupying it, I believe."

"Then be careful, John. You're on their radar now. Anyone they put there will be watching you too."

Marshall smiled slightly and agreed to be careful. He hoped they were watching; maybe one day he could have another look at this strange other world.

*

"Thank God for paranoia," he said to Mark later as they finished the paperwork on their murder suspect. "That was easier than I had any right to expect." And he couldn't honestly see a jury convicting Harril, either, on the evidence they had.

"I wonder what the trick is for getting back there," Mark said thoughtfully.

"I think the whole point of this charade is that they don't want anyone to know."

"Maybe, but I might see if I can make friends with the new Lion," Mark said, "just in case."

Marshall grinned. "You do that. I might join you." After all, he was 'on their radar' now and that might just work both ways.

The Wrong Train

"So what did he have in his pockets, Helen?" Detective Inspector Marshall threw his coat over the back of a chair as he entered the office.

"A train ticket."

"Well there's a surprise. Man found dead on train had a train ticket in his pocket. I meant anything useful, Helen."

She grinned. "I know. Unfortunately, that's your lot."

"A lousy train ticket?"

"Yes and, get this, not even a ticket for the train he was on."

"No?"

"One adult ticket; return fare from London to Nottingham for the twenty-second May, 2000."

"What?" Marshall took the ticket from her. His constable was right in every detail. "A twenty-year-old ticket, for a route that was way off course if it came through Fenwick, and nothing else." Marshall sighed. "It's going to be one of those cases, isn't it? I'll get it checked for fingerprints."

Sergeant Mark Sherbourne arrived with three coffees. "Told him the good news, Helen?"

"She told me. Just once, Mark, I'd like a corpse who has the decency to be carrying a wallet full of ID and, just maybe, a mobile phone on which he's captured a picture of his killer."

"I think I saw that movie," Mark said cheerfully. "So what do we do now?"

"Get a picture of our victim to all the media; let's see if we can identify him. Check any missing persons nationally for the twenty-second of May 2000 or thereabouts. Then see if by any remote possibility British Rail…"

"They're not British Rail anymore," Helen said.

"Whatever. See if the jokers in charge of trains keep any records of who bought tickets."

"Unlikely, sir."

"I know that, Helen. So when you've wasted your time on that, you can interview all the poor sods who were on the train this morning and had to replace the usual 'leaves on line' excuse at work with the more exciting 'corpse in toilet' one. See if anyone noticed anything… anything at all."

"You get out of bed on the wrong side this morning?" Mark said.

"You got me out of bed at five thirty so I could go and stare at a body full of holes in a not-British-Rail toilet; thanks for asking." He smiled at his sergeant who winked back. The two of them had worked together closely for a couple of years, in some very strange circumstances, and were comfortable with each other.

"More coffee needed, I take it?" Mark said.

"And bacon. Two baps or I'll never last 'til lunchtime."

"Should we Google the date too?" Helen asked. "See if anything important happened."

"Like a hole in the space-time continuum, which opened a gate between train toilets in different dimensions?" Marshall smiled at her. "Worth a shot." He headed for his office. "Get me a list of witnesses.

I'll make a start on them, while you and Mark see if you can track down the victim."

"Right-O."

"Leave the search for the wormhole in the fabric of reality until after lunch," he said as he shut his door. He didn't re-open it, to see what had hit it moments later – she might throw something else.

He dropped the train ticket on his desk and relaxed in his chair, happy with his team. It had been a wrench moving from London initially and Fenwick had done its best to throw every weirdness it had in his path, but he had a team here who were more family than mere acquaintances. That meant they all worked well together, however weird or hopeless the case was.

This one had not got off to a good start.

*

Mark appeared several cups of coffee later.

"I've got a missing person from twenty-second May that could be him," he said, delivering a pile of sandwiches.

"Could be?"

"Picture looks like him, if you imagine the body with all of its face. Helen's tracking down DNA or fingerprint information on the Mis Per."

"Details?"

"A Mr Albert Smith, London address, disappeared on his way to Loughborough. I assume he went to Nottingham and had to change, except he never made it."

"Where's he been for the last twenty years?"

"Miracles take a little longer. Any luck with the witnesses?"

"The word 'witness' sort of implies seeing something, which all of these people singularly failed to do… or, at least, not that they're admitting to. Our victim wasn't seen getting on the train at any station, no-one remembers sitting next to him, no-one spoke to him, and so on. He just wasn't there as far as anyone can remember."

"He just materialised in the toilet?"

"So they would have us believe."

Helen stuck her head round the door. "It's definitely Albert Smith. We had his fingerprints on file."

"Why?"

"CND. Got arrested at protests regularly. Snipping fences, blocking roads, you know the sort of thing."

"He must have been early fifties," Marshall said, surprised.

"Forty-eight when he vanished. That didn't stop him holding strong opinions, sir."

"Granted. Mark said he was on his way to Loughborough. Any ideas why?"

"To be a character witness for a fellow protester."

"Probably more help him not turning up then," Mark said.

"He's got a wife… widow," Helen said. "Do we want to go and talk to her?"

Marshall nodded. "I suppose we better. You and I, Helen; I sense Mark may be a little unsympathetic with her views." He clapped his sergeant on the shoulder as they left. "Keep checking these supposed 'witnesses'. Someone must have seen something."

*

Mrs Smith was an upright, elderly lady in her early seventies; her grey hair pulled back in a bun.

"We believe we may have found your husband," Marshall began, once they were ensconced in uncomfortable chairs, in the imposing front room of a huge town house in Kensington.

"That sounds ominous, Inspector. I assume he's not alive."

"I'm afraid not. Have you any idea why he might have been on a train through Fenwick this morning?"

"I haven't seen my husband since May 2000."

"Can you tell us what happened then?"

Mrs Smith drew herself up. "We were at a protest at Aldermaston, Inspector. Albert had agreed to go to court for a friend of ours on the Monday morning, after the concert on the Sunday night."

"Concert?" Marshall felt he was missing half the story.

"Yes, Inspector. Some woman, Monica something who was a famous violinist, came to Aldermaston to play for us. She believed in what we were doing."

"Which was?"

"Blockading the plant. We had to stop them making nuclear weapons."

"Right, so you had a concert and then your husband left?" CND protests and classical concerts was a pairing Marshall found difficult to reconcile.

"He came home and set off early on Monday, to the trial. I stayed at the camp and he was supposed to come back there afterwards."

"And when he didn't come back?"

"It was obvious; the government had taken him."

Marshall caught the words, 'Ah, you're one of those,' before they left his mouth. Instead he said, "Why would they do that, Mrs Smith?"

"To stop our protesting. We were dangerous."

"I see. Did many people 'disappear'?"

"Hundreds. They'd promise to come to marches and so on and then they didn't turn up. We knew they'd been nobbled; told to stay at home." Her faded blue eyes were staring off into an imagined past. "My Albert would never have agreed. So, of course, they would have had to silence him."

Marshall, fascinated, had to ask: "So why did they keep his body for twenty years?"

"To have a hold over me," she said, sounding as if she thought he was particularly thick for not realising this himself.

*

"She's several sandwiches short of a picnic," Helen said once they were back outside. "Do you suppose she believes that rubbish?"

"Some do."

"If you ask me, he got fed up of her and ran away." Helen looked round the crescent of elegant houses. "Or maybe it was an insurance scam like the guy in the canoe that year."

"Except that Mr Smith really is dead."

"There is that."

*

There was a large pink file on Marshall's desk when they returned to Fenwick Police Station.

"Scotland Yard sent up the original notes on Mr Smith's disappearance," Mark said.

"Anything worth looking at?"

"Half a dozen witnesses who saw him get on at King's Cross, two who remember him going to the toilet after about half an hour, then nothing. He was never seen again."

"Wormholes in the toilet-time continuum?" Helen asked.

"Still the most probable answer," Marshall agreed cheerfully.

His phone rang.

It was Liza Trent, the police pathologist.

"John, I've got a preliminary report on this morning's victim for you."

"Fire ahead."

"Died about an hour before he was found. Mauled to death by some very large animal so far unidentified."

Marshall put the phone down slowly. "How long was that train going before it reached Fenwick?"

"About an hour and a half," Mark said. "Why?"

"Our victim was killed by a large animal, probably whilst in the toilet."

"What sort of animal?" Helen said.

"Liza doesn't know."

"There were no large animals on that train," Mark said, "and no way one could get on and off without being seen."

"No," Marshall agreed.

"So?"

"Fuck knows."

He flicked randomly through the wealth of paperwork in the Scotland Yard file. There were large numbers of witness statements from people on the seven-twenty-seven train from London to Nottingham; one from the lady the missing man had been going to help out and one from his wife. Marshall glanced through it. It was full of the same anti-government garbage she'd spouted to them.

"Hey," he said after a moment, "listen to this from Mrs Smith's statement. 'I knew it was the government because I heard a man talking to him at the concert about helping him out and seeing him in the morning. Albert was too trusting, said he'd meet the man on the train even when I told him he mustn't. He said it'd be all right because he owed the man, but I knew they were out to get him.'"

"If we ignore all the paranoia," Mark said, "does that mean he was meeting a man on the train to Nottingham?"

"Looks like it."

"Did he? Was the man found?"

Marshall looked more seriously through the file. "Doesn't seem to have been. There is a photo-fit." He pulled a black and white drawing from the mass of paper. "Surprisingly normal, considering Mrs Smith's fantasies."

The drawing showed a man in his late forties, grizzled and tanned. Marshall thought it looked a bit like Harrison Ford in the Indiana Jones movies.

"Only the one head," Mark said sarcastically. "I didn't see anyone like that on the train this morning either."

"No." Marshall put the picture back in the folder. "We're getting nowhere here. So far we have a man who disappears on a train twenty years ago. He was seen getting on; he wasn't seen meeting any secret government agents, despite his wife's beliefs; he was seen going to the toilet. At which point he vanished entirely until he turned up this morning in a different train toilet. A train – if we believe our witnesses – that he didn't get on to and neither did the large wild animal that killed him, in a room not big enough to swing a cat in. Have I missed anything?"

Helen and Mark shook their heads.

"Unless," Helen said suddenly, "Murder on the Orient Express."

"Explain that."

"It's a book where all the other passengers are in on the murder."

"I know that. So?"

"Well perhaps all the passengers this morning were in on it and no-one's talking."

"It was a packed commuter train, Helen. Not to mention the one he vanished off. We're talking several hundred people."

"Oh, I suppose not." Helen grinned. "Mind you, Mrs Smith would say they'd all been nobbled by the government."

"Luckily, we're not deluded," Marshall said. "Go home, sleep on it. Let's hope we get somewhere tomorrow."

*

Helen was in before him, when Marshall arrived the following morning.

"Anything new on the Smith case?" he asked her.

"Autopsy report from Doctor Trent. Mr Smith was eaten by something large with sharp teeth."

"Still no idea what?"

"Nope."

"Oh well." He headed for his office.

"And I've got a file from the MoD."

"Oh no, please don't tell me Mrs Smith was right."

Helen laughed. "Nothing like that. It's his military record. It seems Albert Smith was in the army."

"Interesting occupation for a CND protester."

"Joined them after he left."

"Which was?"

"After the Falklands," Helen said. "Seems there was a query over his mental state."

"What sort of query?"

"He went missing during the battle for Tumbledown, presumed dead. Then he turned up half a day later, unscathed, miles away from where he should have been with absolutely no recollection – or so he said – of how he got there."

"So, not a stranger to unexplained absences. It's intriguing, Helen, but I'm not sure it helps."

"Morning." Mark arrived clutching three steaming coffees. "Sergeant Wilkes says to tell you there's a man in the front office, wanting to talk to someone about Albert Smith. Seems quite agitated."

Marshall grabbed a coffee and strode downstairs with his sergeant in tow. This could be a break they'd been looking for or, more likely, something of less use than his wife had been.

"I've put him in interview room two, sir," the young PC on the desk told them. "I ought to warn you, he says he's here to collect the body because he put it on the wrong train."

"What?"

"That's what he said, sir. I think he's a bit loopy."

"Join everyone else in this case," Mark said.

*

It was the man from the photo-fit; lean, hard and tanned with a shaggy mop of blond hair and sky-blue eyes. He lounged in the upright chair as if it might actually be comfortable. A wicked-looking knife was jammed through his belt and a gun, of a sort Marshall didn't recognise, was holstered on his right hip.

Marshall made a note to talk to Sergeant Wilkes about armed witnesses and introduced himself and Mark. "I believe you have some news about the death of Albert Smith." He waited.

"A skarall got him." The stranger's English had a faint accent Marshall couldn't place. "I said I'd deliver him home but I got the wrong train."

"A 'what' got him?" Mark said.

"Skarall." There was a pause. "Sorry, they're probably not something you've ever seen. Green; about the length of this room; my height; three rows of teeth and retractable claws. Oh, and a sting in the tail. Real nasty critters."

"Sounds it." Marshall wondered whether the obviously mad man was likely to turn violent and revised his mental note to talk to the desk sergeant about armed, crazy people being allowed into the station. "And this killed Mr Smith, did it?"

"Yes, wasn't supposed to be there. We had the wugbeats under control and then, whoosh, out it comes."

"The what…" Mark began but Marshall waved him to be quiet.

"And where was this Mr..." He left it hanging for the man to supply a name.

An opportunity the stranger ignored. "K'tharl. Three galaxies and two time jumps out."

"And I'm supposed to believe this?"

"Probably not a word of it," the strange man said quite cheerfully. "Doesn't stop it being true. Now, can I have the body to put on the right train, please?"

"We don't usually hand over bodies to lunatics," Marshall said, "even if we kept them here."

"The man on the train said the police had it."

"The pathologist does," Mark said.

"What train?" Marshall said.

"The one I put Bert on."

"That's off limits until forensics have finished with it. How did you get on?"

"With this." The man pulled a mobile phone sized box from his pocket. It had several luminous buttons on it.

"It can take me from my ship to anywhere. Well, it's a little temperamental, hence the wrong train problem."

"Bomb?" whispered Mark.

Marshall gave a tiny shrug. Though the man was armed and plainly deluded, he seemed too relaxed to be dangerous. The device looked more like a mobile phone with things painted on it.

"That will take you away?" he asked.

"Yes."

Marshall hesitated and then decided to trust his judgement. "Prove it."

"Okay." The man pressed a small green button and, much to Marshall's surprise, vanished.

"Fuck!" Mark leapt forwards, waving his hand through the space where the man had been. "He's gone."

Marshall sighed. "I'm having real trouble accepting he was ever here."

"It would explain the getting in and out of a toilet and the twenty-year disappearance."

"Not in any report I'm prepared to write, it wouldn't."

There was a sudden soft buzzing and the strange man was back. He thudded to the ground as if arriving from a height.

Mark leapt backwards to avoid being flattened.

"Convinced?" the man asked.

"I'm not sure where it gets us," Marshall said. "Unless you hang around to do that trick a lot, no-one's going to believe us." He wasn't even sure he believed it.

"Just give me the body and I'll put it back where it should've been and it won't be your problem."

"I haven't got the body. The path lab has it."

"Oh right, yes, you said. I'll try there." The man raised his pad of buttons again.

"Wait," Marshall said, "you can't just—"

"I can."

"But why? What makes Albert Smith special?"

"Nothing really. I happened to end up in the middle of a battle he was in. I'm a bit of a mercenary but no-one wanted to hire me for that one. Anyway, I saved his life so he said he owed me. When I was putting a band together for the wugbeats I thought he might like to help out. He did really well too, until the end. Some people freak when they star jump."

"So you brought him home?"

"Couldn't leave an alien on K'tharl. God knows what that would have done to evolution. Now, I ought to be going."

Marshall closed his eyes. "Go away," he said, "before I have to try explaining this to anyone, or I'm going to lock you up for lunacy and carrying a lethal weapon."

"Okay, I'll grab the body on my way. I guess it wasn't so nice meeting me." There was the strange soft buzzing again and they were alone in the interview room.

*

"So what happens if he does take the body back twenty years?" Mark said as they headed back upstairs. "Will it just never have been here?"

"Will what never have been here?"

"I... what... sorry, John, I totally lost the thread there."

"I... yes, you're right. So where were we?"

"Statements from the drug raids yesterday, I suppose," Mark said.

"God, I hate paperwork." The two of them went to their separate desks. Mark pulled out a file of witness statements and took it in to his superior's office.

"Here you go." He dropped it heavily on top of an old train ticket lying forgotten on Marshall's desk.

PART 3

OTHER SHORT STORIES IN SETTING

The Little Red Book

"Heard about the exhibition, Maggie? Grand opening tonight."

Maggie looked up from her screen. "In case you didn't notice, Geoff, you promoted me to real news some time ago and Jeremy has been doing 'celebrity' these last three weeks." She waved her wooden plaque at him. "See? Margaret Arkwright, News Editor."

"I know, Mags, but it is news. Big exhibition, famous pictures and rumoured to be big celebrities." Geoff gave what she thought of as his 'helpless puppy' look. "I thought our best news hound should be on the job."

"Instead of Jeremy?"

"Well…"

"You want me to go and hold his hand, don't you Geoff?"

"Come on, Mags. You said yourself that he's only been doing the job three weeks and there could be some real stars there."

Maggie closed her eyes in the hope he'd go away but he didn't, just stayed hopelessly smiling at her.

"Oh, Okay. I'll go. Tell him to meet me outside at eight."

She knew she'd probably regret it but none of the books on getting ahead in journalism had mentioned coping with an overwhelming sympathy for your boss. Newspaper owners were supposed to be hard-nosed businessmen in sharp suits. Geoff was anything but.

She finished the article she was working on and checked the contents of her camera bag. One day she was going to work for a paper that was big enough to afford cameramen, so she could spend her time actually listening to the interviewees, rather than considering the photogenic nature of their backdrop.

Taking her kit with her, she went home for an early tea and a nap; it was going to be a late night.

*

Jeremy was early and eager and showed the potential of being a really, really, annoying companion.

Maggie wondered, as he bounded up the Gallery's red-carpeted steps ahead of her, if she had ever been that excited about meeting Fenwick's stars. It wasn't a place that had ever provided the world with a huge number of celebrities or attracted great names of stage and screen to view its delights. She'd given up all hope of a glimpse at an A-lister years ago but she supposed she shouldn't dent Jeremy's enthusiasm.

The gallery had really gone to town. Beautifully tuxedoed waiters handed out champagne in crystal flutes from silver salvers, whilst a string quartet provided refined background music on the first floor. Maggie spotted a couple of Van Goghs, a Constable, Pieter Breughel's 'Fall of the Tower of Babel' and a set of Egyptian exhibits, all on loan from various collections.

In the centre of the main hall, surrounded by more security than she had ever seen in the place, was a plinth holding a small glass case. The only object inside was a red book. There was something discomforting about it though she couldn't identify what; just a desire not to go any closer to the case.

"That's mine," a voice at her elbow said. There was so much suppressed passion in the words that it raised goose bumps along Maggie's skin. She turned in surprise to find herself staring into the pale green eyes of a blond-haired gentleman in his late thirties.

"What? The book? It's kind of you to lend it."

"I didn't. I want it back."

Maggie's antenna went up; this sounded like a story.

"Are you saying this is here without your permission, that it is stolen?"

He looked at her as if she was stupid. "Obviously."

"Would you like to give me some details?" Maggie flipped open her ever-ready notebook. "I could get you a front-page spread."

"Maggie! Maggie! You'll never guess who I just saw." Jeremy came crashing up, his grin a mile wide.

"I'm busy, Jeremy. Mr..." But the man had gone, disappearing amongst the art critics and their bored partners.

"Who was that, Jeremy?" She pointed at the man's retreating back. He looked slightly deformed from behind, as if one shoulder was higher than the other.

"I don't know. Who cares? I just saw..."

"And what's the book? I wish we could get closer." There was a six-foot ring of clear space around the display case.

"Maggie, are you going to listen to me?"

"That was almost a story, Jeremy, and it sounded rather exciting." She sighed and relented. "Oh, go on, who did you see?"

*

She forgot about the strangely lopsided man and his stolen book in the next couple of hours as she hurried along behind Jeremy's whirlwind of enthusiasm. Several soap stars, two footballers, one politician and one bona fide film star later, she saw the man again. He was just standing, staring at the book in its closely guarded case.

Maggie paused and took several surreptitious pictures of him – one bonus of carrying her own camera – and wished she could put a name to the face. Before she could advance to ask him for his tale, the man turned away and was gone.

*

"We've seen everyone there is to see," Maggie told her still-lively companion at two a.m. "I'm going to call it a night. See you tomorrow." She left him happily celebrity-chasing and headed for home and bed. Old habits die hard so she stopped and picked up a catalogue on the way out, even though technically it would be Jeremy's article. He was much too excited to be likely to remember and they needed all the help they could get, in making sure the copy was spelt correctly.

She was also still mildly intrigued as to the identity of the strange red book and the catalogue should tell her; maybe even provide her with a handle on the story she had missed out on.

*

Having gone back to sleep after she had switched off the alarm, Maggie was late for work the following morning.

She was pleased to note that Jeremy's desk was also empty when she dashed in just after ten o'clock. Geoff stuck his head out of the office door and grinned at her. "Not used to the late nights now you're a proper reporter?"

At least he wasn't the sort to fire her for not turning in on time. "I made it before Jeremy," she retorted.

"He had the good sense to phone in sick. Mind you, he sounded fairly ill but I think it was probably self-inflicted."

"Well, some of us believe in doing the work we're paid for." She began to unload her camera bag. "I've got a whole card full of shots here to download and then I suppose you're going to want an article. Unless you want to wait for Jeremy to bother?"

"Let's get it in tonight's edition."

"Well, it's just as well I picked up one of these." She put the exhibition catalogue on the desk.

Having made herself a coffee and checked over various stories that had been sent in and had been put on her desk for editing, she plugged the memory card into the computer and scrolled through the hundreds of shots, to sort out ones worthy of a place in the centre-page spread she was planning.

Nearly the last shots on the card were the half a dozen she had taken of the strange man. He was rather handsome and the slight hump to his right shoulder was less noticeable on the pictures. Again, Maggie had a nagging sense of familiarity but she couldn't place the blond hair and green eyes.

"Geoff, come here a sec, will you?" Having been editor of the Fenwick Advertiser for thirty years, he knew anyone who was anyone. "Do you know who this is? He was there last night and I feel I should know him but I can't place him."

"Wow, years since I've seen him in town. That's Robert Earl, Olympic archer. He won all sorts of medals and I seem to think that we once did a spread on him because he made his own bows or arrows or something. We ran a series on keeping old crafts alive. Had a blacksmith and a thatcher and him and... oh, I can't remember. It's a while ago now. He's not really big on celebrity as I recall, so I'm surprised he went to that sort of thing. He's aged well, I have to say."

"Right, I think I've heard of him, vaguely." Maggie frowned. "He said something really odd last night. They had this red book on display, on a high security stand in the middle of the gallery. I couldn't even get close enough to read the label or anything and this Robert Earl fellow said it had been stolen from him and he wanted it back."

"Any proof?"

"I didn't get the full story. Jeremy was more interested in pictures of pretty women."

"So what was the book?"

"I never looked, just fell into bed." She picked up the catalogue and flicked through it. "It's not in here. All the pictures and so on but no mention of the book."

She looked through the glossy pages again but there was no sign of the exhibit she was searching for. "No, definitely not here. That's odd."

"Worth following up?"

Maggie thought about it but not for long; she loved a good mystery she could solve for her readers. She was also a conscientious worker so she said, "I'll finish the centre spread for you so it can go out tonight and then I'll pop back to the gallery. If there's anything in this then I can do a follow-up tomorrow; a 'behind the scenes' or something."

"What does it really take to put on an art show?" Geoff suggested.

"Yeah, 'Begged, Borrowed or Stolen?'" She smiled at him. "Now, bugger off so I can do the spread for you because now I'm intrigued."

*

By two o'clock, the copy was finalised for the evening paper and she sent it through to Geoff for a last check.

Out of curiosity she ran Robert Earl's name through the paper's archives. It brought up a list of articles on his archery successes and a couple about his craftsmanship. One of these was from the 'Craft

Masters at Work' series. Sure enough, when she brought it up on the screen, the gentleman from last night was shown aiming a rather impressive longbow into the sky. The caption claimed the bow had a hundred pounds of pulling power. Maggie had a flash of understanding; that explained the shoulder.

She scrolled down the list to the other article on craft and stopped in surprise. This second article was entitled 'Master Craftsman at Work' but only a summary appeared on the screen as the article itself was too old and was still listed as on microfiche. Maggie sighed. She realised that putting all these articles on the computer had been a fairly thankless task but any moron could have worked out that this article – supposedly written in 1902 – was in the wrong place. The summary was almost identical to the more recent article – 'Master craftsman Robert Earl spoke to our reporter about his years of making longbows'.

"Bollocks he did," Maggie muttered. She hesitated and then went in search of the original microfiche to find out who the article had really been about.

*

Geoff came in search of her ten minutes later to praise her wonderful spread. "What are you doing down here, Maggie?" The archives were kept in the basement.

"Take a look at this." She moved so he could look. "I found a misattributed file so I came to find it. Who's that?"

He looked at the screen and then at her. Maggie could see the cogs whirring behind his eyes. "Are you all right?"

"Answer the question, Geoff."

"It's Robert Earl. I told you that three hours ago."

"Look at the date, Geoff."

"Sixteenth June, nineteen… nineteen hundred and two? That's

not possible. He looks…" Geoff sighed. "Grandfather, I suppose. God, you really had me going for a moment there. Nice one, Mags. That is really uncanny."

Maggie looked back at the photograph. "No, I'd say that was the same man."

"It can't be."

"Well, I know that but no two relations are that alike unless they're twins." She got up. "I really am curious now. I'm off to the gallery to track down this book and then I might see if I can trace Mr Earl."

*

The woman on the front desk looked rather bleary-eyed but she gave Maggie a cheerful smile. "Hello, you were here last night, weren't you?"

"'Fraid so."

"Got you working today too?"

"Yes." Maggie waved her camera. "I didn't really get a good shot of the red book you had on display last night. I was hoping you wouldn't mind if I went and took a few now."

"Oh, I'm sorry. That was on loan from the Smith Foundation. It went back this morning."

"You mean the place in Museum Street?"

"That's right."

"I might try there then." Maggie turned away and then did a full circle until she faced the desk again. "I don't suppose you know what it was, to merit all that security?"

"What security?"

Maggie blinked. "Well, all the… well." She thought back. In the cold light of day she realised she could remember a six-foot circle of space around the plinth but no cordon or personnel enforcing it. "That's odd," she said, ignoring the other woman's confused look. "I was sure… so what was it?"

"Some sort of ancient diary, I believe, but I can assure you we didn't pay for anything more than the normal security last night."

"I'm going barmy. I could have sworn… never mind." Maggie waved a vague hand and left, still muttering to herself.

Standing on the pavement outside, she considered what to do next. Gradually, she became aware that she was attracting attention. Two men on the opposite side of the road were watching her dithering. Sparing them a cursory glance and flushing slightly, she turned and headed for Museum Street. She would go to the Smith Foundation, because her journalist's nose was smelling something distinctly fishy and it was an excuse to go back to the Foundation. She'd nearly had a story at Christmas, about the strange goings on at the place, which hadn't quite come off, therefore maybe she might get a piece now, if it was involved in this. So it was worth an investigation but, if that was a dead end, then she supposed she'd have to let it go.

It was as she strode down Butchers' Passage past St Mary's that she became aware of being followed. The narrow lane was a quite well-used thoroughfare from the High Street and being followed along it was not unusual but some instinct prompted Maggie to glance back. It was the two men from outside the gallery.

Maggie Arkwright had never shrunk from asking the awkward questions in interviews or in life. She stopped, folded her arms and glared at her pursuers. "Are you following me?"

Close to, they were quite a daunting pair. One was nearly seven feet tall, long of limb and sturdily built. Her imagination supplied him with a limited IQ and quick fists. The other one… Maggie felt her pulse quicken slightly and she resisted the desire to run. The other was a head shorter than his companion, though still several inches taller than her. He had short black hair; rugged, tanned features; and the darkest eyes she had ever seen. He moved with a languid grace that she had seen many a 'wannabe' celebrity attempt without success. He was, without doubt, the most handsome man she had ever met but what raised her pulse was the palpable air of danger. She was reminded of a television programme she had once seen, of a sleek panther stalking its prey.

Swallowing hard, she considered how far she might get if she took to her heels but the pair were now too close.

"I'm afraid we were," the taller one said politely. "We have a friend who wants to talk to you about an offer you made last night. Would you come with us, please?"

He even made it sound like a request though Maggie didn't think refusing was an option. She also needed a swift mental adjustment; this was no idiot.

Mustering all the grace she could, she waved an airy hand. "Lead on, my business can wait." And, if she got out of this in one piece, then it could well be a better story than an unknown book.

She followed the tall man, aware of his companion a step behind, while her mind worked frantically. What offers had she made last night? What hadn't she, would be an easier question. In this job, any chance of an exclusive, in return for flogging someone's latest product or appearance, had to be grasped with both hands.

Her preoccupation was interrupted by the fact that they had arrived in front of a building and stopped. She glanced up and let out a small laugh. "But I was coming here."

"Guessed you might be, that's why we just followed," her guide said. "Come on in."

She was met inside by a young woman, her brown hair pulled back in a ponytail. "Hi, you must be Maggie. I'm Jenny Williams, the librarian here at the Foundation." Maggie resisted the urge to tell the girl that she knew that; she'd done a lot of research on the place after the Christmas fiasco. The huge place they had entered was full of heavy wooden shelving stretching into the distance. "Come through to the office."

The office didn't deserve the description. It had a roaring fire burning in the hearth, a bed in an alcove beyond, and a full-length mirror on the wall, behind a desk covered in a range of weird and wonderful looking objects. A sword hung above the fireplace and cabinets full of curiosities hung in various places on the walls. Several comfortable armchairs were placed around the flames and in one of these lounged Robert Earl.

He smiled at her as she entered. "Good afternoon, Miss Arkwright. Do sit down."

Maggie took the seat closest to the fire and those with her also took seats. "She was at the gallery," the tall one said.

"What were you doing there, Miss Arkwright?"

Maggie frowned. "I'm not sure that it's any business of yours but, as it happens, I went to see if I could get a closer look at the red book you said belonged to you. The receptionist said it had come back here so I decided to see if I could track it down."

"And why would you want a closer look?"

"I had a search in the catalogue from last night and it wasn't in there and I couldn't get close to it when I was there because of..." she hesitated, "...well, actually, I'm no longer sure why."

Robert Earl and the young librarian exchanged a meaningful look which Maggie wished she could read.

"Why did you think you couldn't?" Jenny Williams asked, leaning forward in her chair.

"I got the impression there was a security cordon of some sort but the woman today said there wasn't."

"Interesting. Forceful but crude, lacking in subtlety," Jenny said, which made no sense at all to Maggie.

"Do you mean me?"

"No, sorry, thinking aloud. So they told you the book was here?"

"On loan and returned this morning."

Robert Earl laughed. He nodded to the dark-eyed man. "Will, it's on the desk."

The man named Will retrieved a small, red book from the desk and threw it to Maggie.

It had a red leather cover and was about A5 size. She opened it. It contained nothing; every page was blank.

"That," Robert told her, "was what they returned."

Maggie refrained from stating the obvious; this clearly wasn't what had been lent. On the other hand, other things were less clear. "You told me last night that it had been stolen."

"The 'security measures' you observed led me to the conclusion that they had no intention of returning the book. How shall I put it… as owner of the book, I would not expect to be kept away from it."

Maggie felt there were whole chunks of this story that she was missing and that was not a feeling she liked. "So, I suppose what you want is the front-page story I suggested: 'Gallery steals loaned exhibit' or something like that."

"We were thinking," Robert agreed, "that you might like to run such a story and, being a conscientious journalist… you are, aren't you?"

"Certainly."

"We would expect that you would check out the story by asking Mr Bourne to give his view."

"Mr Bourne?"

"The gentleman in charge of putting the exhibition together, for the gallery."

"You want me to go and talk to him? He's bound to deny it all."

"Mr Bourne is someone who has had his eye on the book for some years now and will be more than happy, I should imagine, to show it off."

"But if you knew that…"

"I did, Miss Arkwright, but it was Jenny, as librarian, who was approached and she is relatively new to the job and was unaware of Mr Bourne's 'interest'."

"All right." Maggie pulled out her notebook. "I better note down your side of the story then, if we're going to do this properly."

"By all means."

Maggie scribbled down all they'd told her so far, aware, as she did so, that the man named Will had moved to read over her shoulder.

"So, you think asking Mr Bourne questions will help you?" she said eventually.

"In order to show you, he will have to remove the 'security' that he has in place. I recommend seeing the article and asking to touch it." He paused and then said coldly, "Once he has allowed that, I will be able to get to it to take it back."

"You're going to be with me?"

"I will be near enough to know. Do not worry about me."

"Don't worry? You're expecting me to be involved in a theft and—"

"I want you to be a good journalist and follow a story, nothing more. I merely express my intentions to allay any shock." Robert smiled though it didn't reach his eyes. "I do not use people unwittingly. What do you say, Miss Arkwright?"

"If I don't?"

"There are other journalists."

Maggie sighed; she could just imagine Jeremy blundering in here. If she looked at it as Robert Earl was expecting, all she was doing was following a story. His objectives needn't concern her.

"All right. I will talk to Mr Bourne but I will have no part in any theft and will deny knowing about it if asked."

Robert Earl seemed unsurprised. "I expected no less. I had Jenny take the liberty of pretending to be you and arranging to meet Mr Bourne at eight o'clock tonight, in his office at the gallery."

"You did what?" She half started from her chair and found a hand very gently pushing her down. She looked up into Will's deep eyes; eyes you could drown in.

He winked.

"Rob has faith in people. He knew you could be relied on." His voice was soft, deep and friendly though she thought that this particular purr had claws hidden beneath it.

"Fine," Maggie snapped. "I'm reliable and I'm conscientious. I do, indeed, happen to be a damn good journalist, so perhaps Mr Earl would care to explain why our archives have a picture of him, with an article written over a hundred years ago."

Will laughed. "Well done, Rob. She's good and you're careless."

Robert joined in though Maggie wasn't sure what they found so funny. "I look very like my great-grandfather, would you believe?" Robert stood up and held out his hand. "Goodbye, Miss Arkwright, and good luck tonight."

"What? What do you mean 'would I believe'?" She found herself shaking his hand. "I... what?"

He pulled her upright. "Will, John, show Miss Arkwright out." Then Will was at her elbow encouraging her to leave.

"But..."

"Until later, Miss Arkwright."

*

Only once she found herself on the doorstep, with the door closed firmly in her face, did she have time to gather her thoughts. "Fuck!" she announced to the world at large. "He didn't even tell me what the bloody book was."

*

"Mr Bourne is expecting you." It was a different woman on reception. "I'm about to close up, Miss Arkwright, so if you wouldn't mind going up. It's the second floor and then turn right."

"No, that's fine."

"Mr Bourne will show you out, once you're done." The woman picked up her bag and coat. "Goodnight, then."

"Goodnight." Maggie followed the woman's directions up the stairs.

Mr Bourne was waiting for her at the top. She had envisaged someone a lot older but Mr Bourne looked to be in his early thirties and she thought he probably visited a gym regularly. His immaculate suit emphasised the broad shoulders and trim waist. He smiled in welcome and grasped her hand firmly. "Miss Arkwright, how lovely to see you. Do come through." He ushered her through a door marked 'private' and down a short corridor to a large office. It was richly furnished and uncluttered, in stark contrast to the library office she had visited earlier.

Mr Bourne sat himself on the far side of a large mahogany desk and indicated that she should take the matching chair opposite him.

"I believe you came to the exhibition last night, Miss Arkwright. A pleasing turn-out, I felt."

"Very impressive, Mr Bourne."

"You had some questions about it?"

Maggie swallowed and nodded. "Yes, may I take notes?"

"Please do."

She flipped open her notebook. "I was wondering about the red book you had on display. I didn't get close enough to have a proper look and I wondered if there was a story to it. In fact, I was wondering if I could get a picture of it for my article." She patted her camera bag.

For a moment she thought he wouldn't answer and then he smiled. "Ah yes, your article. You have been to the Smith Foundation, I believe."

"How…" For the second time that day she found herself wrongfooted.

"What did they tell you?"

Maggie sighed, so much for her interview. "That you have stolen the article in question."

"I prefer to think of it as acquiring some insurance." He leant back in his chair. "So why are you here?"

"I have been asked to publish a story about the theft. I do not write such things without checking the validity of my facts. I hoped to get your side of the story."

"Without telling me of the accusation?"

"I find people are more open and honest if they are not immediately on the defensive, Mr Bourne." As he now was, unfortunately. "I would have raised the allegations later, having made some judgement of your character and the likely honesty of your answer."

"You have remarkable faith in your own ability. I find that… refreshing." Maybe she hadn't ruined this; he seemed quite relaxed. "Ask away and I shall convince you of my honesty. You shall have the truth, though you may well find it unpalatable."

He sounded genuine enough so Maggie took a deep breath and began.

"So, what is this book?" An answer she'd been chasing all day.

"The Diary of Robert, Earl of Huntingdon."

"By?"

Maggie looked up from writing when he didn't answer.

"No, Miss Arkwright, THE diary of Robert, Earl of Huntingdon. Dated in the 11th Century."

Maggie did a quick mental adjustment. "All right, I can understand the value of a book that old." Though she still had the nagging feeling she was missing something and it must have shown in her voice.

"And already you don't believe me."

"It might help if I could see the book. You have to admit that it is quite a claim."

Again, he took a while before answering and then he nodded.

"I don't see why not."

He went to the safe which stood in the corner of the room, fiddled various dials and then muttered a few words that Maggie couldn't catch. He returned with the red book she had seen from a distance the evening before.

"You may handle it, Miss Arkwright, as long as you are careful. It is an ancient book and very precious to me."

She hesitated.

The red cover was blotchy and untitled. It looked as if it had once been brown leather but it had become stained.

"What happened to it?"

"That is blood, Miss Arkwright."

"It wouldn't still be this red."

"You are an observant young woman. This is a most unusual book. The blood remains red."

"How? Unusual in what way?"

"A more pertinent first question, surely, would be to ask whose blood this is."

Maggie hated when interviewees directed the interview themselves but it seemed he wasn't going to answer anything else. "All right, whose blood?"

"That of the author."

Maggie paused, unsure what to make of that, but she might as well continue now she'd started. "And the reason it stays so red?"

"This is where, unfortunately, you will cease to have any belief in my honesty." Maggie decided he wasn't a very good judge of character if he thought she was following him so far. "The blood maintains its colour because the enchantress who caught the blood trapped a part of his spirit within the book as well."

"Really?"

"And, while part of his spirit is caught within the pages of that book, he cannot die and the blood will not fade. While I have that book, I can control if he lives or dies and I can therefore control his every move."

Maggie had a sudden vivid memory of Robert Earl saying, 'That is mine,' in a voice which sent shivers down her spine. Her imagination supplied the rest, filled the gaps and came up with a calculation where two and two most definitely did not make four by any laws of the world she knew.

"I am encouraged by your silence. It suggests a willingness to accept my tale that I hadn't looked for."

Maggie rallied. She hadn't been born yesterday, however plausible parts of her brain were trying to tell her this story was. "It's a while since I did history at school," she said, "but I seem to remember that enchanters and witches weren't real, just old women who were good with herbs."

"A... shall we say... politically correct version of the tale. The church will not admit to their abilities when they worked so assiduously to hunt them down and discredit them. The Earl was found bleeding to death and, in order to save him, this woman used an ancient spell to capture part of his blood and spirit within the book. As long as the book is safe, the Earl cannot die."

Maggie reached out and gently touched the book. "And you think that by having this you control the Earl and can make him... what? Turn up here?" Her tone lacked the incredulity she'd hoped to inject.

"Something like that," Robert Earl said behind her.

He stood in the doorway with a longbow in one hand and a quiver at his belt.

In one graceful, flowing movement he took an arrow, notched it to the bowstring, pulled back and released.

The thud as it pierced Mr Bourne was horrifyingly loud.

"Sorry, Guy." Robert Earl walked forward, removed Maggie's trembling hand from the cover and placed the red book in his pocket.

"You... you killed him."

"I doubt it. He's got something like this somewhere too or he wouldn't be here." He patted the bulging pocket seemingly unconcerned. "What he hasn't got is the common sense to drop old feuds, so we go through this charade occasionally." He patted her shoulder. "Come on, Maggie, time to go."

*

Jenny made her coffee once they were back at the Smith Foundation. The towering John, showing an astuteness she wouldn't have credited him with, added whisky to it.

"So, what am I supposed to write?" Maggie said. "I don't even know what to believe." She shook her head. "I ought to call the police. You just shot a man."

"Do what you feel is right."

"And you…"

"…Will watch your career with interest, Miss Arkwright. You did me a favour tonight. I needed him to remove the spell, to get close enough to retrieve the book. I won't forget."

"And that's it?"

"Unless you want another cup of coffee."

Maggie sighed. She was no nearer to understanding or – rather – no closer to believing what she was being led to understand. She stood to leave. "Do they," she indicated Robert's two friends, "have diaries as well?" She just about managed to make the sarcasm outweigh the curiosity.

Just.

"Ring," Will said.

"Trencher." John smiled and pointed towards one of the cabinets on the wall. "Foundation keeps them safe."

"Indeed." Robert Earl took out the book and handed it to Jenny. "Safely returned. Careful who you offer to lend it to."

The librarian was replacing it in the cabinet as Maggie left.

*

Early next morning, Maggie phoned the gallery.

"Mr Bourne?" the voice on the other end said. "He's fine. He left for the airport about half an hour ago for a tour of oriental galleries. He left a note for you, Miss Arkwright. I'll send it round."

It was written on one of the gallery's own stock of postcards; this one showed the falling Tower of Babel.

"Sometimes," he had written, "it would be illuminating if we all understood each other but the truth is often a difficult language. I expect you will go far." He had signed it simply, 'Guy'.

Maggie thought that he was probably right. Today the truth was an impossible language and one she just couldn't speak.

She put the card away safely and set to work on the slightly easier – but not by much – task of writing something her readers would believe about the gallery exhibition and a small red book.

After the Flood

At fourteen, Mary stopped seeing the harper at the bottom of the garden. It seemed then, a lesser loss against the greater; innocence buried under the soil which rained down on her mother's coffin. Childhood dreams and fancies were so fragile in comparison with the harsh realities she now faced and she almost forgot that it was possible to take that slight sideways step, just as she almost forgot that it was possible to have a mother to hold you.

Neither was totally forgotten but both, seen through the mist of years, became unreal and she found it hard to tell which was the truer memory. Was the hand that had stroked her brow at night any more or less real than that which had showed her harp music? By the age of twenty-four, she could no longer say.

That autumn found her home; a place she had never truly escaped. Behind her lay a broken relationship to a man who, however hard he tried, could not sever ties which bound her to this place. She had loved him and he her – she was sure of that – but she found herself dreading the step which would leave her father adrift with no-one. Or perhaps she feared to lose what connection to the past she had. It was a problem she came home to each night determined to confront and found that nothing ever changed.

In a house where you could still believe a mother lived, her father hung on grimly to memories that were ten years gone. He barely noticed the daughter who had provided for him all that time and who stayed to watch him drown in the past that held them both. Only once had he looked into the future for her.

"Married? You would go? How can I lose you too?" And so, instead, she had handed back the ring and told Tim that things would remain as they were.

"I'll wait," Tim had said and she protested, having visions of another man held in thrall to a dream that could never be.

So, chained to two men, one grasping helplessly at a lost past and one vainly hoping for a lost future, she drifted through a bleak October.

It was on a bright, cold Saturday morning that the sun eventually shone through the clouds and Mary found that the dreams of childhood were closer than she knew.

*

The swollen waters of the Hurne moved sullenly below her as Mary leant over the parapet. The Mortimer Bridge crossed where the ancient Eastgate had once stood, its stone balustrades now strengthened, to take the buses and delivery lorries which thundered past behind her.

She remembered the river flooding in the winter before her mother died, filling Bridge Street with muddy water and reaching as far as the bottom of Museum Street. They had come down to look in awe at the lake that had suddenly appeared.

"Not thinking of jumping are you?" The voice was right beside her and nearly made her drop her handbag into the water. A slim hand flicked out to catch the small square of leather and she turned to face a pair of deep golden eyes set under dark brows.

261

"My apologies." He was slim and lithe with shoulder-length hair as black and glossy as a raven's wing. "I didn't mean to startle you."

"That's okay." She took the proffered bag. "I was miles away."

He turned to look down at the water, side by side with her. After a moment he said again, "You aren't thinking of jumping, are you?"

"No. No, of course not. I was thinking of coming to see the floods with my mother." Her voice cracked slightly on the last word but she hastened on. "The water came all the way up here."

"Then the water all disappeared, leaving just a memory of where it had been and all the flotsam and jetsam of something passed." His voice was rich and deep. "Rather like when someone dies."

"Yes… well… er… I… how…" Mary turned to look properly at him. He wore a long-sleeved black shirt and black jeans which emphasised his pale skin. He continued to watch the water as if unaware of either her scrutiny or her confusion. She had just decided that it was merely a coincidental connection that he had made, when he turned his head to look at her.

"Like when a mother dies." He turned to walk away. As he reached the far end of the bridge he turned back to her as if feeling her watching eyes.

"But memories linger. Like notes plucked on a harp string."

She shouldn't have been able to hear him above the roar of the passing traffic for she was sure he had not raised his voice but the words rang clearly.

She blinked and he was gone, simply vanished, and though she hurried forward to where he had stood there was no sign that he had ever been there. A memory himself, perhaps, to linger in her heart.

*

She walked home slowly, her eyes unseeing, her feet treading paths known since childhood. Different memories kept her preoccupied. Not golden eyes under dark brows but green eyes flecked with brown filled her thoughts; eyes that could twinkle but had also been able to see all the way into her soul. Eyes she hadn't thought of in almost ten years.

Ciaran Silvertongue had stepped into her life one spring day and not left until the week her mother died. Except that wasn't strictly true, he hadn't stepped into her life and he hadn't chosen to go. If he was to be believed, she had stepped into his.

"A slight lessening of the grip you have on reality," he had explained once. "You slide sideways into the place where I live. I see you sometimes, coming here when you're full of the burdens of the living and you cannot step out and come here."

'Here' was the bottom of her garden, except that it wasn't at all. 'Here' was a step out of time; a product of a daydream she had thought at first, a scene born of a ten-year-old's overactive imagination and hormones. Except that wasn't so; Ciaran was as real as any in the world she escaped.

"Can't you come to me?" she had asked once.

"Why would I, child?" Ciaran rarely used her name. "I am of dreams and walk the twilight path. What would I with the everyday? You need to let it go and come to me and I will help you as I can." So she had learnt to let go and to picture the harper with his green eyes and long silver hair, sitting on the grass by a stream that did not exist in the garden she stood in. He was always there, pulling haunting melody from the beautifully crafted harp he bore and that he had taught her to play. Her fingers fumbled at first and then grew nimble and sure until she was brave enough to ask her mum and dad for one in the everyday world. It still sat, gathering dust in her room, not played in ten long years.

She had stood in the garden on returning from the hospital, eyes streaming bitter tears and she had screamed, "I need you. What use are you if you can't be here now?" Screamed it to an empty garden, that stayed resolutely devoid of harpers and streams. As if he had spoken, she answered. "How can I let this go? She was my mum and she's gone and I'll never see her again."

She hadn't seen the harper either and she hadn't tried again. Ciaran and his harping became another memory.

Now, walking home, she worried at it. How could she have deserted a friend? It had never been his fault that her mother had gone. Or had he even existed at all? Was he just another dream of childhood – like the teaching career and the white wedding – buried now in the corner of St Anne's tiny churchyard? If not, what had the man on the bridge meant? She kept returning to him, the man with the golden eyes who knew so much and had said so little.

"Who are you?" she said out loud. "How do you know me?"

"My friends call me Hawkeye." He leant against the wall of number sixty-seven at the corner of her road. "And you would be a harper if you could but find your soul."

Mary jumped in surprise. "How did you do that?"

"I stepped sideways." His smile didn't quite reach the amazing golden eyes.

"You know Ciaran?" She grasped at the familiar phrasing.

"Release is in music." Which, though not an answer, said enough.

"He used to tell me that."

"A shame it was a lesson you never learnt. There is more to harping than the touch of the strings."

"I know, Ciaran told me that as well." She paused, feeling tears welling up. "How is he?"

"That is something you could find for yourself." She didn't feel there would be anything of sympathy in this slim, dark man with eyes of molten gold but he surprised her. "Life moves on, child, and it can be hard to put away your anger and find space to play."

"Anger? My mum died."

"I know. Did you grieve?"

"Of course." There had been nights of tears as she lay and cursed God for taking her mother away; ranting and sobbing at her dad for no longer being able to go to university because she couldn't leave him alone. She remembered Tim's look as she handed his ring back and her own fear of stepping into the future.

She remembered and yet saw it as if for the first time.

She had screamed at Ciaran, at his absence.

"There was anger too," she admitted, and then realised that she was speaking to herself. The strange man had gone again.

*

She let herself in thoughtfully through the front door. Everything was the same but now, with insight – through golden eyes? – she realised that this was something she could have changed too. This dependence on staying the same was not merely her dad's fault. He had needed her and she had failed him in so many ways.

She lifted her mother's coat down from the hook on the wall and held it to her face. She could smell the perfume her mother used to wear but now she realised she could also smell the dust and decay. Looking around she could see it everywhere, the dust of years settled over what had been a shrine but was now just a grave that had buried them, along with the woman they loved.

Clutching the coat, she made her way to the back room where her dad sat slumped in front of the snooker on television.

He looked at her briefly and then again, more sharply. "That's..."

"...Mother's coat. I know. I think it's time to move on. I'm going to clear her things out." After all, after a flood you had to clear out the flotsam and jetsam to carry on with life.

"But…"

"And then, if he'll still have me, I'm going to marry Tim and see if I can become the teacher I always wanted to be."

"Mary…"

"I'm sorry, Dad." She sighed, seeing – or imagining – a pair of golden eyes reflected in the silver on the mantelpiece. "If I'd known how – if I'd been less scared – I should have done this years ago. I failed you when you needed me."

"Failed me?" Her dad seemed truly startled. "You've always been here for me."

"But if I hadn't been, maybe you would have gone out, had a life. I told myself you needed me but I think the truth is that I needed you, needed things to stay the same."

Without waiting for an answer, she went down the hall to the kitchen, collected the roll of bin liners and headed upstairs. On the landing, instead of heading for her mother's wardrobe, she found herself standing in front of the harp.

Gently she lifted it down and ran her fingers across the strings. Awkwardly at first and then with remembered skill, she tuned the strings, listening for the rich tones. Once she was satisfied, she began a slow air, picking out the notes with growing confidence.

"I never thought I'd hear that again." Her father stood in the doorway.

"Something else I should have done years ago." She began a livelier tune, feeling her shoulders relaxing as Ciaran had taught her; pouring all her concentration into the fingers dancing across the strings. She barely noticed when her dad picked up the bin liners and moved away purposefully down the landing.

*

It was late, nearly twilight, when she stepped into the garden. All her mother's things sat in bags piled in the hall and her dad – at her instruction – had gone to the pub. It was darts night and she hoped that some of the old team would be there to welcome him. It was a first step on a long road but he had eventually taken it. She would admit to bullying him slightly but had done so without anger for the first time in years, pushing him gently to move on, rather than berating him for standing still.

Now she stood amongst the windfall beneath the apple tree, cradling her harp. She was nervous but determined. Sitting carefully on the damp grass, she took a deep breath and began to play.

"I'm sorry, Ciaran," she whispered as she formed his image in her mind.

Without fuss, the world slipped sideways and she found herself sitting in a green meadow on the banks of a gurgling stream under a sinking summer sun. A scene that never changed in all the times she had been here or in the decade since her last visit. Only in one way was it different to how she remembered. Not one man, but two, awaited her and, with no surprise at all, she saw that the eyes of the second were golden.

She stilled her strings.

"You again."

He smiled and, this time, it reached the eyes, crinkling the corners. "Well done." He came forward and helped her to stand, his grasp cool but firm. Before she could respond he had turned to the harper. "Two tunes, I think. One for loss, my friend, and one for future possibilities."

"From the heart." Ciaran smiled.

"Always." The dark man turned back to her and swept a bow. "I shall be listening." With barely a ripple in the evening air, he vanished.

Ciaran came forwards and took her gently in his arms, holding her for a long moment and she noticed that he was as she remembered. Ten long years had passed him by and wrought no change; he was as timeless as the scene.

"A tune," he said eventually. "Play from your heart and I shall follow. Release your loss to the music."

So she played and then he played while she cried tears for love remembered and gone, and ten years' friendship wasted and lost.

In the end, under a rising full moon, she played again; a dancing tune of hope for the future, sometimes following him and sometimes leading the soaring tune. And once, she was sure she saw a pair of golden eyes reflected in the moonlit waters before the music ended and reality called her home to a world moved on and full of future possibilities.

The Enemy Within

Cara cursed as the first effects of the drug took hold. As the room swam and lurched and her legs buckled, she loosed a stream of slurred invective at her uncle.

The betrayal hurt.

Robert had always been there for her. Now, with enemies flocking outside, it seemed that even he could not be trusted.

The curses didn't move him. He merely smiled sadly as she slumped onto the handwoven rug. "I'm sorry, child. You would not leave. Forgive me when you wake."

Cara struggled against the darkness, bitterness battling with love. This was her uncle's way of getting her to safety when all else had failed. The curses would no longer come, though her heart ached. She had told him she would not run to safety; that she would fight beside him. She had thought this argument won, weeks ago. How dare he treat her like a baby when she could fight just as well as he? Her last thought, as the dark claimed her, was that he had no right to deprive her of the chance to die beside him. With Simeon gone, who else would hold his hand into the dark? And how was she to live without them?

Her head fell forward and dark dreams claimed her.

*

The walls were white and empty and the lights unforgivingly bright. Karen blinked several times and sighed; she had believed herself free of this place. The door was firmly shut and there were restraints on the bed though they currently hung loose. She pushed herself upright and listened closely. The voices in her head were silent now but with them had gone the memories. She wondered what she'd done this time to send her back.

There was a policeman on the door just like last time – that had been a frightening experience. All the interviews and demanding questions about an assault she couldn't remember and here, with the voices silent, she'd had no help to get her through.

She tried to take stock. The clock on the bedside table told her it was 2:30 and the daylight through the window suggested it was afternoon but she had no way of telling what day it was. How long had she lain, adrift on a drug-induced sea? She was sure she could have them running fast enough, if she tried to leave the room, but all she wanted was to know where and when and why and she wasn't yet annoyed enough to create panic for the sake of an answer. The anger was coming though, she could feel it rising. It always did when she was stuck in these bare white rooms waiting for someone to decide that she was sane enough to leave. Patience was not a virtue she had ever mastered.

She swung her legs off the bed, still feeling slightly groggy, and staggered to the window. They'd put her on the second floor of The Nightingale; no easy escape route offered. The trimmed hedges and neatly manicured lawns below told her nothing beyond the fact that it was a nice summer's day. The bedside table, upon examination, was empty apart from the clock and no clothes were piled on the regulation plastic chair.

Karen shook her head. How did they expect her to lie quietly and submissively if they deprived her of absolutely everything?

Still unsteady, she made her way to the door and wrenched it open.

The effect was immediate. The policeman leapt to his feet and the nurse on the ward station hurried towards her then stopped as Karen smiled slightly and went back to sit on the bed.

They sent two further nurses who stopped, confused, in the doorway on discovering her sitting calmly on the bed.

"Did you try and leave?" one demanded.

"I wanted to see someone."

"Dr Roberts said you'd still be asleep."

"Well, I'm not." Karen pointed out the obvious. "I want to know why I'm here."

"You don't remember?"

Karen sighed and wondered just who was in need of treatment. "No," she said slowly and clearly, "I don't remember."

"Brought in yesterday, you were, in a terrible state." The second nurse seemed to take some sort of perverse pleasure in this pronouncement. "Doctor'll tell you all about it, I'm sure."

"But I'm asking you." Karen could feel the familiar anger waiting to pounce. "Why can't you tell me?"

"Now, now, there's no need to work yourself up. You need to calm down. Doctor said you had to be properly calm."

"I would be if you'd just talk to me." Karen pushed herself from the bed, her fists clenched.

The two nurses exchanged glances. "I think you need to rest a little more, Karen." She said it as if talking to an infant, her tone exaggeratedly calm. "But we'll send for Dr Roberts."

They encouraged her back on to the bed and sat her down gently, both doing so with a care that Karen thought was probably genuine, if misplaced.

The policeman moved his chair inside the room and Karen resigned herself to going nowhere for a while and lay down, her eyes struggling to remain open – probably a continued effect of whatever they had given her to calm her down. As she sank back into sleep she reasoned that it had been an utter waste of effort just to discover that it was probably Sunday.

*

Cara fought off the effects of the drug to find herself being carried in the pitch black down an underground corridor. The walls, narrow and hewn from solid rock, showed in the flickering torchlight of someone ahead.

Cara twisted her head but couldn't work out who held her or how many there were. She relaxed and concentrated on gaining some clarity in her thinking and vision. She had known the passages under Fenwick Castle since she was small and might be able to work out which way Robert was sending her.

The man carrying her stopped. "Which way?" he hissed. Cara grinned to herself. She might have known.

"It's all right, Rafe, I'm awake. If you put me down I might be able to help."

Rafe almost dropped her in surprise but then carefully set her on her feet. "My lord said you'd sleep all the way."

"Well, I haven't." She smiled at him. "I told Robert I wasn't going to leave him."

"He couldn't bear to see you die, lass, you know that. He wanted you safe."

Cara nodded. And here was another who wouldn't want her dead. Rafe had been her personal bodyguard for as long as she could remember. He had spent long years grumbling about 'babysitting' and 'a job demeaning to a soldier' but Cara had long since seen through him. He had stood beside her father on the day he fell and had lost the use of his left arm protecting his fallen lord. Since then he had given her the same unswerving loyalty.

She looked at the second of the men.

"Hello, cousin." Simeon grinned, his blue eyes twinkling in the torchlight.

Cara gaped at him, feeling as if the world had taken a sudden lurch sideways. "I thought you were lost. You have been mourned."

"Publicly." He laughed. "Lysette was none too pleased about the deception but it is amazing what a ghost can discover."

Cara frowned but then left it; she had more urgent concerns. "I can't leave." She put her hands on her hips. "This is my fight."

"And one you might win in another place, on another day, but not here and not now."

"You can't know that, Simeon. We are holding out and the prince is on his way to relieve us."

"He will come too late, Cara. He has too far to come and too many enemies in his way." He paused and then sighed. "I'm sorry but some of your men have been bought and the secret of these ways revealed."

"Bought?"

"My father suspected a plot of some sort, hence my death. I discovered the ringleaders last night and none too soon. The castle will be betrayed tonight, through these very passages. He had to get you away."

"But surely if you discovered it you could stop it and—"

"There are too many, Cara."

"How could they?" Her voice rose in indignation.

"Cara, hush. Any man, however loyal, after so long on short rations, near to starving and seeing only a slow death, may choose to survive any way he can."

"You think they are right?"

"No, but I understand that not all men may be loyal to the death when death turns out to be so hard. We need to go, Cara. These passages will be full of the enemy before long."

"Are you going with me? Has he sent us both away?"

Simeon paused and then sighed again and shook his head. "How could I leave him? I mean to see you safe to the entrance and then return."

"You expect less of me."

"Maybe I expect more of you."

"I'm not going." She said it firmly, a decision she had made weeks ago. "What loyalty do I show if I run now while men starve and die for me?"

They stared at each other in the flickering torchlight. "No arguments, Simeon?"

"No more, cousin. In truth, I expected no different. I suggested drugging to my father as I knew what your response would be to any other persuasion. I would have rejoiced to see you safe but I think better of you for staying."

Rafe interrupted, "But my lord…"

"…Will understand." Cara knew her uncle well. "After all, it was he who taught me to be who I am." What she knew of loyalty came from Robert. Not a father she could barely remember, who had died fighting in the first rush of victory to install the new king, but her uncle who had held fast in stubborn loyalty to a dream of a brighter future despite the attacks of an old guard determined to cling to the past.

The three of them turned and set off back the way they had come, climbing the twisting stone passages through the rock.

They had gone about half the distance when Simeon stopped. "Hush." Clearly they all heard the sound of men coming down.

"Who is it?" Cara mouthed.

"Come to lead the enemy in," Simeon said, leaning in so that his lips almost brushed her ear. "Back a way there's a different route up that we could try."

They slipped back to the side turning but Cara paused just within it. "I want to see who."

Simeon looked as if he would argue but then nodded. He sent Rafe further along to hide their light and then waited in the dark with Cara. Half a dozen men soon appeared. They walked easily and chatted in low voices, obviously without fear. Cara noted that all were men she had known since childhood. Three had fought, side by side with her father, in the battle at Crook Bridge which had put Owain on the throne.

"Is that all there is? Can't we take them?" she whispered into her cousin's ear.

He shook his head. "I wish, that's just the ones coming to let the enemy in. Even there, it's two against six and Rafe crippled."

"He fights as well as you do with two hands." Which wasn't true, nobody fought as well as Simeon. He was a master with two swords, filled with deadly grace. But Rafe was as good as many who only fought with one weapon. "And I can fight."

"With what, Cara?" She had no sword on her tonight.

"You were sending me out there with no weapon?" She almost forgot to keep her voice low.

"We were sending Rafe with you." Simeon smiled. "He fights as well with one hand, you know, as most do with two."

Cara could have slapped him, had done so repeatedly whilst growing up, because his ready wit and sharp tongue always seemed to be one leap ahead. Robert had left them to it, smiling indulgently whenever he was eventually called in to separate the pair of them. If

Robert had taught her loyalty, then Simeon had taught her to fight and to think. Only recently had she realised how much she loved and respected him too. Like father, like son.

"They've gone." Simeon noted. "We might as well continue up this way." He called Rafe back and they hurried on.

It was sheer misfortune that the seventh of the betrayers had stopped to relieve himself on the way down. As they rounded the next corner, they came face to face with him as he hurried after his fellows.

Simeon drew his swords. His opponent, not quite as fast, found a blade buried in his chest before he had a chance to lift his own. He fell, lashing out as he did so and catching Cara across the calf.

She stumbled and then caught herself. "A flesh wound, don't fret. Let's move. They'll know there's something up when he doesn't follow." She pushed past Simeon and had gone five paces before her leg buckled under her.

Rafe swept her up in his arms and the three of them continued on up the passage.

*

The walls were as glaringly white as before when Karen stirred a second time. The curtains were drawn now and the clock said it had reached late evening.

After a brief glance she closed her eyes again and lay still trying to control the ever-present anger. Her brother was getting married and she needed to be there for him. Here her train of thought derailed; she'd come in yesterday and the last thing she knew it had been Saturday morning so now it was Sunday so she'd missed Saturday – missed the wedding.

Or perhaps not.

She couldn't bring anything to mind but sudden dreadful premonitions were lurking, back where the voices should have been.

Something must have happened at Simon's wedding but try as she might, she couldn't recall what.

While one part of her brain worried at this problem, another part realised that, though most of the drug had worn off, her left leg seemed to have no feeling. She wriggled her toes which shot stabbing pains up her leg.

Suddenly she was wide awake staring in horror at the crimson stain spreading across the white sheet, her leg afire with agony.

Karen screamed.

It was Doctor Roberts who arrived to the policeman's frantic call.

"What have you done to me? What have the bastards done to my leg?" Karen erupted before he had made it completely through the door. She had known Dr Roberts for some years now, had spent a lot of that time yelling at him.

The doctor stared in amazement then ripped back the sheet to reveal a six-inch gash down Karen's calf which was bleeding profusely. "You didn't do this?"

"Of course not." Self-harming had never been one of her problems whatever she did to others. "I've been asleep."

The policeman nodded. "She's right. She's been out of it and she's got nothing on her to do something like that. We checked."

"Well, something in this room or someone who has entered this room has done this. Find me a junior who can sew this up and Karen needs fresh sheets. Then do a thorough search." He sat in the chair. "Can you tell me why you're here, Karen?"

She shook her head. "Simon was to be married on Saturday, but I can't remember."

"I'm afraid Simon didn't turn up."

Karen blinked as memory came flooding back. Simon hadn't come, had left her alone with the black swelling and crashing inside and the voices loud and imperious.

It was Lynsey's fault; it had always been Lynsey, clutching at Simon and trying to drag him away from where he should be by her side. It wasn't going to work. She wouldn't let the bitch take him away from her. Whirling, she slammed her fist into Lynsey's bewildered face sending crimson flooding down the pristine white of her dress. Then she grabbed her by the throat and began slamming her head back against the altar again and again and…

Firm pressure on her wrists brought her back to the present.

"Karen!" The doctor sounded as if he had been shouting for some time. "Stop it!"

"He wouldn't leave me! That bitch stole him and…"

"Of course he wouldn't leave you and a shame you couldn't see that on Saturday. A shame he didn't think either. Once he realised what he'd done, he came straight here. He's here now and once we've got that leg sorted I'll bring him through."

"What happened to my leg, doctor?" She paused, unwilling to confront what might have happened to Lynsey.

The doctor looked worried. "I'm not sure, Karen. We'll check the room carefully."

"The voices will know." She tapped her head. "They know everything. But you need to stop the drugs because they make the voices go away and then they can't protect me."

Doctor Ranald sighed. "We've had this argument, Karen. These voices of yours aren't good for you but, for now, Karen, as long as you stay calm, I won't sedate you again. Now slip out of those sheets and let's deal with that cut."

Her leg buckled under her as she tried to stand and the doctor caught her and sat her in the chair. "I think we need to get some proper food into you as well," he commented dryly. "My nurses have been wearing rather too much of your meals in the past twenty-four hours."

Karen smiled weakly and closed her eyes again while the doctor and his staff bustled round her.

Simon arrived once they'd stitched and bandaged her leg. He was clutching a tray of food and looked rather sheepish. "Hi, sis. I guess this is my fault."

She shrugged sullenly, unwilling to forgive him yet.

"I was having second thoughts about Lynsey and I never thought what my not turning up might mean to you. I should have taken the time to explain." All his life he'd been protecting her, Karen thought reluctantly. Always there, always careful of her fragile state of mind.

"Second thoughts?"

His turn to shrug. "We just weren't compatible, wanted different things." Which meant, if the others were anything to go by, that Lynsey had wanted a house and a marriage without a Karen in it. She had probably argued that Karen would be better off in a white room like this one all the time.

"I'll not have anyone who can't love you too." Simon followed her train of thought as he so often did. She wondered, sometimes, whether it was part of him that spoke to her in the back of her head, telling her what she needed to do.

"I'm sorry." She'd lost count of how often she'd had to say that. "You'd be better off without me."

"Never, don't say it. Not now Lynsey's gone. I need you more than ever."

"Gone?" Karen felt cold; maybe she was going to end up forever in a white room.

"She left. Didn't wait around for me to show up and explain. It'll be just the two of us again for now, when you come home."

Except it never was just the two of them, not with the voices that were her near-constant companions.

She smiled for him. "Yes, just the two of us."

*

Cara finished hurriedly bandaging her leg tightly under Simeon's watchful eye. "It'll hold for tonight," she assured him.

"There may only be tonight," he pointed out.

Lord Robert turned from where he had been watching the courtyard below. "We could surrender."

"After holding out so long?" Cara was appalled.

"A lot of good men will die tonight, Cara. We may all die tonight. If the enemy has a way in then we cannot win in our weakened state and with a third of the men turncoats." He cupped a hand to her cheek. "I don't want to see you die, child. Neither my son nor you who I have loved like a daughter."

"You always taught us to stand true to what we believed."

"I did." He smiled at her fire.

"So why change now?"

"I'm not sure my beliefs are worth the loss of all I love."

"Can you say," Simeon asked quietly, "that surrender will guarantee our lives?"

Robert was silent and Cara, remembering tales of the past ten years, knew the answer all too well. Owain had won himself a throne and a life spent on horseback putting down one rebellious lord after another, bailing out his faithful time and time again. No quarter was ever given.

"No, my son, I think only a total reneging on our loyalty to Owain and a pledge to join the fight against him is likely to grant us the possibility of life." He paused. "And maybe not even then. We are known to have supported him openly for too long."

"I, for one, will not fight my king or go back on my oaths,"

Simeon said calmly.

"Nor I," Cara agreed.

"Then we will die fighting," Robert said. "I put him on that throne and swore to be his man. I'll not bow my knee for any other, whatever the cost."

The three of them drew their swords and went out to order what was left of the garrison and to stand ready with them for the attack. Not from outside this time but from below; an enemy within.

The first of the attackers came surging from the underground passages as the three of them reached the courtyard. In front came the six men that Cara and Simeon had seen heading down a short time earlier. They carried a white flag.

Robert waved his men to hold and stood forward. "What do you mean by this?"

"My lord, we do not wish for your deaths but we can see no way out. Owain has not come and we are starving. We have invited the enemy in, on condition that you are given opportunity to surrender the castle without further loss of life. You will be honourably treated, my lord."

"As honourably as chains will allow?" He smiled. "The king will come."

"We will have died gnawing at each other's bones by then," the spokesman retorted. "We must have food."

Robert nodded. "I understand, Geoffrey. Will you offer such honourable treatment to any as do wish to surrender?"

"Yes, my lord. I was told to so offer."

Robert raised his voice. "You are all hereby delivered from any oath to me and mine. I will not surrender nor betray my king but I hold no man or woman at fault for wanting to avoid this death. Any who wish to, may leave. I would ask merely that you refrain from bearing arms against me. Is there an arrangement, Geoffrey?"

"Lord Ranald has promised to refrain from any attack until second watch. You may safely open the lychgate to allow people out." Geoffrey paused and then made one last plea. "He will not attack at all, my lord, if you were to join us in leaving."

"I will not be joining you," Robert said softly. "All who wish, may leave now." He turned away so as not to watch and know who deserted him but Cara noted every one and was surprised at just how few chose to go, who had not already changed sides. A few soldiers, a slightly larger number of servants and two of the priests followed Geoffrey to the gate.

"Hold!" The voice was clear and imperious. "Do not shut the gate yet."

Lysette descended the steps from the keep and picked her way across the courtyard until she stood in front of Robert. Her once fair features looked pinched and frail through lack of food but her expression was as haughty as it had ever been. Cara had always thought that Owain's sister had not Owain's grace.

"For my brother's sake and my husband's, my lord, I have stayed in this hell hole and suffered but I will do so no longer. Only an idiot would turn down such a generous offer. Come, Simeon, we will be leaving."

She was fully halfway to the gate before she realised that she walked alone. Her proud stride faltered and she turned back. "Simeon?"

"I am sorry, my lady. I remain here."

"You will die here."

"At least I will not be foresworn, Lysette."

"And I will not starve!"

Simeon sighed. "Never fret. I release you from all ties. You never promised to starve and die with me. Make your own peace with

Owain, I have no quarrel with you. Go in peace, Lysette." He turned away and only Cara, beside him, saw the effort it cost.

Lysette paused for a long moment, obviously torn, and one of the enemy stepped forward slightly. "My lady, I am sent to escort you to Lord Ranald and to thank you for the guidance which showed us a way in here." He made his voice loud enough to carry to all corners of the courtyard.

Lysette glanced at him, then at Simeon who had turned back, his face a stony mask. After a frozen second she picked up her skirts but still she hesitated, as if unsure which way to run. In the absolute silence, as all held still, Cara tore her dagger from her belt and threw it, end over end, at her sister-in-law.

"No!" Simeon pushed her arm, throwing her off balance. The knife missed and clattered harmlessly to the cobbles. "Leave her, Cara."

"She betrayed us."

"I was saving our lives," Lysette snapped, picking up the knife. "If you'd just had the sense to see. We will all die here. My brother is not worth that and we help him not at all if we are all dead."

Before she could say more, second watch rang crisp and clear from the encampment beyond the gate.

Rafe shrugged helplessly at Simeon from where he stood by the gate. "I'm sorry, my lord, they're coming." He slammed it fast and barred it, leaving Lysette within the courtyard.

With barely a pause, those enemy who had emerged from the tunnels began the attack and Cara forgot all else but the opponent in front of her.

*

"I thought I might find you here." Lynsey appeared in the doorway. Karen looked up, startled by the bitterness in the soft voice.

"Lynsey?" Simon turned. "I'm sorry, this all…" He shrugged vainly. "It wasn't quite what I intended."

"I don't know." Lynsey came in and perched on the end of the bed. A plaster across her nose marred the symmetry of her face and her blouse hung provocatively open at the neck to show the bruising beneath. "I think it demonstrated your argument perfectly; she really can't cope without you."

"Not intentionally."

"Oh Simon, I know that. You spend your life protecting Karen. Of course you didn't intentionally drive her in here or try and get her to kill me. You do, though, need to think about yourself sometimes. A point which I believe I made."

"I was thinking about you, actually."

"So answer me one question, Simon, and then I'll go. Did you leave me stranded at the altar with your sister going stratospheric because you don't love me or because you think she needs you more?"

"Look…" Karen began, focusing their attention on her, when something slapped her across the face. "Ow, what was that?" She put her hand to her cheek and it came away wet with blood. "What happened?"

Lynsey was staring at her, eyes wide. "That just appeared. That's not possible."

"It happened to her leg too. Doctor Roberts seemed to think she'd done it to herself somehow." Simon got up and started looking around pointlessly.

Another sharp pain, this time across her upper arm, made Karen cry out. Blood began to seep through the hospital gown.

"What the hell?" Simon pulled open the door. "Doctor! Help, someone! Doctor!"

Doctor Roberts appeared at a run. "What is it?"

"That!" Simon pointed. "Lynsey and I both saw. It just appeared, from nowhere."

"How?"

"I don't fucking know!" Simon exploded. "Something's attacking my sister and it's in your bloody hospital room."

"Hush!" Karen ordered, hearing something altogether more recognisable. "The voices are back."

The three of them stared at her.

"Saying what?" Simon asked curtly.

"We have to get upstairs," Karen said, listening hard. "Now!"

"And how the hell will that help?" Lynsey asked.

"We've got to go up."

"Go up? I think we need—" Doctor Roberts headed for the door.

"No! You mustn't open that. This way." Karen pulled open the door behind the bedside table sending the small cabinet crashing out of the way as she did so.

The fact that the door hadn't existed until she opened it bothered her not at all.

*

Cara rushed up the circling stairs, her breath coming in short sobs. Simeon followed her up, his sword stained red. She bled freely from a cut to her cheek and another to the left arm where her blade had not been fast enough. Her leg had stained its bandage and only her strength of will kept her climbing.

Behind them, on the steps to the door of the keep, Robert was dying; holding off the enemy to allow them time to escape. Except there was nowhere to go but up and that no help. Above them, Lysette scrambled hastily upwards as well, much to Cara's disgust; she had wanted to leave her in the courtyard.

"They're in," Simeon gasped from below. "Faster. If we make it to the roof we can hold the door against them."

They pushed on, collapsing eventually through the stout oak that let them on to the keep roof. From here, Cara could see the entirety of the castle and its surrounding army. Figures like toys littered the courtyard below, bodies piled in awkward heaps.

Simeon pushed the door to and jammed one of his swords through the handle. "It won't hold long."

*

Karen pushed ever upwards, ignoring the various stabbing pains and the amazed exclamations from her companions as they followed her up a circular stair that shouldn't have existed. Instead she listened to the insistent voices in her head. *"Faster, if we make it to the roof we can hold the door against them."* Unclear who she needed to hold against, but certain that the voice was talking to her, Karen headed for the roof as fast as she could manage.

The door on to the roof was unlike any fire exit in the rest of the hospital and the roof seemed to be small and circular despite the fact that the hospital building stretched out below over several acres of land. Amongst the nicely manicured lawns below, Karen could see the corpses piled in haphazard shapes and the stench of death mixed unhealthily with the disinfectant of hospital corridors.

She turned to Simon and Lynsey who had staggered onto the roof behind her. The door still swung open beyond them.

"Shut the door! We've got to hold it against them."

"Against who?" Simon said as Lynsey replied. "The doctor hasn't made it up yet."

"Shut the door!" Karen screamed, seeing the blades of those following already appearing around the first curve. She dashed past the two of them and slammed the door shut, holding it closed with all her weight.

*

"Just a little while," Cara said, watching the distant slope where a phalanx of horsemen had appeared over the crest. Even over such a distance the royal blue of their surcoats could be seen. Owain, against all the odds, had made it. Behind the horsemen, moving slower but no less surely, strode a wave of marching men who gradually turned the hillside blue.

Simeon gave them a swift glance and went back to the door. "It will be close, Cara, they're almost to the top and this won't hold."

Cara nodded and went to join him, her sword gripped firmly. "What about her?"

Lysette answered. "I can speak for myself, Cara. I'm sorry I let them in. If I'd known Owain was so close then I would have survived another day but I didn't and we were starving to death while my husband hid in dark corridors pretending to be already gone. Tell Owain what you will."

"I meant," Cara said coldly, "whether you could be trusted to hold the door with us."

"I can't fight, but I won't hinder," Lysette snapped.

"Leave her, Cara," Simeon ordered. "Watch for Owain, Lysette, and we'll hold here."

*

Lynsey looked at Karen in amazement. "What? Are you mad?"

"No, you need to watch for us, over the edge. So we know when we will be rescued. Simon and I will hold the door."

"Rescued! You've absolutely lost it. You were the idiot who led us up here, you can bloody well get us down. We don't need rescuing, unless it's from you."

Simon looked slightly sick.

"Karen, we don't need rescuing, sis. Let's just go down."

"No! We're dead if you open that door." Karen fought Simon away from the door. Then she stopped in horror. Behind Lynsey she could see the archer peering around the crenulations on the top of the north tower.

*

Cara opened her mouth but was stopped by the sudden jarring on the door at her back. The enemy had made it to the top. She turned to face the door beside Simeon, her sword held fast.

"Simeon," Lysette said behind, "I think they're up the tower."

"We can tell that," Cara snapped, deliberately misunderstanding. "It's the way the door is shaking."

"I mean..." Lysette's voice tailed off and Cara risked a brief glance over her shoulder in time to see the arrow arch across from the north tower.

Time split.

Karen saw the arrow suddenly in both realities. Lysette was about to fall. She looked at Simon, at Simeon – at the horror etched on both faces. Simeon watching the woman he loved, Simon watching his sister descend into a maddening spiral that made no sense, totally unaware of the arrow speeding towards Lynsey.

With sudden realisation she understood. She'd had him last time round, this time she had to let him go.

The arrow hit with a hollow thud and Lysette slowly spun and fell to the roof as Karen threw herself across time and distance and hurled Lynsey out of the way, taking the arrow high up in her chest.

"No!" Down the years Simeon, or possibly Simon, cried for the loss of a woman he loved. His voice echoed across two rooftops and in the recesses of Karen's mind as her voices finally stopped.

Midnight Treat

The unicorn wasn't supposed to be there.

Well, that was somewhat of an understatement.

The unicorn wasn't supposed to be, full stop.

They were imaginary, fantastical creatures who had never existed.

Not something you could see in the zoo, or might even have been able to once upon a time.

Found in the average kitchen in Fenwick? Definitely not.

So, how to account for the unicorn who was – quite definitely – in his parents' kitchen.

Will rubbed at his eyes, just in case, but the unicorn stayed resolutely solid, its horn scraping the ceiling as it moved its bent head.

"Am I dreaming?"

The animal pulled back its lips from its teeth, giving Will the distinct impression it was laughing at him.

"You don't exist," Will tried.

Without taking its eyes off him, the unicorn lifted one hind leg and smashed its hoof through the door of the washing machine.

"All right, all right," Will waved his hands frantically, "you're here." He paused. "Why are you here?"

"Good question," a voice said behind Will. "This isn't what I was expecting."

Will whirled round to confront a young man, about his own age, who was clutching a lethal-looking sword and dressed in a large amount of leather and fur.

"What were you expecting?"

"King's Copse."

"Oh," Will paused, thrown by the answer, "that's right." His parents had been impressed by the royal name of the new estate above West Cross. The houses all had gardens, double garages and massive ground-floor living spaces, which combined kitchen, dining and sun room. Large enough, it now transpired, to contain a unicorn.

"It is?" The strange young man looked round and repeated, sounding less sure. "King's Copse?"

"Edward Road, King's Copse Estate, West Cross, Fenwick," Will clarified. The streets were all named after royalty.

"No," the other said, "King's Copse, his favourite hunting ground, site of his death and where he is buried."

"What?" Will had his own look round. The unicorn was still there and now had its head in the fruit bowl and the young man with the sword was looking increasingly aggressive. "What king?"

"Our king."

Will briefly considered mentioning Queen Elizabeth the Second and then settled for, "You said he's buried."

"That is a mistake."

"You mean he's alive?"

"Of course not," the young man snapped, "but his death was not foretold and can be reversed."

"Really?"

"I will take his steed, his sword," this was waved vigorously and narrowly avoided taking out the trinket cabinet, "and his champion to him and he will rise again."

"You're his champion?" Will did his best to keep the scepticism out of his voice.

"No," the young man said, "you are." He totally failed to restrain his own scepticism.

Will opened and closed his mouth a couple of times and eventually settled for a strangled, "What?" which totally failed to convey any of the thoughts going through his head but did give him time to try and figure out where he'd left his phone, if he could get to it without being skewered, and what the police might make of the situation if he phoned them. Any plea for help, he decided, would have to concentrate on intruders and swords rather than unicorns. The animal had moved on to eating the dried flower arrangement on the table.

"The shaman said I would come first to the champion and then we would go to the king to save him."

"Well, your shaman is talking bollocks," Will said bluntly. "Firstly, I'm no 'champion'. I'm quite good at snooker and I play for the medic's football team at The Nightingale but that's about it." He ignored the confusion crossing the other's face. "Secondly, I'm not going anywhere with you."

"You must help save the king."

"No, I must go and get my phone and call the police and, quite possibly, the RSPCA."

After a short pause while the young man obviously totally failed to understand what Will had said, he raised the sword slightly and repeated, "You must help save the king. You will come with me."

Will sighed. His phone was by the bed because he hadn't considered he might need it while he grabbed a midnight snack. The young man was between him and the doorway to the hall and the unicorn was preventing him reaching the range, where there was a large frying pan which might serve as a shield of sorts. The knife block was also beside the range but nothing in it was long enough to go up against the metre of metal the young man was adeptly brandishing.

Will looked round again but couldn't come up with anything else useful as a weapon. The unicorn had finished the table centrepiece and was watching Will as if considering if he was edible.

"Go where?" Will said tentatively. "How? And do you bring me back here afterwards?"

"The king will want to reward you."

"By bringing me home," Will said firmly, wondering if he ought to mention any clauses as to what happened if he didn't save the king.

"Of course," the young man deflated slightly, "if that's what you want."

Will nodded vaguely, backed himself against the fridge and wished he hadn't been tempted by the last piece of lemon meringue pie. He considered his options.

He had no phone, an armed young man between him and it, and a unicorn taking up a large part of the kitchen. There were three possibilities.

One, there was a dangerous criminal in his kitchen so he better do as he was told. This failed to account for a large horse-like beast with a horn on its forehead so he rejected this as an option.

Two, he was dreaming so he might as well go with it because he would wake up sooner or later.

Three, he really was being asked to go and save some king.

Accepting the situation seemed to afford less opportunity to end up on the sharp end of a sword or horn, Will decided he had very little choice.

"Go on then," he said. "How do we save a king?"

This didn't create paroxysms of joy in the youth who was looking positively underwhelmed about his 'champion' but he withdrew a stone, glowing with a green light, from the leather pouch at his belt. "I have found the champion," he said, speaking into it as if into a phone and sounding totally unsure. "Send me to the king."

The light grew brighter and spread across the kitchen. Will tried to push himself through the fridge door, away from the approaching circle of emerald and shut his eyes as the light became too bright.

There was a brief, disorientating jolt, everything became colder, and Will sat down heavily as the fridge behind him vanished.

His eyes flew open and he leapt to his feet again as his senses registered hard earth beneath him.

He was outside, in a copse of trees. It was full dark of the night, illuminated only by a banked small fire in the centre of the small clearing he was in. A man was clutching at his neck and making slightly strangled noises in the middle of a group of dangerous-looking men. The tone of the raised voices in the group suggested a measure of panic going on as the man at the centre made various incoherent noises.

"Possessed," Will heard before the medical student in him took over. He leapt forward, ignoring the weaponry on display and hands trying to grab at him, and pushed his way through the ring of men.

The man he was approaching – who he assumed must be the king – had sunk to his knees. He was a middle-aged, bearded man. His receding, long hair was greying. What caught Will's gaze, though, was that the man's lips looked like they were swollen. The hands were scrabbling at his face and throat which were reddening as he watched.

"What's he eaten?" Will demanded, ignoring the hands attempting to pull him away. When no answer was forthcoming, he decided it wasn't worth asking it again; the king had had an obvious reaction to something. What it was hardly mattered.

"Who are you?" one man demanded as the youth who had brought Will tried to explain. "He's King's champion. I was sent for him. The shaman said…" This obviously had some effect as the hands grabbing at Will fell away slightly.

The king hung his head as his breathing became more laboured. "I need to see your tongue," Will said firmly, kneeling beside the wheezing figure.

The king looked blearily at him and then raised his hands to pull his mouth open as if he couldn't manage it without. The fingernails were beginning to go the same blue as his lips; the tongue he revealed was overly large.

Will held the gasping form still as best he could and had a hard look at the king's tongue, face and neck.

"I need an EpiPen," he said, aware that this was probably a pointless thing to say. "I know where I can lay my hands on one." The first aid kit in the Highwayman contained at least two because Madge Cartwright had alcoholic tendencies and a peanut allergy. He'd recommended the landlord had included a pen after one near-fatal evening. Will glared at the young man who was hovering at a distance. "Can your shaman get me there?"

As the young man simply stared at him in incomprehension, Will leapt to his feet, pushed his way out of the circle and grabbed at the pouch, "Give me the bloody stone," he ordered, "or I can't save your bloody king."

This seemed to get through to the youth who grovelled in the pouch and retrieved the stone. Will grabbed the glowing green gem off the fumbling lad and, feeling a little stupid, yelled at it. "Look, whoever is listening to this, I need the first aid kit from behind the bar of the Highwayman. Can you manage that?"

There was a second swelling of the green light until it was

blinding, another disorientating jolt and Will found himself back in the kitchen holding the stone.

He was alone.

So, now what? He was home; no strange man, no sword, no unicorn, just a slightly glowing pebble.

And a patient he had begun to treat was dying – possibly in another time, maybe another reality – but he'd signed up to be a doctor to heal people.

"Bugger!" Will stuck the stone in his pocket, grabbed the torch from by the back door and headed out.

The Highwayman was several streets away, in the centre of the old village, so he ran.

Luckily Martin – the landlord of the Highwayman – was nocturnal and still clearing up so came immediately to Will's frantic knocking.

"Epipen," Will gasped, "emergency."

Martin was fast on the uptake – a benefit to a good landlord – and he darted back in to grab the first aid kit with no further explanation.

"Here, lad, take it," he said. "Bring me the story back with it. Go!" He pushed Will out of the pub.

"Got it!" Will yelled at the stone, dragging it out of his pocket.

Nothing happened.

Perhaps he needed to return to the kitchen. He pelted back the way he'd come.

"Got it!" He tried again as he burst through the kitchen door clutching the stone in one hand and the first aid box in the other.

This time the light flashed immediately and the world swam in a, by now, familiar way. Will found himself back in the clearing.

Very little had changed. Some men were crouched round the weakly struggling king. The rest were shouting at Will's companion who had backed behind the unicorn in a defensive way. Will got the impression they were questioning his own reliability or ability. They all immediately turned on him as he reappeared.

Will pushed his way through those gathered around the recumbent figure; the king's breathing was now see-sawing in a most alarming way as he struggled to get enough air through his swollen lips.

Will dropped the stone and flung open the box. He scrabbled through its contents, ignoring the exclamations going on above him until one of the larger men dragged him forcibly to his feet.

"What are you doing?"

Will waved the EpiPen he had grabbed from the box as he was lifted. "I'm saving your king's life."

"The Shaman said—" the young man began though Will noted he was doing very little to help.

"Magic maker, is he?" demanded the man holding Will off the ground by his shoulders.

Will opened his mouth to tell them he was a doctor and hesitated. This wasn't the twentieth century and he didn't have time to explain modern medicine and EpiPens. So, maybe he needed to go about this a different way.

"Yes, and this is my... er... wand," he said, cringing inwardly but couldn't think of a better word. "Now, let me heal the king."

He twisted violently from the man's grasp, fell to the floor, yanked the top from the EpiPen and jabbed it into the king's thigh. There then followed the longest ten seconds of his life as he waited for the pen to take effect, whilst shielding it with his body and hoping no-one was going to try and take it off him.

Gradually Will relaxed; the king's breathing seemed almost immediately easier. The men around hesitated but he could feel the tension still in the air, perhaps he needed something else. Feeling a little stupid he said, "Bore da, sut wyt ti," which was the start of a

Welsh nursery rhyme his mum had on a tea towel, and waved his hand over the king's face. This seemed to have a calming effect and one or two of the men took a step backwards.

Will threw more contents out of the first aid box until he found a second pen. He breathed a silent thanks to Martin for keeping it stocked.

"You cured the king," a large, muscled man growled at him. It sounded like a threat.

"Yes," snapped Will, and added to himself, 'and if his breathing doesn't start to improve in the next five minutes, I'm going to have to do it again, so I stand a chance of getting out of here alive.'

"Are you really a shaman?" one of the others asked.

"A doctor," Will said, and then quickly added, "a shaman too, a healer."

Watching the swelling, Will tried to judge if it was beginning to recede. The breathing was still fairly laboured, and he wasn't going to find ambulance or hospital out here. After a further couple of minutes of watching the king whilst trying to pretend several dangerous-looking men weren't glaring at him, Will repeated his Welsh nursery rhyme, adding a couple more words, and plunged the second EpiPen into the king's thigh.

Gradually, the swelling and redness began to abate and Will could hear that the king's breathing was truly beginning to settle. Those standing round him eased and took hands away from swords while Will refilled the first aid box.

In the slightly awed silence, Will was pushed out of the way by a gentle muzzle as the unicorn reached its head over to nuzzle at the king. The king stirred weakly and lifted a hand to stroke the soft, white fur.

"I think I was in time," Will said, trying to pretend he was talking to a ward of concerned relatives. He picked up the stone from where he'd dropped it and offered it towards the young man who had come forward behind the unicorn. "Tell your shaman fellow I think the king is going to survive and that I'd like to go home."

"But—" one of the men began, making a grab for Will.

Will raised the spent EpiPen and the man immediately backed away.

"No," he said. "Give your king air and space and he'll be fine. I'm going home."

"But the king will want—"

"Tough," Will said. "I'm going home." He lifted the stone the young man hadn't taken. "Take me home, your king is safe," he ordered it.

After a brief pause where Will worried if he was stuck there, the light flashed and the familiar bewildering lurch put him back in his kitchen.

The young man was with him and caught the stone as Will let it fall in relief.

Will staggered to the table, dropped the first aid kit, and collapsed in a chair. The adrenalin, which had kept him going for the last half an hour, was draining from him.

"How can we ever thank you?" The young man was hovering by the kitchen door, as he had when Will first saw him.

"You don't need to," Will said.

"I'm so glad we found you."

"Not sure I agree," Will said drily, "and any good first aider would have done."

"The shaman said it was fate," the young man went on as if he hadn't heard, "a champion living in the very spot the king fell. You are linked."

"If he says so," Will shook his head. "For all his prophecies, I don't think the 'steed' or the 'sword' were a lot of use."

"They got *you* there," the young man said, silencing Will. "You had to believe. The shaman said they were necessary."

Will looked hard at the young man and then shook his head. "Just go." He waved the other man away and resolutely ignored him until the flash of green told him he was alone; the youth vanished.

He rested his chin on his hand and looked round the kitchen at an empty fruit bowl, a ruined table decoration and a hoof print in the washing machine.

Eventually he decided his mum couldn't be any more mad at him, so he might as well eat the last piece of lemon meringue pie too.

ABOUT THE AUTHOR

Emma Melville lives and works in Warwickshire. She is a school teacher of students with special needs who writes in her spare time, concentrating mainly on crime and fantasy short stories, often inspired by her involvement with folk dance and song. She has had several short stories published in anthologies and won several literary prizes. Many of her stories involve Inspector Marshall and fantastical crimes in Fenwick.

Also available on Amazon in
AN INSPECTOR MARSHALL MYSTERY series:

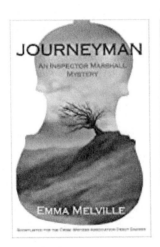 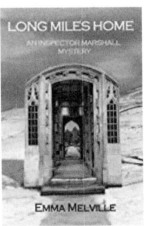